THE FRANKLIN'S FELONY

Sandal Castle Medieval Thrillers

Book Three

Keith Moray

SAPERE
BOOKS

THE FRANKLIN'S FELONY

Published by Sapere Books.

20 Windermere Drive, Leeds, England, LS17 7UZ,
United Kingdom

saperebooks.com

ISBN: 978-1-80055-243-2

Keith Moray is represented by Isabel Atherton at Creative
Authors.

For Rachel, my fellow traveller and best friend.

A FRANKLIN was in his company.
His beard was white as a daisy;
As to his temperament, he was sanguine, thereby dominated by the humor
blood.
He well loved a bit of bread dipped in wine in the morning;
His custom was always to live in delight,
For he was Epicurus' own son,
Who held the opinion that pure pleasure
Was truly perfect happiness.
He was a householder, and a great one at that;
He was Saint Julian (the patron of hospitality) in his country.
His bread, his ale, was always of the same good quality;
No man had cellars better stocked with wine.
His house was never without baked pies
Of fish and meat, and that so plentiful
That in his house it snowed with food and drink;
Of all the dainties that men could imagine,
In accord with the various seasons of the year,
So he varied his midday meal and his supper.
He had very many fat partridges in pens,
And many a bream and many a pike in his fish pond.
Woe was his cook unless his sauce was
Hotly spiced and sharp, and ready all his cooking equipment.
In his hall his dining table always
Stood covered (with table cloth) and ready all the long day.
He presided as lord and sire at court sessions;
He was a member of parliament many times.
A dagger and a purse all of silk
Hung at his belt, white as morning milk.
He had been a sheriff, and an auditor of taxes.
There was nowhere such a worthy landowner.

The Franklin's Portrait, *The Canterbury Tales*

With us there was a DOCTOR OF PHYSIC.
No one alive could talk as well as he did
On points of medicine and surgery,
For, being grounded in astronomy,
He watched his patient closely for the hours
When, by his horoscope, he knew the powers
Of favourable planets, then ascendant,
Worked on the images of his patient by natural magic.
The cause of every malady you'd got
He knew, and whether dry, cold, moist or hot;
He knew their seat, their humor and condition.
He was a perfect practicing physician.
These causes being known of what they were,
He gave the man his medicine then and there.
All his apothecaries in a tribe
Were ready with the drugs he would prescribe
And each made money for the other's guile;
They had been friendly for a goodish while.
He was well-versed in Aesculapius too
And what Hippocrates and Rufus knew
And Dioscorides, now dead and gone,
Galen and Rhazes, Hali, Serapion,
Averroes, Avicenna, Constantine,
Scotch Bernard, John of Gaddesden, Gilbertine.
In his own diet he observed some measure;
There were no superfluities for pleasure,
Only digestives, nutritives and such.
He did not read the Bible very much.
In blood-red garments, slashed with bluish grey
And lined with taffeta, he rode his way;
Yet he was rather close as to expenses
And kept the gold he won in pestilences.
Gold stimulates the heart, or so we're told.
He therefore had a special love of gold.

The Doctor of Physic's Portrait, *The Canterbury Tales*

PROLOGUE

Kilkenny, Ireland, Saturday, 3rd November, 1324

Wind! Oh, how I have longed to feel it on my face.

Petronella had felt a glimmer of relief when she was taken from the dank dungeon cell deep in the bowels of Kilkenny Castle. As she was thrust out of the main castle into the courtyard, she blinked, as even the light of this dismal winter day dazzled her eyes, so accustomed had she become to darkness.

And is that rain I am feeling?

She took a deep breath and a fleeting memory of her childhood home in Meath was kindled by the smell of animals in the castle undercroft, the smell of the rain on the cobblestones beneath her feet and the sound of people beyond the castle walls. It was so different from the stench of the cell with its rotten straw and her chamber pot that was only taken away once a week. It felt like a blessing to be away from the horror of the rats that came at night and nibbled any of the stale bread she left in a corner to deter them from boldly crawling over her face as she fitfully slept, attracted by the smell on her lips of the gruel she had occasionally been given when the turnkeys felt kinder than usual.

'It … it's so cold!' she said to no one in particular, knowing that no one was going to feel any pity for her.

She felt a stab of pain as the handle of a lash was shoved into her back to urge her forward. It made her cry out as it inevitably struck one of the open wounds on her back from the many floggings the Bishop of Ossory had ordered her to be subjected to over the past five months. Each one had been a punishment for failing to deny the charges against her and the others who had been accused of witchcraft. The last one had been the worst, when she had been forced to walk the path that linked the six parishes, being whipped along the way. The flesh from her back had been torn to pieces, and she imagined that there was barely an inch of it that had not felt the lash.

Her scalp itched and burned from the crude shaving she had been given that morning, and the long black shift that she had been given chafed her back. Even putting that on had been difficult for her, as her thumbs were useless after their earlier treatment with the thumbscrews.

'Move, witch!' the jailor growled at her. Then with a chuckle, he added, 'Don't worry about the cold. You'll soon enough be warmed up. At least you've been spared a flogging on the way.'

Petronella felt her bowels tighten and her heart started to thump. As she was shoved across the castle drawbridge towards the street, she saw the crowd and cries went up.

'There she is, the witch!'

'Beat her!'

'Burn her!'

'Send her to hell!'

Then stones, vegetables and clods of mud were aimed at her. Most missed, but then a ball of horse dung hit her full in the face, much to the amusement of the crowd.

She was driven along the high street, forced to endure the spitting, shouting and cursing and the physical pelting by the throngs on either side. The jailor and the soldiers that accompanied her did little to stop her humiliation until they reached the high wooden platform in the town square on which a huge stake stood, surrounded by piles of wood. Then they cleared people away from the steps and prompted Petronella to mount them.

Alongside the executioner, a burly fellow wearing a leather mask to conceal his face apart from two slits for his eyes, Richard Ledrede the Bishop of Ossory, her persecutor, was there along with the great and the mighty of Kilkenny. Even Sir Arnold le Poer, who was her mistress Dame Alice Kyteler's brother-in-law by her last marriage, was there. There was one of the Black Friars from the nearby Black Abbey; Brother Fergus, he was named. She had seen him many times before when he had been with the bishop, whispering in his ear, prompting him to ask certain questions. He stood watching her with a look that seemed to convey disgust and yet also triumph, his arms crossed and hidden inside his wide sleeves.

Petronella was forced to stand before the braying crowd while the bishop made an invocation as he approached her, before declaring in a mix of English and Latin, showing off both his learning and his bigotry, 'Petronella de Meath, *heretica, una de sodalibus dictae dominae Aliciae.*'

Almost delirious with fear, she dimly understood him. He called her a heretic, and a member of Dame Alice's brood. Immediately, she felt a pang of fear. Not for herself, but for those she loved. Yet she knew that there were seven others who had already gone to their deaths, strangled or hanged and buried in an unmarked hole somewhere. Dame Alice, though, she had fooled them.

The bishop droned on, raging about the Devil, hell and the demons that waited to feed on the souls of the damned. All the time he pointed at Petronella until he took a step nearer and leaned close to her, his breath stinking of onions and wine. He shouted in her ear, 'Tell them, witch!' To encourage her, he gave her a back-handed slap across the face. 'Loud, so that they can hear.'

Fearfully, as he raised his hand to strike again, she cried out, 'It is true. My mistress Lady Alice and I and ten others are guilty of witchcraft.'

The friar came forward at this point with his rosary and his cross. 'Shall I take her confession, my lord?' he asked, a look of disgust on his face.

But the bishop shook his head and waved him away. 'She is bound for hell and eternal damnation. Rather, spit on her, Brother Fergus.'

The friar filled his mouth with spittle and did as he was bidden.

The bishop took a roll of parchment from his robe, unfurled it and began to read out the sins that they were all supposed to have committed and to which she had finally confessed when the pain of the torture had been too much. Pointing at her again, he went on, 'It appals me to recount the depravity of this woman, but you good people must know the depths to which she had sunk. She had renounced the Christian faith and on three occasions sacrificed to the Devil.'

The crowd hissed and cried out angrily as he referred to the parchment again.

'She has brewed philtres composed of adders, spiders, the herb cinquefoil, the brains of an unbaptised babe and other ingredients for love or hate. She has consulted and consorted with demons and familiars. She has performed diabolical ceremonies with a ritual of lighted candles and spittings to cast a spell upon her enemies — aye, even upon her own husband and son. She has boasted that she was a mere novice in comparison to Dame Alice, who taught her every secret of this craft; she averred there was not a more cunning witch in the realm of Ireland itself, nor England, nor the whole world. Glorying in her iniquities, refusing the Sacrament of Penance, spurning —'

He droned on in his pebbly voice, telling them of the trial of Dame Alice that was of necessity held in her absence as she had absconded with her wicked familiar, the spawn of the devil, and none knew of their whereabouts. Growing more passionate with every sentence he uttered, the bishop incited the crowd to more expostulations of disgust and revulsion and calls for her death.

His voice rising above the noise of the crowd, he finally bellowed, 'I excommunicate you and condemn you to hell and the eternal damnation you so richly deserve!'

And when he was finally finished, he and the dignitaries filed away to watch from safety as Petronella was secured to the stake at the ankles, waist, shoulder and throat. She had heard earlier from the kindlier of the two jailors that the executioner might spare her the agony of the flames by strangling her before he lit the fire. But when the executioner spat at her feet and walked away, her heart sank. She pressed her head back against the stake in dejection, left to her final thoughts as the torch was prepared.

Look at them all. How cruel to come out in droves to watch one poor wretch go to her death. Enjoying themselves, being entertained, feeling righteous and smug.

She felt she should hate them all, only she had no energy to do so. She was only aware of the terror that was already causing her heart to gallop so fast that she thought it might burst, like a bag of blood. The thought almost made her smile.

Then she thought of Dame Alice. She who had promised them all so much. Who had promised that she would protect them, save them if things went ill for the group. But Petronella knew there would be no saving. Dame Alice had vanished. She had used her powers to disappear. It was for that reason that Bishop Ledrede had taken out the wrath of the Church on her, Dame Alice's servant. And she had kept silent for so long, recanting only under the severest of torture, when her spirit was finally broken.

But there were others that she pined for. She hoped against hope that they would be safe.

The executioner approached with his torch, shoved it hither and thither, lighting the pyre. Soon, smoke was curling up from the wood. Fanned by the November breeze, tongues of flame started to lick around her ankles. Then her shift caught fire and the heat became dreadful as the flames seared her flesh.

Through the smoke she saw the braying crowd, jeering at her, wanting her death, her agony.

But then as the smoke parted in the breeze, she saw in the crowd one that she did not expect to be there. There was no joy on that face, but sorrow. And determination.

Do I see my avenger? No! You must go! she thought. *It is too dangerous for you here.*

The flames closed in and the smoke grew dense, curtaining her from the sight of the crowd.

May you be the hand that will avenge me, was one of her final thoughts.

Her lungs burned as she inhaled the searing hot air and she screamed. But it was not just a scream of pain; it was an unrecognisable utterance, a plea: 'Remember me!'

But none heard it above the crackling of the burning wood. The flames began to char her flesh and the air was sucked from her, suffocating her instantly and sparing further torment. The executioner continued to stoke the fire, and the crowd watched with varying degrees of fascination and revulsion as her blackened body spouted blood that bubbled and evaporated in a purple haze, simultaneously filling the air with the stench of burning flesh.

The bishop, the dignitaries and the crowd watched the conflagration until the stake and the platform itself was no more than ash. By then, the face that Petronella had seen had long gone.

CHAPTER ONE

Sandal Castle, Wakefield, 1327

'Get out and don't bring me that pigswill again. Bring me ale!'

There was the sound of crockery smashing on wood and then the rapid opening and closing of a heavy door and the sound of running feet on a floor high above.

Sir Richard Lee raised a cautionary hand as the clatter of footsteps reverberated down the stairwell of the barbican. 'One moment, Doctor Flynn. It sounds as if Sir Thomas has sent Wilfred packing.'

The Irish physician Doctor Brandon Flynn tugged at his long, well-groomed red beard, and holding his medical satchel against his chest he flattened himself against the wall lest the person rapidly descending the stairs should career into them. He was a man of about forty years dressed in a long red and purple striped robe with a furred hood typical of his profession.

'Your pardon, Sir Richard,' said the wide-eyed Wilfred, the castle steward's head servant. 'I'm afraid that breakfast was not to Sir Thomas's liking.' He raised the tray with shards of a bowl, a mess of pottage and fruit and fragments of a clay goblet on it, and he shook his head worriedly. 'I hope you can cure him of his melancholy, Doctor Flynn. I cannot get him to eat a mouthful of food.'

'If it is God's will, I shall surely cure him,' replied the physician reassuringly in his Irish brogue.

Wilfred looked uncertainly at Richard and the physician. 'I pray it will be, sirs. All of the castle staff were distraught when

Lady Alecia was taken from us, but this fit of melancholia that Sir Thomas has sunk into does not seem to be lifting.'

Richard nodded. 'It has also been hard for my wife, Lady Wilhelmina, to lose her mother so suddenly. Especially when she is with child. She wanted to come to nurse her father, but I did not want to risk the effect of his melancholic nature upon her baby.'

Wilfred sighed. 'If I might say so, Sir Richard, I think it is good that Lady Wilhelmina is safe in your manor at Durkar. Some of the women servants with experience of such things have told me that ladies with child need to be spared from being too close to sorrow.' He bent his head and added, 'And from fits of ire.'

'Sir Thomas has always been subject to ire,' Richard explained to the physician.

'Shall I bring him a jug of ale as he commanded, Sir Richard?' Wilfred asked.

The physician interjected. 'I will assess Sir Thomas first and tell him whether I permit him to drink ale or not.'

Wilfred grimaced doubtfully, but perfect servant that he was, he bowed deferentially. 'I will dispose of this and then I will return and wait outside his chamber to take your instructions.' He bowed again and continued his descent of the stairs.

'Tell me, Sir Richard, before I see the patient: I know that Lady Alecia died suddenly, but how soon after did Sir Thomas sink so low in his mood? It will help me to know something of his temperament and of his recent history.'

'Then let us tarry a few moments,' Richard said, pointing to a door leading off the stairs. He opened it into a small chamber ordinarily used for storing pikestaffs. The two men sat down on a bench.

'Well, you should know first that my late mother-in-law was a lovely lady, and it broke many hearts, my own included, when the Lord took her in her sleep five weeks ago. She had suffered from rheumatism for many years, but her mind was ever nimble and she kept Sir Thomas's temper on an even keel, which was not easy.'

Richard went on to explain that much had changed in the four years since he had come to Wakefield, when he was appointed as the Circuit Judge of the King's Northern Realm by the monarch, King Edward the Second of Caernarvon himself. Prior to this, the Wakefield Manor Court had been held by Sir Thomas Deyville, the Steward of the Manor of Wakefield, a man who had a very different idea about justice to Richard. As Sir Thomas was not versed in law, he had dispensed what he considered to be appropriate sentences, although they had little legal precedent.

'Sir Thomas did not appreciate me assuming control of the Manor Court. He thought that my judgements were overly lenient, and we had a stormy beginning to our relationship. That animosity did not concern me overmuch, except that I was forced to stay at Sandal Castle, effectively as a guest of the steward.' Richard smiled as he thought of his wife. 'The fact that Sir Thomas and Lady Alecia had a comely daughter added another complication. Sir Thomas typically adopted an aggressively protective attitude as it became clear that Wilhelmina and I were falling in love. Lady Alecia recognised our feelings and blessed our courtship, which softened Sir Thomas's attitude. Eventually, we forged a good and mutually respectful relationship.'

'So when you took over the court, he was still the steward of the castle?'

'Indeed, Sandal Castle is the centre of the Manor of Wakefield, which extends for thirty miles or so across the country from east to west. With twelve graveships and almost one hundred and twenty towns, villages and hamlets, there is a considerable amount of overseeing necessary. John de Warenne, the Earl of Surrey, was the Lord of the Manor until King Edward the Second confiscated it after his favourite, Piers Gaveston, was executed under the orders of the earl and other nobles.'

The physician puffed out his cheeks and slowly blew through his lips. 'So much bloodshed this poor country has had these last few years. When Queen Isabella returned from France with Roger Mortimer the Lord of Wigmore, everything changed. The King was taken and imprisoned and deposed. Then, first the elder Hugh le Despenser, the Earl of Winchester, was beheaded and then most brutally his son, the Lord of Glamorgan, the King's latest favourite, was hanged, drawn and quartered.'

Richard nodded. 'Sir Thomas has taken all this news badly. He was a staunch supporter of King Edward the Second.'

'Then that may have had a bearing on his emotions and humours. What did he think of the deposition of the King and the coronation of his son, a mere stripling of fifteen, as King Edward the Third?'

'He has accepted it, for now Sandal Castle and the Manor of Wakefield belongs to King Edward the Third. Sir Thomas, as the Steward of Sandal Castle, runs it on his behalf. It is in his interest to make it profitable, which he ordinarily does with an iron fist.'

Richard said nothing of his own feelings, since as a sergeant-at-law who had been appointed by King Edward the Second and who had performed services for him and Hugh le

Despenser, he himself had felt saddened by the recent political change throughout the land. He was not at all sure that he supported Roger Mortimer and Queen Isabella, King Edward the Second's wife. He disapproved of their love affair and of the way they were ruling England on behalf of the new King. He was careful not to verbalise any such feelings, since he did not yet know the physician well.

'So by that do you mean that Sir Thomas is a disciplinarian?' Doctor Flynn asked.

Richard clicked his tongue. 'He is, although these last couple of years he has become mellower. However, since Lady Alecia's death he has shown very little interest in his administrative duties, much to the chagrin of his clerk. When I first arrived at Sandal Castle, he was a real stickler for orders and had trained the castle servants like dogs. They all had their own bells and had to come running when theirs was rung. He carried a stick with a small leather lash on the end, which he used on hands and buttocks. With some difficulty, Lady Alecia, Lady Wilhelmina and I persuaded him it would be better to use respect rather than the lash.'

Doctor Flynn had been sitting with his medical satchel on his lap, but now he laid it at his feet on the stone floor and idly ran a finger along one of the pikestaff poles. 'I must say that I am surprised to find that his chamber is in the castle's barbican.'

Richard clicked his tongue again. 'He had a room prepared at the top, so that he did not have to sleep in the chamber in the steward's lodge that he and Lady Alecia had shared all those years.'

The physician nodded. 'He ordered Wilfred to bring him ale. Does he drink much? If so, does his temper vary with the amount he imbibes?'

'The answer is yes to both, although I have never seen him drunk. He is fond of both ale and mead, rather than wine.'

The physician frowned. 'So his system has become hardened to it.'

'Since Lady Alecia's death, he has sunk into a fit of melancholy and ire. He refuses food and he drinks mead and ale all day until he retires to bed. As you will have gathered by his shouting and the way he threw his breakfast at Wilfred, his temper is extremely short.'

Doctor Flynn stroked his beard with his finger and thumb as if ensuring that it had remained well groomed. He stood up. 'That is all very helpful. Perhaps you could now let me see him.'

Richard led the way to the topmost floor of the barbican and tapped on the iron nail-studded door. 'It is me, Richard; I have brought a physician to see you, Sir Thomas,' he called out before the steward could bark out some curse or rejoinder at being interrupted.

They entered the large room with a bed in one corner and a washing bowl upon a table under a tall slit window. They saw the steward slumped in a chair behind an old oaken desk, which was covered in an untidy heap of parchments, tally sticks and ledgers. His full beard was unkempt, his beaver hat was askew and his eyes were bloodshot.

'Come in, if you must,' he grunted. 'But not for long, Richard.' He pointed at the desk. 'As you can see, I have much work that awaits me.'

Richard smiled. 'This is Doctor Flynn, come to see you and make you better.'

The Steward of Sandal Castle looked dispassionately at the two men. 'I have no need of a doctor. I am not ailing.'

'Nonsense,' Richard replied firmly. 'You have been in a dark mood since Lady Alecia died. You are rageful and you are drinking far more than is good for you. Wilhelmina is with child and she is worried sick about you. I will brook no discussion, father-in-law. Doctor Flynn will look at you and you will take whatever treatment he suggests.'

Sir Thomas was about to argue, but seeing Richard's set jaw he slumped down in his chair resignedly. 'What learning have you, Doctor Flynn?'

'I am an Irish physician trained in physic at Oxford and in surgery and accoucheurship at Montpellier in France.'

Richard sat down and folded his arms, feeling it best to remain during the consultation lest his father-in-law should refuse to cooperate. He listened as the physician proceeded to ask the steward a series of questions and then examined his tongue and felt his pulse. Every now and then, the doctor stroked his beard or harrumphed to himself.

'Have you pissed in a chamber pot overnight?'

Sir Thomas nodded in the direction of the bed. 'That fool Wilfred should have emptied it, but he had forgotten my ale and went off in a hurry.'

Doctor Flynn did not comment but opened his satchel and took out a matula, a glass uroscopy vessel for examining urine. He scooped up a sample from the pot and swirled it around as he walked to the slit window and held it to the light. 'It is the green of a stagnant millpond,' he mused, 'with a froth tinged with yellow.' Then, wafting it back and forth under his nose, he sniffed it. 'A sharp aroma, too.' Finally, he dipped a finger in and licked it. 'It is bitter, but not sweet, which is the only good thing so far.'

Richard found himself having to suppress a smile as Sir Thomas glowered at the physician and opened his mouth to retort, only to be silenced by a series of questions from Doctor Flynn about where he was born, the exact date and the time of day.

Various strange metal devices were hanging from his belt. He selected one which consisted of a series of moveable wheels and arranged them to perform a calculation. He stroked his beard as he interpreted the pattern on the device. 'Your humours are badly out of balance, Sir Thomas,' he pronounced. 'You are suffering from acute melancholia after your wife's demise as the result of both an excess of black bile and an abundance of stagnant blood. If we get the humours — your vital fluids — back in balance, then your spirits will rise.'

He selected another metal device, which Richard recognised as a volvella, a device used by physicians to calculate the amount and the time when a patient should be bled. A physician had explained this to him when he had been ill himself from a poisoned arrow after the Battle of Boroughbridge, five years before. He'd told him that the four humours, blood, phlegm, yellow bile and black bile, were the vital fluids that ran through the body, each associated with different organs, the balance between them accounting for the temperament of the individual. Imbalance resulted in disease, and the physician had to know how the mysterious planets and the twelve constellations of stars affected them.

Doctor Flynn expertly moved its workings to align them with the information that he had ascertained from Sir Thomas. 'I will have to purge you to remove the black bile,' he said as he reached into his medical satchel and took out a parchment scroll, which he unrolled to reveal the drawing of a man, with multiple points dotted around it, each with notes attached by arrows. Comparing the readings on both his lunar dial and the volvella with a table on the parchment, he nodded to himself and then turned to the steward. 'I will give you a purgative to take this afternoon and then again this evening at sundown, each with a jug of milk. Then tomorrow at cockcrow I shall return and bleed you.'

'At cockcrow?' Sir Thomas repeated incredulously.

'This chart is called "the bleeding man" and indicates the part of the body where a vein must be opened to remove the blood. Tomorrow the moon is in the ascendant at cockcrow, so I will take blood from behind your knees at that moment. I will take varying amounts of blood every day for five days, during which time you will drink only milk. You will eat porridge with rhubarb and —'

'Milk!' Sir Thomas bellowed.

'Only milk and absolutely no wine, ale or mead,' Doctor Flynn said, his voice firm and his gaze penetrating so that the steward wilted before him. 'I will have an apothecary in Wakefield make up a flask of *aurum potabile* to be taken seven times every day. It is an excellent tonic and restorative from melancholia.' Richard thought that he saw a shrewd gleam in the doctor's eye as he explained further. 'It is made from gold, which is needed to restore the glitter in your life. If you drink ale or mead with it, you will poison yourself and may die. It will be expensive, Sir Thomas, but it will cure you.' Once more, Sir Thomas was about to protest, but was silenced when the physician authoritatively raised his hand. 'Finally, I need to take a cutting from your beard and a lock of hair from your head.'

'Whyfor?'

'I need to make a model image of you which will assist in bringing you back to health.'

As Richard held the door open for Doctor Flynn, he heard his father-in-law mumble to himself, 'Pah! Sounds more like witchcraft than physic to me.' Part of Richard agreed with him.

Half an hour later, Richard and his right-hand man, Hubert of Loxley, rode out from Sandal Castle accompanied by Doctor Flynn. The physician was returning to Wakefield and planned to visit the owner of the tannery by the River Calder and some other patients on the Birch Hill and around Cheapside before seeing patients in the consulting room of his house at the top of the Warrengate. Richard and Hubert were journeying so that Richard could take the court session that morning.

The road from Sandal Castle towards Wakefield took a meandering course down the hill, passing the village of Sandal Magna with its hostelry, the ancient Church of St Helen's and surrounding hotchpotch of timber-frame houses and wattle and daub dwellings. Some had animals in small enclosures and others devoted their attention to vegetable patches during the growing seasons where they grew carrots, turnips, rhubarb or liquorice, for which the dark soil in the area was famous.

'Will Sir Thomas get better, do you think, Doctor Flynn?' Hubert asked.

The physician nodded confidently. 'Assuredly, as long as he obeys my instructions. The trouble is that such afflictions of the mind can make a person contrary and fail to follow the doctor's orders.'

'Sir Thomas must stop drinking ale and mead,' Richard explained.

'That I would not welcome if it was I that was being treated,' Hubert replied. He thought for a moment. 'If it would help, I could let him wear my crusader's arrow.'

When the physician raised his eyebrows questioningly, Richard explained, 'Hubert wears an arrowhead that he bought some years ago.' He did not add that he had purchased it in a tavern, or that Hubert was extremely superstitious about it.

'Apparently, it was removed from a crusader's back at the Siege of Antioch.'

'That was over two centuries ago,' Hubert interjected. 'The crusader survived what should have been a mortal wound. He wore it for the rest of his long life on a chain about his neck. It has protected each wearer after him, and since it fell into my hands I can swear to its power. It can deflect arrows from their path.'

'Strange as it may sound, Doctor Flynn,' Richard went on, 'more than once Hubert has indeed seemed to have escaped serious injury, including a dagger blow to his chest which would undoubtedly have slain him had it not fortuitously struck the arrowhead under his tunic.'

'Aye, and I have never ailed since I hung it about my neck. Not even a sniffle.'

Richard and Hubert were of about the same age and had been through battle, hardship and many adventures together. Hubert had been a man-at-arms in the service of Sir Jasper Loxley, the father of Richard's first wife, Eleanor. After her death, Sir Richard had answered his sovereign's call and fought against the Marcher Lords at Hereford, Pembroke and Shrewsbury. Later, they had been involved in the rout of the Earl of Lancaster's army at Boroughbridge, as they had tried to cross the River Ure. Richard had taken an arrow in his calf during the battle that went straight through the muscle into the belly of his horse. It fell and pinned him under it, leaving him at the mercy of a couple of Lancaster's infantry. Fortunately, Hubert was always at his side and outfought and dispatched them with his broadsword, saving his master's life. Afterwards, Richard was taken to the Abbey of St Mary in York where the poison on the arrow fulfilled its evil purpose and he lay raving in fever for two weeks, all the time watched over by Hubert, who was distrustful of the potions the Benedictine monks plied him with.

Upon his recovery, he was ordered to attend upon His Majesty, King Edward the Second at York Castle. There he was given his special commission as Circuit Judge of the King's Northern Realm and Coroner to Wakefield and the five towns around. This effectively made him the Judge of the King's Bench in the North with jurisdiction over the Manor of Wakefield and the Demesne of Pontefract.

Hubert reached a hand under the neck of his tunic and pulled out the arrowhead on its chain for the physician to see.

'A talisman like that will indeed be very powerful,' Doctor Flynn remarked. 'It still has its barbs intact, and the tip looks undamaged. The surgeon who removed it knew what he was doing. The planets must have been favourably aligned that day on the crusader's horoscope chart to have given him a lucky escape and to have imbued it with such power. It must have been that and the fact that his humours must have been in perfect and righteous balance.'

Richard had always regarded Hubert's absolute faith in his arrowhead as simple superstition, but hearing the highly educated doctor's view on it made him feel he perhaps ought to reconsider. 'I know something of the humours,' he said to Doctor Flynn, 'yet can they explain all about the way that we feel? Indeed, do they colour the way that we think?'

The physician tugged his beard reflectively. 'Not exactly, Sir Richard. We think about the events that happen, but that thinking can affect the overall flow of our humours. The great Aristotle himself taught that these humours are associated with the elements of air, fire, earth and water, and in turn they are linked with the paired qualities of hot, cold, dry and moist. So, earth is dry and cold, water is wet and cold, fire is hot and dry and air is wet and hot. The way they are linked means that one element can transform into another. Then Hippocrates the father of physic taught the importance of maintaining the balance of the humours in the body. Each person has a temperament that is the result of their particular balance. Thus a sanguine person has an excess of blood, choleric individuals have excessive yellow bile, melancholics have too much black bile and phlegmatics have too much phlegm.'

'So in Sir Thomas's case he has an excess of black bile, causing him to become melancholic?'

'Exactly so, but he also has stagnant blood, from his heavy drinking. I need to purge him to get rid of the excess black bile, and I need to bleed him to remove the stagnant blood in his liver and spleen.'

'And by working out his horoscope and the planetary positions, you can tell when the best time to bleed him will be. I understand now. Sir Thomas will have a tendency to melancholia and to anger. The grief that he is going through will have tipped the balance of his humours?'

'Quite correct, Sir Richard.'

'But can the humours also respond to other emotions, like jealousy and guilt, for example?'

'They can, just as the seven deadly sins can all upset the balance and the person will experience the symptoms, emotions and illnesses linked to their temperament. And the reverse can happen, when an imbalance can predispose one to feel guilt or jealousy.'

Hubert gave a short laugh. 'It all sounds too complicated for me. I think I'll just trust to my arrowhead to keep me safe.'

They had reached a crest in the trail and began the descent towards the Sandal Magna fishpond. Some hundred yards before it, the trail divided and Richard pointed to the way on the right. 'We will leave you now, Doctor Flynn. Hubert and I shall take the road through the village of Agbrigg and then continue into Wakefield along the Pontefract Road.'

They bid farewell and rode on. Richard was conscious that Hubert was wondering why they were taking the less direct route, just as they had done several times recently.

'I have much on my mind at present, Hubert, and I would like to take this path which is more scenic and conducive to my thoughts before I have to concentrate on whatever cases are presented to me in court.'

'Of course, my lord,' Hubert replied, not presuming to question his master, despite his knowledge of what lay ahead.

At the edge of the village they skirted a small copse of trees. Almost immediately they were assailed by the stench of putrefaction. Both horses snorted and made as if to shy away from what lay ahead, but Richard and Hubert said nothing and simply urged them on.

Rounding the edge of the copse, they saw the decaying corpse hanging from the gibbet as it had for the past ten days.

A young urchin of about ten years was reaching up and holding onto one of the dead man's feet. He had a knife in one hand and was sawing through a big toe.

'Hey!' bellowed Hubert. 'Stop that!'

He was about to spur his mount towards him, but Richard raised a hand to restrain him. 'Gently, Hubert. He is just a boy, but I am intrigued to know what his intentions are. Fetch him.'

The urchin had rapidly pulled his hood up and scurried away, running along the unploughed balks that divided the ridge and furrow fields.

Hubert guffawed. 'To tell you the truth, my lord, I only intended to frighten him.' He spurred his mount and caught up with the lad, reaching down and dragging him up by his hood to lay him over his horse's neck. 'Here we are, my lord. A dangerous felon if I ever saw one. Shall I tie him up and take him to the Tolbooth before you try him in court?'

'Pl-please, masters, I meant no harm.'

'So what is the meaning of that?' asked Richard, pointing to the hanged man's toe that the lad was clutching in one hand and the crude knife in his other. 'Why have you hacked off that big toe from this felon's corpse?'

The lad bent his head lower to avoid looking at Richard. 'Please, sir,' he said tremulously, now visibly shaking with fear. 'I … I need it to help —'

'Calm yourself, lad,' Richard said in a softer voice. 'Just tell me why you have desecrated a hanged man's body? Tell me why you needed such a disgusting thing and what you were going to do with it?'

When the boy started to sob and snuffle, Richard nodded to Hubert and pointed at the ground.

'Come, lad,' said Hubert, dismounting and lifting the youngster by his collar to deposit him on his feet in front of Richard's horse. 'Don't try to run, for I have a tight hold on your hood. Now answer Sir Richard Lee the Judge of the Manor Court. Keep in mind that you have committed a felony.'

'Not a felony, Hubert, merely a misdemeanour,' Richard corrected. 'A felony is a much more serious crime. Now speak, boy.'

Tears welled up in the young lad's eyes and tumbled down his cheeks, drawing a trail through the patina of grime that covered them. He looked up at Richard and took a deep breath before blurting out, 'I needed it for my mother, sir. She has a huge wen on her chest, so she tells me. It's making her ill, and she's not able to work for more than an hour before she has to lie down. There's only her, me and my little sister Emily.'

Faith, a common enough story, Richard thought. *It does not sound like a simple wen if it is so big it makes the mother ill.* 'What is your name, boy?' he asked. 'Have you no father?'

'Hal, sir,' he replied, then shook his head. 'My father died when I was still a young 'un, sir.'

And you still only look about ten. 'Well, Hal, what work does your mother do?'

He shrugged. 'Whatever she can, sir. Washerwoman, stick gatherer. She helps with the harvests in the summer, mucks the pigs, anything.'

'And what were you going to do with that toe you cut off?'

Hal suddenly looked terrified. 'I wasn't going to do anything, sir. Some ... somebody else was. They were going to use it to get rid of my mother's wen.'

Hubert sucked air through his teeth. 'Sounds like witchery or something, my lord. Should I get this person's name?'

Witchcraft? Richard thought. *Or just simple folk's country medicine? It will be one of the old women of Agbrigg, I imagine. One of the wise women, as they call them. In truth, it is probably little different from Doctor Flynn's treatments. Probably much cheaper, though.* He shook his head. 'No, Hubert. I don't need to know that yet. I want to learn more about Hal's mother's wen. So I want you to go home with him and find out as much as you can about how she feels, and where she has this wen. Then meet me at the court.'

'Very good, my lord,' Hubert said as he bowed his head and then hoisted Hal up to sit in front of his saddle. He pointed to the toe still clasped in Hal's small hand. 'What about that?'

'Let him take it. The corpse has no need of it now, and perhaps it will be useful to this person who is going to help Hal's mother.'

Hal tugged his forelock and muttered his thanks to Richard as Hubert rode off.

Once on his own, Richard dismounted and stood looking up at the corpse hanging from the Agbrigg gibbet. *So here I am again. I cannot get this out of my head. Was I right or was I wrong? First Lady Alecia's sudden death, then Sir Thomas's fit of deep melancholia and the effect it was having on Wilhelmina. Clearly, I was not in the best of humours when I heard the case against you, Quinn of Ryhill.*

A slight breeze caused the corpse to sway slightly, making the rope and the wooden gibbet frame creak eerily. Richard gazed up at the empty sockets where crows had pecked out the eyeballs and started to tear away the flesh, so that not many of the man's features remained and few who knew him would now recognise his face. Once again, the gut-wrenching feeling of despair and guilt flooded over him.

Was I too hasty to sentence you? Did I hang a man who was not wholly guilty?

CHAPTER TWO

Wakefield was an ancient town built by the Saxons on a limestone ridge that sloped down to the River Calder. It was surrounded by a number of villages that were actually Viking settlements. It was not a pretty town, in comparison with the great cities of London or York, yet it was clearly quite prosperous and not without its own charm. Indeed, throughout the north of the land it was called the Merrie Town, probably because it boasted several hostelries and bawdy houses.

Richard crossed the bridge over the River Calder and rode up the southern road into town, passing through the Kirkgate tollgate and following it up the steep hill to the Birch Hill, where it met the other three main roads. Within this area there was a pond, a market cross and a large circular space called the Bull Ring. This was so named because bull and bear-baiting regularly took place there when fairs were held.

On market days such as this day, the whole area was covered in stalls and booths, temporary animal pens for the cattle and sheep that were driven from miles around to fetch the best prices they could for their owners. Accordingly, the streets were bustling with people.

Richard made his way up the road that was rutted by oxcarts and packhorses. On either side there were gabled wooden houses with roofs of thatch or reeds, and crude wattle and daub dwellings, most with undercrofts for animals and supplies. Dung heaps and refuse of all kinds had to be negotiated along with the flocks of animals, carts, donkeys and trudging humanity.

Not far from the Bull Ring was the Tolbooth or town prison, and close to it was the Moot Hall where the Manor Court was held. As he crested the hill, Richard could see the Church of All Saints with its mighty spire.

The Moot Hall was a large timber-framed building capable of holding up to two hundred people. It had been built a century before by William de Warenne, the fifth Earl of Surrey. Since then, the Lords of the Manor of Wakefield and their appointed stewards had used it for the various types of court heard throughout the year. Above its doors was the emblem of the de Warenne family, and above that was a small sundial. A stream of townsfolk were entering the main door, but they soon stood to one side at the sound of Richard's horse. A young ostler was already waiting for him to arrive, and he rushed forward as he dismounted and led his horse away to the nearby stable beyond the Tolbooth where prisoners and those awaiting trial were held. Carrying his saddlebag, Richard entered the Moot Hall.

A long corridor led to a lockable room called the Rolls Office, which was furnished with a large desk and chair and several stools. Taking up a corner of the room was a large locked chest with numerous pigeonholes, containing the Manor of Wakefield court rolls. Dating back to 1274 and written in a mix of English and Latin on fine vellum scrolls, they recorded all of the dealings of the Manor Court.

John of Flanshaw, the town bailiff and the main officer of the court, was sitting at the desk writing on vellum when Richard opened the door. 'Ah, Sir Richard, I was just making out the list of the court proceedings,' the bailiff said, replacing a quill in the holder beside the large pewter inkpot. He was a well-fed man in his late thirties with porcine eyes and a square-cut black beard that was flecked with grey. Richard knew him to be a stickler for routine, an able court clerk and an efficient bailiff. Picking up a pounce pot containing powdered cuttlefish bones, he sprinkled some on his list, tapped the vellum and then blew the loose particles away. 'It will dry in a moment, sir.'

Finally, in the obsessive manner that so amused Richard and which was characteristic of the man, he straightened the vellum on the desk and stood to vacate the chair for Richard.

'A goodly crowd seems to be attending today to hear justice served,' Richard said as he sat down to look over the bailiff's precisely written list.

John of Flanshaw nodded. 'There are a couple of cases that people have been talking about for some days, Sir Richard. As usual, they will be hoping for some sport by the Tolbooth. And after the hanging of Quinn of Ryhill ten days ago, there is talk that you have — er — decided to take a sterner approach in your sentencing.'

Egad, has the country become bloodthirsty, since the King was deposed in favour of his son? Do they want to see hangings and amuse themselves seeing people punished? 'If the jury finds a person guilty, then I shall apply the sentence permitted under the law, but I shall do so fairly.'

The bailiff smiled thinly. 'You are always fair, sir. As is the law, provided a person does not break it. The people of Wakefield like to see justice served.'

'You mean they never tire of throwing horse or pig dung at poor wretches in the stocks or the pillory?' Richard replied.

'If they deserve it, sir. A punishment to fit the crime, be that felony or misdemeanour.'

It is not so simple as they all think, Richard thought. *Most crimes are misdemeanours and can be dealt with by a fine, some time in prison or even time in the stocks or pillory. Felonies, though, they almost always*

the court roll chest. I will lock it up before I come through and I will bring the key.'

Once the court official left, Richard rose and unlocked the chest and took out the latest roll and returned to study it at his desk. He had been over the case numerous times in his mind, but he wondered if seeing it written on vellum in John of Flanshaw's precise, unemotional manner might help him to see it dispassionately, as he believed he had during the case as it had been presented ten days previously.

Et capta es ad supplicium suspensi usque ad locum et mortuus es. He heard himself passing the sentence of death: 'You will be taken to a place of execution and hanged until you are dead.'

On the face of it, the case was clear. Bryce-a-Green had been caught in the act of stealing a cow from Quinn of Ryhill. He'd been described as 'a notorious thief', which John of Flanshaw had meticulously written in Latin: '*fur erat notorium*'. A hue and cry had sounded in the hamlet and four local Ryhill men had pursued him when he'd fled. These men were Quinn and three neighbours. Bryce-a-Green had turned on them and brandished a knife. They'd overpowered him, beat him and then Quinn had decapitated him with a scythe.

Richard had heard the case and questioned Quinn and the three neighbours. Their testimonies did not agree. Quinn angrily claimed that they had acted as one, killing Bryce-a-Green because he had been intent on killing them all. The other three claimed they had tried to stop Quinn, but he'd been incensed and out of control. It was his scythe, his hands upon it and his crime.

The jury were unanimous in their guilty verdict of Quinn, but not of the three others. Richard felt that an example had to be sent out, for as he had declared in Latin, '*fecerunt sibi iudicat*' which John of Flanshaw had transcribed on the court roll along with his helpful translation into English: 'they made themselves judges.' Accordingly, he sentenced Quinn to death and the others to twenty lashes each and a week in the Tolbooth to consider their part in the affair and their failure to stop murder being done.

The sentence had taken place at the Agbrigg gibbet. Quinn was bound and taken there from the Wakefield Tolbooth on a horse-drawn cart, followed by a procession of folk who wanted to see the execution. Richard and Hubert had attended to see that the sentence was correctly carried out, and he was surprised to see how many local dignitaries, including guildmasters, franklins, clergymen and even a fair number of respectable ladies from around the area had come to watch the spectacle. It saddened him to see so many people regarding it as an entertainment to watch as the noose was placed about the condemned man's neck and the cart was drawn slowly away, leaving him to dangle and jig from the gibbet, being slowly strangled over a quarter of an hour.

As was part of the sentence, *putredo ossium usque ad cadunt*, the body was left to rot until the bones fell.

A week later Richard heard from Hubert, who had picked up local gossip in one of the Wakefield taverns that Bryce-a-Green had had a long-term feud with Quinn. There was also a whisper that the three men from Ryhill were known as the type who would do anything for money. He wondered if that meant they would be willing even to take a flogging.

Richard felt that surge of uncertainty as he read over the case before finally rolling it up and replacing it in the court roll chest. He could not stop himself from thinking that if Quinn was not wholly guilty, then there had been a miscarriage of justice.

Until I am sure in my mind, I must make certain that I do not make the same mistake again.

Again he had that hollow, disconcerting feeling, and thinking back to his conversation with Doctor Flynn he wondered whether he had been in an ill humour himself that day and whether the decision to make an example of Quinn of Ryhill could have been influenced by an imbalance in his own vital humours, from worry about his wife Wilhelmina and her unborn child and Sir Thomas's melancholia after the death of Lady Alecia. From his conversation with the physician, he was of the opinion that these humours could effectively sway the way one thought.

He slapped his forehead with the flat of his hand. *I must control my thoughts and my emotions*, he thought. *I must be a good and fair judge.*

With that determination fixed in his mind, he put his coif on his head and picked up his mallet and the pile of vellum sheets that John of Flanshaw had prepared for him and left the Rolls Office.

The court chamber of the Moot Hall was as large as a barn. There was a dais at one end, upon which was a large oak table with a chair for the judge of the court and a few others for visiting dignitaries, such as Sir Thomas Deyville, or occasionally if Richard saw fit, one or other of the local guildmasters. On the ground opposite and below the dais was a three-sided wooden pen which was used by those addressing the court or being addressed by it. To the side was another pen called the dock, which was raised to a slightly lesser height than the judge's dais, for the accused in a case, but this had a gate to secure the person until the judge and jury were satisfied of innocence or convinced of guilt. Then it was up to the judge to pass sentence.

On the left hand of the chamber, twelve local men of various social standing were sitting on stools.

The chamber was full of men and women either sitting in the few seats at the front or standing behind, chatting noisily while they waited for the court to begin. On hearing Richard's familiar tread from the corridor, John of Flanshaw swiftly obtained silence by rapping a pole on the first wooden pen.

'Silence! All rise for Sir Richard Lee, Circuit Judge of the King's Northern Realm and of the Wakefield Manor Court.'

Richard came in, mounted the dais and took his place behind the desk upon which John of Flanshaw had placed a sheaf of blank vellum sheets, an inkpot, a pounce pot and a selection of quills. He cast a look around the great hall at the standing folk, mainly tradesmen, shopkeepers and their wives. Those sitting at the front were of higher status, or able to pay a coin or two for the privilege and comfort of a seat during what could be a lengthy session of court. Among them he espied Master Geoffrey Hopwood of Kirkthorpe, the franklin who had wanted to see him.

He was a distinctive-looking, well-dressed fellow. Although he was probably only in his early forties, he was one of those men who had aged before their time, for he had a full white beard and luxuriant white hair that crept out from beneath a fine brown beaver hat. He sat in the middle of a row of equally sumptuously dressed men and women of his class. They were leaning towards each other, obviously whispering and nodding about something. Richard had not seen several of them in his court before, and their presence intrigued him.

One man was bent over, presumably looking in a bag or something at his feet. When he straightened up in his seat,

Richard was surprised to see that it was none other than the Irish physician Doctor Flynn.

Curious, Richard thought. He bowed his head to the court and rapped his gavel on the desk. 'I declare the court open. Bailiff, swear in the jurors and then let us have the first case.'

The court proceeded much as Richard had expected from the list of cases that John of Flanshaw had provided him with. He heard a succession of disputes over land, arguments about payment for goods, accusations of theft of things such as grain, a brace of rabbits, a couple of turnips, loaves of bread and a sack of wool. In addition, there were a few cases of arrests by the town watch for breaking the curfew or being found drunk or caught in some sexual act, either natural or otherwise. In the less trivial cases, the two burly constables would force-march a shabby and bedraggled figure into the lockable pen to have the charges read out and to listen to witnesses to the charge before being subjected to questioning by Richard.

Richard generally felt more sympathetic towards those who pleaded guilty and were prepared to receive his judgement than towards those who vehemently proclaimed their innocence and yet were found guilty after almost irrefutable evidence or witness statements were received. Nonetheless, he did always endeavour to make the sentence no more than that prescribed under the law, for that to him was the most precious of things.

As it happened, Richard considered all of the cases seen that morning to be mere misdemeanours under the law, to be reflected by appropriate judicial sentencing. He was aware of murmurings of discontent when accused people were merely fined. Thus far, none of the cases had occasioned corporal punishment or merited custodial sentences in the Tolbooth.

The court audience responded to his use of Latin with murmurings of approval and sage nodding, as if they all understood each and every one of the terms.

In the case of Ham of Kettlethorpe, charged and found guilty by the jury of stealing eggs from his uncle's henhouse, Richard knew that there was an expectant hush as he summed up.

'Ham of Kettlethorpe,' he addressed the frightened-looking lad of twelve years of age, 'this was *actus reus*, a deliberate theft of eggs. But you pleaded guilty and claim that you were trying to feed your younger brothers and sisters, so my sentence is *ad valorem*. That means you will pay back the value of the eggs. You will work in your uncle's pigsty for two days.'

This was received by mumbled words of approval, for the lad was well known and popular, whereas his uncle was regarded as a gruff old bully who begrudged allowing his dead brother's son a few eggs for the family. When the uncle started to mutter complaints, a section of the crowd started to sway and several threats to him were overheard by one of the two burly constables who had been standing by the dock and now advanced towards the threat-makers.

Richard rapped his gavel and shook his head at the constable when he looked round. With a deferential bow, the man returned to the side of the dock with his fellow constable. They stood facing the court audience with folded arms and unsmiling, severe expressions on their faces.

Richard waited until John of Flanshaw finished writing at his small desk and then called to him. 'Let us hear the last case.'

As he said it, he glanced over at the row of seated figures around Geoffrey Hopwood, the franklin. He had noticed some of them dozing during the previous cases, but now they were all attentive.

The bailiff stood and called out in a loud voice, 'Bring in Peter Plowman.'

The large double door at the side of the judge's dais opened and the Tolbooth turnkey, Judd of Alverthorpe, a tall man with a thick black beard, wearing a leather skullcap and a leather tunic with a belt from which hung a number of heavy keys, came in holding another fellow by one arm. This was a young lad of no more than sixteen or seventeen years, who walked with a limp and whose head was a mass of cuts and bruises. One eye was swollen closed and his jaw looked lopsided.

Sir Richard watched as he was led to and shut in the dock, where he slumped forward to rest his elbows on the wooden edge.

John of Flanshaw went to stand before him. 'Prisoner in the dock, identify yourself to the court and to Sir Richard Lee, the judge of this court.'

The youth was visibly anxious as he looked round at the court, opening his good eye as wide as he could. He was hoping, Richard had no doubt, to see some friendly face in the crowd. Then turning to look at Richard, he nodded his head vigorously. 'Aye, sirs. I am Peter Plowman, son of Peter the Plowman. I should not be here.'

'You'll speak when you are spoken to by Sir Richard,' snapped the bailiff. 'Finish identifying yourself. Where do you live?'

'I live with my mother in our cottage at the Half Moon Beck.'

John of Flanshaw turned and addressed Richard. 'Shall I read out the charges, Sir Richard?'

Richard nodded and the bailiff went on, unfurling a scroll and reading from it.

'Peter Plowman is charged with killing and stealing a sheep belonging to the yeoman Cedric of Sharlston. Cedric and two of his men caught him in the late afternoon before dusk as he made off with it upon his shoulders. They had followed a trail of bloodspots alongside a hedgerow. The accused put up a fight and wounded Cedric with the knife he had used to slit the sheep's throat, before the yeoman's servants overpowered him and tied him up.'

'How do you plead to this, Peter Plowman?' Richard asked.

The youth had been hanging his head, but now he stood up, swallowed hard and looked straight at Richard. 'I took the sheep, sir, but it weren't stealing. It was a debt that villain Cedric owed my mother and wouldn't pay. She can't afford that, being a widow, and we need to have money to eat.'

Richard was well aware that many poor tradesfolk often went unpaid and hungry as a result of non-payment by their so-called betters. 'A debt, you say? For what?'

'For six bushel baskets, sir. My mother is a basket weaver, and she made him half a dozen large baskets, but he wouldn't pay. So I took a sheep from him; that's fair, I reckon.'

Richard shook his head. 'It would be fair if you honestly bartered for it. If you just took it, then it is theft, a serious crime. And if you did indeed wound your accuser, then these are two felonies of which you are accused.' He turned to John of Flanshaw. 'Call the accuser, Cedric of Sharlston.'

The bailiff did as bidden and a surly-looking man dressed in a green coat and hood stood up from the seated row and followed John of Flanshaw to the witness pen. He swore an oath to tell the truth upon the Bible presented to him.

'Cedric of Sharlston, you have accused Peter Plowman of stealing one of your sheep and of wounding you.'

'He did, sir. I and my men caught him and he tried to stab me.' He held up an arm and pulled back his sleeve to reveal a heavily bound dressing. 'The physician, Doctor Flynn, sitting there can prove this.'

Richard had wondered why the physician was present in court and why he hadn't told him that he was coming. He told the physician to stand and answer.

Doctor Flynn stood and bowed. 'Yes, Sir Richard, I was consulted by Cedric of Sharlston.'

'Tell the court about this,' Richard instructed.

'I was in my surgery two days ago, Sir Richard, when Cedric of Sharlston and his men brought Peter Plowman to the Tolbooth. Cedric of Sharlston called upon me to treat his wound. It was the type of flesh wound that bleeds a lot, but was not severe. A blade had shaved the topmost layer of skin only.'

'I was defending myself,' Peter Plowman cried out. Richard silenced the lad with a firm stare but did not reprimand him. Instead, he looked hard at him for a while, noting his looks, distorted though they were by his bruising. He also noted his hair colouring, which struck him as most curious for one of his age, for there were a few streaks of white amid his shaggy black locks.

'Do you owe Peter Plowman's mother money for six bushel baskets?' Richard asked the yeoman.

Cedric of Sharlston shrugged his shoulders. 'A paltry sum, perhaps.'

Richard dipped a quill in the inkpot and wrote something down. 'And you know Peter Plowman?'

The yeoman nodded. 'He works the fields and tends animals for Master Geoffrey Hopwood, the franklin.'

'He says that he took the sheep as payment for your debt.'

The yeoman's cheeks grew red with anger. 'He stole a sheep and killed it and wounded me, my lord. He should be hanged.'

Richard rapped his gavel. 'The jury shall decide if he is guilty or not. And I as the judge will be the one that passes sentence if he is found guilty.' Once again, Richard felt that cold feeling run up and down his spine. He could not stop himself from thinking about the corpse of Quinn of Ryhill hanging from the Agbrigg gibbet. Turning to the youth in the dock, he went on, 'Do you understand the seriousness of these charges, Peter Plowman? Crimes are either misdemeanours or felonies. A misdemeanour may be dealt with by imprisonment or a flogging or some such, but a felony is serious and under the law will result in a more severe punishment. Perhaps the most severe penalty.'

Peter visibly trembled and looked round pleadingly upon the audience. He turned to Richard. 'That man is a villain, my lord. He had his men beat me. I can't see out of my left eye and I think they broke my jaw.'

Richard looked at the notes the bailiff had prepared, while he thought about the case. He was already troubled, but there was something disconcerting about this matter. Then he set about examining Cedric of Sharlston in more detail, before he again questioned the accused.

Finally, he turned to the jury. 'You have all heard the evidence. In a few moments, I will ask you to consider if Peter Plowman is guilty or not. But before I do, you must understand this about the law, because the outcome of your decision could be most serious for the accused. Firstly, before an act is considered a felony, there must be *mens rea*. That is Latin and it means that there must be evidence that he had a guilty mind and was intending to commit a felony. This is vital, since Peter Plowman intended merely to exact payment for a debt unpaid and he claims that was his single intention. He did not wilfully steal the sheep. He wilfully intended to collect the debt owed to his mother, no more than that.'

'But, my lord, he killed my sheep. That cost me money,' protested Cedric of Sharlston. 'Far more than the paltry sum I owed for those shoddily made baskets.'

Richard rapped his gavel. 'Do not interrupt!' He turned again to the jury. 'Secondly, for this second charge to be considered a felony, he must be found *de aliqua felonia felonica facta*, meaning that he acted in a felonious manner, knowing that he was committing a felony.'

The foreman of the jury raised a hand. 'I don't understand, Sir Richard.'

Richard nodded. 'It means that you have to decide if he knowingly wounded the yeoman, meaning to injure him, or if he was acting in self-defence as he claims.'

When the foreman and the other jurors conferred and then all nodded, Richard went on.

'Is there anyone in the court that would say anything in the accused's defence?'

Immediately, the franklin, Geoffrey Hopwood, stood up. 'Sir Richard, I am Geoffrey Hopwood of Kirkthorpe, a franklin and a knight of this shire. I have known Peter Plowman all of his life. His father was a ploughman of mine before him, and his mother and he live and work in my employ on my land at Half Moon Beck. I know him as a good, industrious and honest fellow. He would not steal, knowing that he was stealing and he would not commit violence other than to defend himself. I would be willing to pay recompense to Cedric of Sharlston, my good neighbour, for his sheep, for his discomfort from the wound and for any fee he had to pay the good physician, Doctor Flynn.'

I wondered if I would hear such an intervention, Richard thought. And looking from the franklin to the accused youth in the dock, he found himself being most intrigued. 'I shall take this into account,' Richard replied. Then to the jury: 'How say you, members of the jury? Is Peter Plowman guilty first of theft of a sheep? And secondly, of wounding with intent to do serious bodily harm?'

The jurors stood and crowded together, discussing in whispers for some moments, before returning to their seats.

'We find the accused guilty of both felonies, my lord,' the foreman said upon being asked by Richard.

Peter the Plowman gasped and staggered, supporting himself by grasping the edge of the dock.

Richard saw the smug expression on Cedric of Sharlston's face as he looked across at the franklin, whose cheeks had paled as he slouched in his seat.

The courtroom was suddenly filled with noise. Half seemed in favour of the verdict and half against.

'Hang him!' went out cries from the courtroom.

'Flog him first!'

'No! He's just a lad.'

'The yeoman is a bastard!'

'Let him go.'

Richard banged his gavel and nodded to the Tolbooth jailor and the two constables, who stepped forward, hands going to the cudgels tucked into their belts. The crowd went silent. 'I am not convinced by this,' Richard said. 'And I invoke the article of the law, *non obstante veredicto*. That means that for the time being, I overturn this verdict. I shall consider the case further, but there will be no hanging or flogging. Instead, I sentence Peter Plowman to be incarcerated in the Tolbooth until I have made further study of the evidence.'

The murmurings from the crowd went on, but lessened as Judd of Alverthorpe the Tolbooth jailor and the constables took yet more belligerent steps forward.

'And the court will pay Doctor Flynn's expenses to go to the Tolbooth and examine the prisoner's wounds,' Richard added. 'Take the prisoner away.'

At a sign from the bailiff, Judd of Alverthorpe went to open the gate and led the prisoner from the dock.

Richard surveyed the courtroom and the movements and reactions of many of the people present. In particular he noted the flushed, angry face of Cedric of Sharlston and the smiling face of Geoffrey Hopwood as he shook hands with Doctor Flynn and several of the people who had been sitting with him, both men and women.

It looks as if the franklin himself has just won a case and been exonerated, Richard thought. *There is more to this case than meets the eye, and I shall find out more before I deem the case to be over. One thing is certain, though. This lad does not deserve the noose.*

After closing the court session, Richard went back to the Rolls Office and found Hubert standing outside the door waiting for him.

'Did you find out about Hal's mother?' he asked as they entered the office ahead of John of Flanshaw.

'I did, my lord. She is the Widow Clegg. I am no physician or apothecary, but I can tell that woman is unwell. She says she has a wen upon a breast, which has been getting bigger. I did not ask to see it, of course, but said that I would report to you. They are poor people, my lord.'

Richard nodded. 'It is as I feared. What of the toe of Quinn of Ryhill, the hanged man?'

Hubert looked uncertainly in the direction of the court clerk, who was standing at the desk arranging his notes from the court for Richard to go over. 'I said that he could give it to the other person and let them do what they had to do.'

'Did you find out who that was? Man or woman?'

Hubert shook his head apologetically. 'I did not think you wanted to know that, my lord. I can go back and find out.'

'No need at this stage. But after we have finished here, I want you to seek out Doctor Flynn, who was in court today. Take him to see Hal's mother and we will have his opinion. Tell him the court will pay his fee for this also.'

He nodded to John of Flanshaw and sat down at the desk to begin reading the notes. Picking up a quill, he dipped it in the pot and made certain alterations, all of which the bailiff acknowledged deferentially. Hubert sat on a stool and watched him with interest.

'I apologise for my lack of learning, Sir Richard,' John said. 'I wish that I had more Latin than I have and yet more ability in transcribing the spelling of it.'

'No apology needed, John. It is ultimately my responsibility to ensure that what is written is a correct version of the judgements I have given. These records will be there for others to see over the centuries.'

There was a knock on the door and one of the constables opened it upon the bailiff's order to come in.

'Master Geoffrey Hopwood of Kirkthorpe craves an audience with Sir Richard Lee,' he said to John of Flanshaw.

Richard nodded to the bailiff and the franklin was ushered in. He was a fairly stocky fellow with a paunch that protruded slightly above his belt. He bowed extravagantly and swept off his hat. As he did so, the sheath of a bollock dagger hanging from his belt struck the white silk purse next to it and made a chinking sound. Intrigued by the sound of the dagger on a full purse of coins, Hubert looked up with interest. Folding his arms, he languidly watched the franklin, having already formed the opinion that he was something of a popinjay.

'Sir Richard, I wanted to thank you for your leniency over the case of Peter Plowman,' said the franklin. 'He is a good lad and in my opinion does not merit death by hanging. It would be the death of his mother, a good woman.'

'I have not yet decided his case,' Richard replied. 'I have merely overturned the guilty verdict. I agree that death for stealing a sheep is a harsh sentence, yet it is a punishment within the law. I am not convinced that it should be considered a theft, but a reclamation of a debt, as he maintained. Although the way he did it does not justify what he did. I intend to ponder over this.'

'Indeed, I understand that, but I am glad that I do not need to pay a visit to his mother to tell her bad news, for I like to look after all my tenants and servants. I would also like to invite you to my manor house at Kirkthorpe tomorrow. I have arranged a small feast to celebrate St Julian's Day. I would be pleased if your wife would also do me the honour of coming.' At this Hubert's interest was piqued, and he shifted on his stool. The franklin turned at the sound and smiled ingratiatingly. 'And your man is also welcome. I have some most excellent ales and wines, and there shall be merriment and amusement aplenty.'

'Unfortunately,' said Richard, 'Lady Wilhelmina is with child and must stay at my manor in Durkar. Also, I have to pay a visit to a reeve in Wragby tomorrow. My father-in-law, Sir Thomas Deyville, is unwell and I am overseeing some of the affairs of the Manor of Wakefield.'

Geoffrey Hopwood looked crestfallen. 'I am sorry that your wife cannot come, but she must take care of her child to be.' Then he beamed. 'But actually, this may yet be a most fortunate happenstance. You must mean Gembert Cooper, the reeve of Kirkthorpe and of Wragby. He does much work for me. He and his aunt are coming to the feast, and you could see him there.'

Richard pouted thoughtfully, then seeing Hubert's look of disappointment, he smiled and nodded. 'As you say, that is indeed fortunate. I accept your offer of hospitality tomorrow.'

The franklin nodded affably. 'Then perhaps you will attend a service beforehand at the Church of St Peter in Kirkthorpe at the ninth hour. Then I will look forward to welcoming you to my humble home.' He bowed and left.

Once he had gone and Richard had finished his work with John of Flanshaw, Hubert and Richard left the Moot Hall and made their way to the stables to collect their horses.

'I saw how your eyes filled with enthusiasm at the mention of Hopwood's ale, Hubert.'

'Aye, my lord. I look forward to sampling it, but I must say that I am not sure if I trust the man.'

'How so, Hubert?'

'It is his dagger, my lord. He dresses in all that finery, with a full purse of white silk, and yet he wears a crude wooden-handled bollock dagger. But did you see the size of the two bollocks? They are larger than you would normally see. It is as if he is saying, "look at how rich I am, but if you try to take my purse, I will stick my bollock dagger in your ribs. I am a man!" If his weapon was just to show his wealth and rank, then a baselard or an anelace like yours would be a fitting dagger for a gentleman.'

Richard lay a hand on his friend's shoulder. 'Is there nothing that you do not know about weaponry, Hubert?'

'I learn every day, my lord. I do not want to arrive at the day I have a fight when my opponent knows something that I do not.'

Richard laughed. 'A good philosophy to hold. And I take your point about the dagger that he carries. I had not spotted it myself, but I will observe later.' He told him of the case of Peter Plowman and of his overturning of the verdict for the moment. 'To tell you the truth, Hubert, there is something about the case that puzzles me, although I cannot put my finger on it. It may be as you say, that there is something about this franklin that is not quite as it should be.'

CHAPTER THREE

Richard had softly kissed Lady Wilhelmina's brow and left her sleeping the following morning to ride by moonlight to Sandal Castle to meet the physician Doctor Flynn so that he could be present when he bled his father-in-law.

The Steward of Sandal Castle was not in a good temper as the physician opened the wooden shutters of the slit window in his chamber to allow moonlight to add to the light thrown out from the trio of candles that had been lit for the procedure.

'A plague on that physic you gave me,' Sir Thomas grumbled as he lay on his stomach on his bed while the physician prepared his paraphernalia to open the veins on the backs of both knees. 'I was on the garderobe half the night.'

'Exactly as I intended it, Sir Thomas,' Doctor Flynn replied, placing a metal basin beside the knight's legs. 'As I told you yesterday, you have a humoral imbalance with too much black bile and also too much stagnant blood. The purgative has been working to remove the black bile, and now I shall take off some of the morbific blood.'

Richard sat on a chair at the head of the bed so that he would be able to talk to his father-in-law to help distract him. He noticed the embossed lines inside the metal bowl indicating quantities of blood when they were reached. 'I am sure that you will begin to feel better once your humours improve, father-in-law.'

Sir Thomas harrumphed. 'I would feel better with a tankard of ale or a mug of mead rather than that milk and sops that this leech insists I take.'

The physician reached into his sleeve and withdrew a small waxen model that he had made. He had moulded it into the shape of a man and wrapped Sir Thomas's hair round the head like a beard and scalp hair. 'This is the image I said I would make of you, Sir Thomas. It will work in sympathy with you and help to restore the balance of humours.'

Sir Thomas looked at Richard, who tried to disguise his own scepticism. The Steward of Sandal Castle frowned and then shrugged his shoulders. 'What care I if it is nothing but sorcery, as long as it works.'

Doctor Flynn gave him a haughty look. 'It is not sorcery, but a legitimate part of the art of physic, Sir Thomas, and you will see that it works.' After laying the model on Sir Thomas's back between his shoulder blades, he took out a leather case from his medical satchel and laid it on the bed. 'Once all of the elements of the treatment work together, your ill humour will improve and life will not look so bleak, Sir Thomas. Now, prepare yourself, for the moment of bleeding is nigh upon us.' He removed a lancet with a double-edged blade from the case and appraised its sharpness with the tip of his finger. With his free hand, he palpated the veins in the back of Sir Thomas's right knee.

From the bailey of the castle far below, they heard a cockerel crow.

'Cockcrow, father-in-law,' said Sir Richard. 'Hold my hand and grip hard if it will help.'

'Pah! I am no maid that needs a hand held. Do your worst, Doctor Leech.'

The physician gave a short laugh. 'Patients usually ask me to do my best, Sir Thomas. And actually, that is exactly what I shall do, for this skill that I possess in bleeding has been long-learned, and each time I open a vein is better than the last and that is to your advantage.' He stretched the vein between finger and thumb so that it bulged and then deftly incised it along its length for half an inch. Immediately blood spurted out, and he positioned the basin to catch the small fountain where it hit the metal bowl with a zinging noise. 'I have made the cut along the vein so it will bleed as much as I need and will stop when I apply pressure on it. It will heal rapidly,' he explained. 'I will bleed the other leg in a few minutes and then tomorrow an hour after cockcrow I will do the same. From the third day onwards, I shall use leeches upon the appropriate bleeding points to remove smaller amounts of blood.'

'Why a different time?' Sir Thomas asked with a hint of sarcasm. 'Is it that you need an extra hour in bed?'

Doctor Flynn smiled thinly at Richard and patted the volvella hanging from his belt. 'No, Sir Thomas, it is because I have consulted my charts and calculated the time and amount of blood to be taken.'

'The art of physic is amazing to behold,' said Richard as he watched the physician then nick the backs of the wax model's legs with his lancet, leaving a drop of blood on each. *Do I dare ask the physician to help restore my humours to stop my guilty ruminations about Quinn of Ryhill?* he wondered. *Can this wax doll really take a bad humour away and bring happiness where there is sadness and grief?* But instead he told Sir Thomas of his intention to go to St Peter's Church in Kirkthorpe before going to Kirkthorpe Hall to enjoy Master Geoffrey Hopwood's planned feast to honour St Julian's Day.

'Ah, a capricious fellow is Hopwood. He was as staunch a supporter of King Edward the rightful sovereign as I at one stage, but as a knight of the shire he voted at the last parliament in favour of the King's deposition and his son's coronation.'

'It would not be easy to vote otherwise, father-in-law,' said Richard, 'not when Queen Isabella and Roger Mortimer have seized power and imprisoned King Edward the Second.'

Sir Thomas grunted. 'What say you, Doctor Leech?'

'You mean, Doctor Flynn,' the physician replied, suppressing any testiness from his voice. 'I, sir, am a mere physician and keep clear of politics as much as I can. I would only say that whoever can bring peace to the realm would have my backing and my blessing. Just as long as there is no bloodshed or persecution. As an Irishman, I have seen what persecution can do to people and it is to be avoided at all costs.'

Sunlight was streaming into the chamber and the moon had all but vanished by the time the bleeding was done and the incisions bound with bandages.

'I will leave more purgative for you to take this evening, Sir Thomas,' Doctor Flynn said as he came back into the chamber from the garderobe, where he had disposed of the blood. 'And I will leave a bottle of *aurum potabile* with Wilfred, your head servant. He will give you a dose seven times a day.'

Sir Thomas grunted as Richard and the physician left him alone.

As they had done the day before, Richard and Hubert rode out of Sandal Castle with Doctor Flynn. On this occasion, all three took the turning for Agbrigg and passed the gibbet from which hanged the corpse of Quinn of Ryhill.

'Poor fellow,' remarked the physician.

'He was a felon, found guilty of murder,' responded Hubert.

'I don't doubt it. I just feel sorrow for a soul to be deprived of a grave in consecrated ground.'

Much the same thought that I have, thought Richard. But instead he said, 'The law is the law. If such a felony is committed, the perpetrator's life is forfeit, their possessions and wealth are to be confiscated, and whether or not the soul enters heaven or goes to hell is up to the Lord and St Peter.'

As they rode on, the conversation turned inevitably to the boy Hal and his mother's wen.

'As I am sure that your man Hubert told you after we visited her yesterday, this woman's problem is not a simple wen, but a canker.'

'Can you cure it, Doctor Flynn?' Richard asked.

'I fear not, but I may be able to shrink it with cautery and help her pain and her tiredness with physic. It would be as well if her priest begins to prepare her for the journey that lies ahead of her.'

Hubert frowned. 'Then young Hal and his sister will be alone in this world. It will be difficult for them.'

Richard sighed. 'As it is for many folk, Hubert.' Then to Doctor Flynn: 'I was surprised to see you at court yesterday.'

The physician stroked his red beard as if to ensure that no hairs were out of place. 'It was something of a surprise for me, too, Sir Richard. I had intended to visit a few more patients after I had seen Robert Jenkin at the tannery, but the franklin, Master Geoffrey Hopwood sought me out, since I had treated Cedric of Sharlston. He thought that it would be as well if I attended the court, since his injury could be important in the case of Peter Plowman.'

Ah, so the franklin was keen to ensure that Cedric of Sharlston did not exaggerate the severity of his wound. Interesting! 'Hubert and I are going to enjoy his hospitality now,' Richard replied.

'I know, Sir Richard. I heard you say so to Sir Thomas.'

I did indeed, but I just wanted to see if you would feign surprise or show any other reaction.

59

The physician pointed to a humble house some distance off the main trail. 'I bid you enjoy the franklin's feast. I will begin my treatment of Hal's mother, the widow Mistress Clegg. You did say that the court would pay my fees, Sir Richard?'

With an inward smile, Richard affirmed the payment and they parted.

'I told Doctor Flynn that yesterday, my lord,' said Hubert. 'Yet he asked me again after we left her and he asked you just now. I think the physician has a partiality to coins.'

Richard smiled as they rode on, but he said nothing. *And you, good Hubert, are a good judge of character, methinks.*

Kirkthorpe was a small hamlet three miles from Wakefield, in the middle of the considerable estate owned by the franklin, Geoffrey Hopwood. It had a scatter of simple wattle and daub homes, some animal pens and stacks of dried cow dung cakes circling a small duck pond. The Church of St Peter was an old Saxon timber-built structure with a thatched roof and a small square tower which looked more like a little barn than the more substantial stone Norman churches. It was clear that people from the hamlet had come, together with folk from surrounding holdings and farms, for the St Julian's Day celebrations.

An ostler had taken Richard and Hubert's horses and the franklin himself greeted them at the door and personally led them to the pew at the front of the church where several gentlefolk were already sitting. The nave was full of people of all classes, from nobles to yeomanry, servants and working folks. Richard recognised many as having come from as far as Wakefield and Pontefract.

'This is my daughter, Rowena,' Geoffrey said, introducing an attractive young maid of about sixteen or seventeen in a wimple and a green gown, who was sitting demurely next to an older man.

Richard immediately saw that she was holding a long staff and seemed to be looking straight ahead. As she turned at his voice, he saw that the pupils of her eyes were not black but dull white. She immediately rose and curtsied in his direction.

'Rowena has been robbed of most of her sight since early childhood,' the franklin explained. 'I have been her eyes ever since her poor mother passed away when she was young.'

Rowena nodded. 'I can see a little, Sir Richard. I mostly see shadows, but you would be surprised how much you can tell about a person's shadow.' She lifted her staff and added, 'My stick also tells me if anything is lurking in the shadows.'

A clever maid, of that I have no doubt, Richard thought. 'A pleasure to meet you, Rowena,' he replied and received a dainty smile and another bob of her head in return.

'Sir Basil de Roxford and his wife, Lady Katherine,' Master Hopwood said next, introducing Richard to the older man, who was in his late fifties and his younger wife, a handsome woman of around forty years.

As Richard and Hubert bowed to them, the franklin gestured to a very tall man and a woman sitting beyond them. The man had a pinched nose and a beard cut in a very severe manner that made him look totally humourless. By contrast, the woman had a naturally smiling visage.

'Matthew Drewitt, the manciple of St Leonard's Priory and his sister, Mistress Myrtle Drewitt.'

Another couple sitting at the far end of the pew bent forward to smile and nod at Richard.

'And finally, my very good friend, Gembert Cooper the reeve of Kirkthorpe and Wragby and his aunt, Mistress Mary Wisley. You said that you had to have discussions with him.'

Introductions completed, the franklin sat beside his daughter and Richard and Hubert took their seats at the end of the pew. 'Father Alban is our priest and an enthralling orator. His services are always a joy to listen to.'

'Your priest, you say?' Richard asked in surprise, for the only Father Alban he knew of was the priest of the Church of All Saints in Wakefield. He had only held the office for a year after the departure of the previous incumbent, Father Daniel, who was also known as the Wakefield Master, the playwright of the Wakefield Mysteries, and had left to take up a post at the University of Oxford.

'Well, he is not exactly our priest,' Master Hopwood returned. 'He is also the priest at the Church of All Saints in Wakefield, but he is always happy to take services here.' He leaned towards Richard and gently nudged him with his elbow. 'He and I get along very well, even if we do have slight differences of opinion now and then.'

Richard smiled knowingly. 'I know Father Alban and have heard him preach at All Saints. I understand what you mean.'

A man of mixed humours, I imagine Doctor Flynn would say. He either bores one to sleep or he is all inflamed about something. I am not certain that I would have called him an orator.

A small handbell was rung from the back of the nave and all present turned to see Father Alban striding up the aisle. He was a skeletally thin man in his mid-forties with a slight stoop, who was already balding so that his tonsure consisted only of a half circle of hair round the back of his head from ear to ear. He was wearing a brown hooded habit and carrying the handbell. A pace behind him was another cleric, a man more than a decade younger, with black hair and a neat tonsure, wearing a black mantle over a white habit. A patina of dust and mud marks suggested that he had been travelling and had not had time or opportunity to change into fresher clothes. He was carrying a cross.

Again, Geoffrey Hopwood leaned closer and whispered to Richard, 'Father Alban is coming to the feast, as is Brother Fergus.'

'A Dominican friar, I see,' said Richard.

'Yes, from the Black Abbey at Kilkenny in Ireland. He is on his way to St Leonard's Priory at Ackworth Moor. Matthew Drewitt had arranged for him to stay with Father Alban in Wakefield last night before travelling on to the priory. I met him yesterday and extended my invitation to the feast today. It was Father Alban's idea that he should help him worship at the service here today.'

Reaching the altar, Father Alban rang the bell a final time and laid it on the floor, and then he and Brother Fergus kissed the altar. Turning to the congregation, he welcomed them and introduced the other priest, before beginning the mass and leading prayers.

Once complete, he mounted the pulpit and surveyed them. With his slightly hooked nose and stoop, he had the appearance of a bird of prey. He held his arms out as he addressed them.

'Welcome everyone on this great day when we celebrate St Julian. But what do you know of our saint?' There were murmurings, but no one had the chance to speak, as he went straight into a description. 'I will tell you the history. Julian was a nobleman in the south of the country, who loved above all else to go hunting boar with a lance or deer with bow and arrow. One day, he chased a stag over many miles and shot it. But for some reason his aim was not as good as usual and he wounded the beast, which led him some miles more before collapsing. When Julian finally approached it, he was amazed to hear it talk to him.'

Hubert let out a soft whistle of amazement, just as many of the congregation also expressed incredulity in one way or another. The priest watched them and waited for silence before continuing.

'The stag was dying, but it asked why Julian was so intent upon killing it. "Is it that you are starving and want me for food, to feed a family?" it asked. Julian shook his head. "No, I hunted you for sport." The stag was indignant. "For sport, you would take a life," it replied. "In that case, as I look into death I can see what lies ahead in the future for you. You will indeed become a famous hunter. You will gain riches and honours from the King." Julian was pleased to hear this and almost regretted having shot the beast. "But there is more," said the stag, as it lay breathing heavily. "One day, great hunter that you will be, you will kill your mother and father." The stag died there and then, and Julian carried it back to his castle and had his servants prepare its hide and sent the body to be butchered. He put the head upon the wall of his hall and he forgot all about the stag's prophesy, preferring to tell himself that exhaustion after the hunt must have made him drowsy so that he'd wounded the animal rather than killed it outright, and that drowsiness had made him see and hear things that were not possible.'

Father Alban slowly turned his head this way and that, surveying the congregation before going on.

'As time went by, he did become a great and famous hunter. The King rewarded him richly and bestowed many honours upon him. He married a rich widow and his estates prospered. One week he went away on a hunt, and while he was abroad, his mother and father arrived at his castle, seeking him. His wife knew nothing of the prophesy, yet knowing who the couple were, she put them up for the night in the master's bedroom. When Julian returned unexpectedly later that night and saw a man and a woman in his bed, he suspected the worst. He thought that the woman was his wife and that she was committing adultery with another man. He killed them both.'

Rowena the franklin's daughter gave a gasp of astonishment and covered her ears, horrified at the tale of adultery and death. Her father put a comforting hand on hers and squeezed it reassuringly. Others had similar reactions, and once again Father Alban waited for silence before continuing.

'His wife had gone to church, but when she returned she found him drunk. He saw her and at first thought she was a ghost and fell to his knees in terror. He told her that he thought he had killed her and a lover and, dragging her, showed her the horrific scene in the bedroom. By torchlight he recognised his parents and, overcome with remorse and guilt, fled the castle. He resolved to do a fitting penance.'

Father Alban looked about the congregation. He slowly repeated the words, 'remorse and guilt.' He looked at all the people, his eyes widening as if he was looking into their souls and seeing the sins they had committed.

Richard felt the guilt that had been nagging at him resurface again, and he tried to dismiss it from his mind.

Father Alban continued, 'So Julian travelled far away, where no one knew him, but his wife found him and they built an inn for travellers near a wide river, and also began a hospital for the poor. One day a leper came, begging for food and a bed. Julian let him have his own bed. He knew nought that the leper was in fact a messenger from God who had been sent to test him. He was forgiven and he became the patron saint of hotel keepers and travellers.' He pointed at the franklin sitting on the front pew. 'And today, this twelfth day of February, on St Julian's Day, our good franklin, Master Geoffrey Hopwood of Kirkthorpe has invited all to the feast at his manor house, Kirkthorpe Hall. For this we thank him, but I want you all to think about your own sins. The things that you feel guilty about. The things that tomorrow you will want to make a confession about.'

Yet again he surveyed the people in the church, like a bird of prey, swivelling his head right and left, as if sensing quarry in the flock. His voice rose in volume as his passion seemed to increase. 'In the story of St Julian, we can learn about sin! Think of the sin of pride!' He slapped the pulpit with his hands to emphasise the word. 'And we think of adultery, that is a deadly sin!' Pausing, he slapped the pulpit a second time. 'Which can lead to murder!' Another slap on the wood. 'And the guilt and regret that must follow and eat into your soul.'

All around the church, people were nodding and muttering affirmations of agreement. Many made the sign of the cross over their hearts. Richard noticed Hubert had placed his hand flat on his chest, over his precious arrowhead.

The priest's eyes again seemed to enlarge as his fervour for his speech rose. Little flecks of spittle had formed at the corners of his mouth, and he wiped them away with the back of his hand. 'And there is much to feel guilty and yet angry about in this land. The King was forced to abdicate and he is held prisoner. His son is now anointed as sovereign in his stead, even though he is but a child.' He paused again, to take a deep breath. 'And an adulterous couple now hold the reins of power in this land.'

This time, stunned silence greeted him.

Dangerous talk from Father Alban, thought Richard. *Some would even call it treasonable.*

'There is evil in the land, spreading like a canker,' Father Alban continued. 'Malign forces threaten to destroy everything we hold dear, everything we hold sacred. All of us must guard against the forces of darkness that creep into every city, town and village. That threatens to taint every hamlet, every home and ultimately reach and corrupt every person in the land — if you allow it!'

Richard looked sideways at the franklin and at the other people sitting on the pew beside him. Every one of them looked shocked and unsure of how to react.

'Do you wish me to do anything, my lord?' Hubert whispered, but Richard raised a finger and waggled it from side to side.

'And now,' Father Alban went on, his voice reverted to normal volume, 'I want you all to meet Brother Fergus of the Black Abbey in Kilkenny, which is in Ireland. He is a Dominican friar who has been sent to St Leonard's Priory on Ackworth Moor. I have asked him to tell you about the darkness that is creeping over our land, for he comes to St Leonard's on a mission from Bishop Ledrede of Ossory in Ireland.' He climbed down from the pulpit and the Dominican friar took his place.

'I thank Father Alban and I thank all of you for listening to me,' Brother Fergus began in an unmistakeable Irish brogue. 'I am a humble friar of the Dominican order, sent by my bishop to St Leonard's Priory to assist and pray for the good people of this area. There is indeed evil creeping over the land. My bishop told us about the witchcraft and sorcery that broke out here four years ago in Pontefract. Spells were cast against King Edward the Second and against the Earl of Winchester and his son, the Lord of Glamorgan. As I am sure you all know, the earl, the elder Hugh le Despenser, was executed upon the orders of Queen Isabella, King Edward's wife, and Roger Mortimer, Lord of Wigmore, this October past. Then his son, the younger Hugh le Despenser, was executed last November. It seems that those spells have worked.'

People shifted uneasily in their seats and again the church filled with anxious mutterings and gasps.

The friar paused and raised his hands until there was silence again. 'His Holiness Pope John, the twenty-second of his name, had an attempt on his life by witchcraft and ten years ago issued a papal bull called *Super Illius Specula*, which makes the practice of sorcery and witchcraft a heresy, punishable by excommunication and then by death. Our own Bishop Richard Ledrede was appointed to Ossory by His Holiness in Avignon and discovered four years ago that witchcraft was being widely practised. A coven of these wicked creatures was uncovered and he brought them to trial, and wrung confessions about spells they had cast, murders they had caused and carnal orgies they had had with demonic familiar spirits.'

The congregation became more agitated on hearing all of this; many began mumbling prayers, signing the cross and covering their eyes.

'It was my privilege to assist Bishop Richard, so that eight of these creatures were executed, either by hanging, drowning or burning at the stake.' His face contorted in revulsion as he described all of this. 'Only two escaped. They vanished and no one knows where they disappeared to.'

'To hell!' someone bravely cried out.

'As we have had experience of witchcraft, Bishop Ledrede has sent several brother friars to other priories and abbeys of our order throughout Ireland and England to ensure that it does not start up again. He has sent me to St Leonard's Priory, which is a subsidiary of St Richard's Friary in Pontefract, for he is concerned that since this area has been badly affected once so it could be again. So, good people of Kirkthorpe, you must all be alert to the danger that witches pose. If you suspect it is happening, if you believe there are witches or sorcerers practising their evil art, you must report them. I will be found at St Leonard's Priory and I have authority to bring such evildoers before the Ecclesiastic Courts. Remember, the Bible says that one must not suffer a witch to live.'

In front of the altar, Father Alban stood with his hands hidden in the crossed sleeves of his habit. He called out loudly, 'All adulterers, thieves, heretics, and all who practice unholy arts of any type shall be revealed and will receive God's punishment. The gates of hell await those who sin.'

Richard noted that almost everyone in the congregation was alarmed and agitated, including the franklin and his daughter. Rowena had reached out for her father's hand, and he cradled it in both of his.

He was not aware that someone in the church had already decided that there would be a death by the morrow.

Kirkthorpe Hall, Geoffrey Hopwood's home, was a large two-storey mansion inside a high-walled enclosure about two furlongs from the church. The main guests who had been sitting on the front pew travelled on horse, pony or donkey, or by covered coach, which had been tended at the church gates by a couple of ostler boys. Richard noticed that Sir Basil de Roxford, looking quite grizzled and lame, was helped up into his saddle by a male servant who had been waiting at the rear of the nave. Lady Katherine then allowed him to help her onto a covered coach, which he climbed in to take the reins of a horse.

Gembert Cooper, the reeve of Kirkthorpe and Wragby, helped his aunt Mistress Wisley, and the maniple Matthew Drewitt aided his sister Mistress Drewitt. Once Geoffrey Hopwood had helped his daughter Rowena onto a donkey and himself mounted a grey mare they set off, the franklin leading his daughter's donkey and the procession.

'A strange service, my lord,' Hubert said in a hushed voice as they took up the rear of the mounted guests ahead of locals who made their way on foot. 'I did not like hearing that friar talk of witchcraft and sorcery. I thought we had enough of that four years ago. I wondered if you might —?'

'Challenge them?' Richard anticipated. He shook his head. 'A church is not the place for it, Hubert. The people were stirred up with fear enough. I imagine that if the franklin is as hospitable as you have heard, then there may be much ale, mead and wine drunk to soothe their qualms.'

'I hope so indeed, my lord,' Hubert replied with a grin. 'I can smell woodsmoke and roasting pig, unless my nose deceives me.'

As they approached Kirkthorpe Hall, the gates of the enclosure wall were suddenly thrown open and music was played on drums, tabards, trumpets and bagpipes.

'Welcome, my friends,' cried out the franklin, turning in his saddle. 'As a devoted follower of St Julian, this day my home is your home — for all of you. There is food and drink aplenty, and today you will be merry.'

As the procession entered, tumblers, jugglers and a fire-eater appeared and the musicians mingled with the guests. A pig was indeed being roasted on a fire and tents and booths were set up in front of the manor house, where all manner of drinks and a huge variety of food could be obtained.

'It is my pleasure to treat the people who work my land, tending my crops and animals, and those farmers who rent my fields,' Master Hopwood proclaimed as he led his main guests into the great hall of his home.

At the threshold, Hubert asked in a whisper, his tone hopeful, 'Shall I stay outside, my lord?'

'Yes, indeed. Find out what these folk thought of the service and of the things the two priests talked about.'

A long table was laid out with places set for eleven people. Geoffrey Hopwood stood at the head of the table and directed people where to sit. His daughter Rowena sat on his left with Father Alban opposite her. Next to them he put the lame Sir Basil de Roxford with Lady Katherine across from him, next to Rowena. Mary Wisley sat next to Sir Basil and her nephew, the reeve Gembert Cooper, sat beside Lady Katherine.

'Sir Richard, you will please sit next to Mistress Wisley, and Brother Fergus will sit opposite you.'

Richard stood behind the chair allotted to him and smiled at Myrtle Drewitt, the manciple's sister, as she took her place beside him, across from Matthew Drewitt.

The men assisted the ladies to sit before taking their own seats.

'My friends,' said the franklin. 'It is my honour to entertain you at this meagre feast in praise of St Julian. As you will soon find, I am an unashamed devotee of St Julian and I like to think of myself as a son of Epicurus. Those outside are this day being rewarded with a fair and a feast, entirely at my expense,' he said, tapping his white silk purse, and he beamed as the guests at the table politely applauded and congratulated him on his generosity.

'No, you are too kind,' he went on, waving his hand modestly. 'But I do want you to savour and enjoy the ten courses that my cooks have prepared for you. There will be roast meats, baked pheasants, geese, wildfowl — all bred for the table on my lands. There will be pullets and pork, peacocks in pepper sauce, lobster and crayfish in vinegar, fried eels in sugar and mackerels in —' He paused, his cheeks rosy as he enthused about food, clearly a passion of his. 'Well, let me leave you with some surprises! And there will be wine from my cellars, and ale or porter for those who prefer it, or even milk from my very own cows.' He turned to his daughter and placed a hand on her shoulder. 'My dearest daughter has actually arranged the order of the dishes and supervised the cook. For this I thank her.'

Rowena was looking straight ahead, but raised a hand to pat her father's. Richard thought that the smile she gave seemed somehow contrived.

Master Hopwood continued. 'But before we begin, I will ask Father Alban to say grace.'

Father Alban rose and surveyed the guests in that hawk-like manner he had exhibited while standing in the pulpit in the church. He enunciated a grace in Latin and then in English before sitting down.

Taking his seat, the franklin laughed and reached for a handbell beside a goblet and rang it. Instantly, doors opened, and a team of servants filed in, led by a butler who began directing his subordinates with almost military precision. A pantler and his assistants began serving trenchers for all, and finger bowls for every two people. A stream of serving women followed with salvers of cut meats, steaming pots and jugs of wine and ale.

Father Alban raised a hand when he was approached with wine. 'Milk only for me, and I shall only have bread to eat and mayhap some cheese and an apple.'

From further down the table, Brother Fergus also piped up. 'I would like to applaud Father Alban's abstemiousness, yet I have travelled far, journeyed across the sea, ridden and walked more miles than I care to recount, but as this feast day is in honour of the sainted Julian, I can honestly say that I am looking forward to indulging myself to the limit.' He raised his goblet, which had just been filled by a serving maid. 'I drink to you, Master Hopwood, to your lovely daughter Rowena and to all the fair ladies at this table.'

The franklin immediately thumped the table with his empty goblet several times and chuckled. 'Well said, Brother Fergus. I have heard that Ireland is inhabited with people who have the gift of speechmaking. Once Father Alban has his milk and everyone has a beaker or a goblet filled with the drink of their choice, we shall drink your health and the success of your mission.'

Richard looked along the table and noted the steely look that Father Alban bestowed upon the Dominican friar.

The meal progressed, and as one delicacy followed another, the gathering began to converse. As was his habit, Richard kept an ear out for what was happening along the length of the table. Father Alban's sonorous voice made it obvious that he had not finished discussing St Julian, hospitality and overindulgence. He heard the franklin protest, and he heard Rowena chirp in an intelligent remark here and there. And he heard Sir Basil de Roxford and Lady Katherine remonstrate and disagree with him.

Richard looked at the knight and his wife and wondered how the couple so different in age had met and how long they had been married, and if they had children.

He immediately found himself talking with Gembert Cooper and his aunt, Mistress Mary Wisley. The reeve was a slender and quick-witted fellow with a closely trimmed beard and hair shorn short to give him an overall well-groomed appearance. He was ready with answers about his duties as the village reeve and swift to praise his host, the franklin.

'Master Hopwood gives me a free hand in village matters and is always generous with his advice when asked,' he volunteered. 'He was kind enough to provide materials for me to extend my house when my aunt here came to live with me after her husband died.'

Mistress Wisley was also of a cheerful disposition. A pretty woman, also slim of waist and with an almost permanent smile on her cherubic lips, she was equally complementary about Rowena. 'She is a most able young woman. Such a shame that she is almost blind. Her father has schooled her well. She can speak two languages, plays the lute and has many accomplishments. I have never known one so young have such a knowledge of plants and herbs. She is forever making potions and creams for her father's tenants.' She pursed her lips and leaned towards him to whisper. 'I do not know if I should say it, but there is talk that her lack of sight is the result of a curse.'

'A curse on her?' Richard queried, speaking softly.

'On her father, from someone he once wronged. A witch.'

Gembert Cooper leaned across the table to hear them. 'What is that you are saying, Mary?' he asked, beetling his brows.

'Oh nothing. I was just saying to Sir Richard that Rowena is very accomplished and is nearing the age when I was betrothed.'

I think the reeve heard her and did not think that she should have told me what may be mere village gossip. That is interesting, since such gossip often holds a kernel of truth. 'I am sorry to hear that you lost your husband, Mistress Wisley,' said Richard. 'Yet I am confused. You are Master Gembert's aunt, yet you do not look —'

Gembert Cooper slapped the table. 'Everyone says that, Sir Richard. Mayhap it is because I look older than I am?' he said jestingly, as if to cover up the consternation that Richard thought he had detected in his face a moment before.

'Nephew, I shall scold you later,' Mary Wisley replied. 'No, Sir Richard, the truth is that I am the youngest of thirteen children and Gembert is the first of my eldest sister's children. We are actually of a similar age.'

Mistress Myrtle Drewitt on Richard's other side sipped her wine and then dabbed her mouth with her napkin. 'I would not be so swift in marrying Rowena off, Mistress Wisley. Not all women want to marry, especially if they have many interests. I, for example, am perfectly happy to support my brother, the manciple at St Leonard's Priory. I too have cultivated many interests and have been permitted by the prior since I arrived and showed my knowledge of herbs and physic to run our dispensary and help in the hospital, which is free to all who need it.'

Richard thought that everything about Mistress Drewitt seemed prim and direct. She sat upright and used her personal food knife with precision, cutting food into delicate, even amounts which she ate with great care. He did not think one would call her a beauty, but she had a strangely austere sort of charm.

'My sister has a rare aptitude for plant lore, Sir Richard,' offered Matthew Drewitt the manciple. 'I am fortunate to have her, just as St Leonard's is benefitting from her skills in physic and herbs.'

Brother Fergus finished chewing on a sweetbread and took a hefty swallow of ale to wash it down. 'Well now, that is wonderful, Mistress Drewitt, but have you not considered entering our order as a nun?'

Myrtle Drewitt and her brother exchanged glances before she turned to the Irish friar. 'I think I can be of most service as a lay person.'

Brother Fergus smiled at her. 'Of course, Mistress. I understand, as taking holy orders demands many things of us. But I look forward to living at the priory and seeing your dispensary myself.'

Richard had noted the wary look that had passed between the Drewitts. 'You talked about witchcraft in Kilkenny,' Richard said to the friar. 'I had heard about a witch being burned at the stake a few years ago.'

'Three years ago,' replied Brother Fergus, becoming more serious. 'We sent her to hell and eternal damnation as she deserved. Petronella de Meath was her name. She was an acolyte of Dame Alice Kyteler. Dame Alice was a usurer, a moneylender, which itself is a crime. Worse still, she was a murderess as well as a witch. She poisoned not one, but four husbands!' His voice had risen and his face had flushed. 'She was again put on trial for witchcraft with her minions when Bishop Ledrede discovered her demonic activities. We will never know how she did it, or where she went to, but it is my belief that she used witchcraft to disappear herself along with her familiar spirit, a demon they sometimes called Robin Artisson and other times Robin, son of Art. It is likely that she is practising her art somewhere in the country to this day. But she is just one of a legion of witches that are now blighting our country. That is why Bishop Ledrede has sent friars like myself to our holy priories and monasteries all over the country.'

Everyone at the table had turned, startled by the sudden vehemence in the friar's voice, especially as he talked of murders. Richard asked him to enlighten them and he did, recounting how Dame Alice Kyteler had married four times, each time accumulating more wealth. It was claimed that she had poisoned four husbands and succeeded in killing the first three. When John le Poer — her fourth husband — survived, he and the children of her previous husbands claimed that she had caused the men's deaths. She was put on trial, but she was acquitted and exonerated.

'Undoubtedly, she did it through charms,' said Brother Fergus. 'She even bewitched her fourth husband's brother, Arnold le Poer, who is now the Seneschal of Kilkenny, during her trial for witchcraft so that he aided her against Bishop Ledrede.'

'But the law is the law,' said Richard. 'If the court found her innocent, that is the end of the matter.'

'Then what use is the law?' Father Alban erupted angrily from the other end of the table. 'Wrongdoers should be punished if they offend God's laws. Murderers, thieves, adulterers. All of them should get the punishment they deserve. The Bible says so.'

The franklin leaned forward in his chair. 'The law should be just, but it can be justly lenient. We saw that yesterday with our good Sir Richard Lee and the case of Peter Plowman.'

'Pah!' expostulated Father Alban. 'The law should be consistent. Just over a week ago, the law hanged Quinn of Ryhill after he slew Bryce-a-Green. Whyfor was Peter

Plowman not also executed?' He stared hard at the franklin. 'What say you to that, Master Hopwood? Why should there be leniency? I would not want to be tried in such a court that is not consistent.'

Richard felt that cold, uncomfortable, hollow feeling as guilt and doubt swept over him again. *Is the priest saying what others must be thinking? That I hanged one man and yet have been too lenient with another?* 'As I said earlier,' Richard replied, not allowing himself to show any temper, especially when he was feeling doubtful about his own decision-making. 'The law is the law, and the court can make its judgement based on that.'

'The jury found Peter Plowman guilty and you overturned it,' Father Alban persisted.

Has the priest been drinking? I thought he was only having milk.

Geoffrey Hopwood tried to placate the priest. 'Calm yourself, Father Alban. As a religious man, you need have no concerns about the courts. You could always claim Benefit of Clergy. All you need to do is recite some piece from the Bible.' He grinned at everyone seated. 'I have always ensured that I have enough Latin at the ready, for I would claim Benefit of Clergy and be tried by an Ecclesiastic Court, where the sentences are lenient.' He gave a chuckle, then spoke out loudly and clearly, '*Amen dico vobis quia unus vestrum me traditurus est.*' Then with a smile, he gave the translation in English: 'Truly I say to you that one of you shall betray me.'

Father Alban snorted derisively. 'Spare us your party tricks, Master Hopwood. If you have a secret, then be prepared to be betrayed.' Then he pointed at Brother Fergus. 'But even ecclesiastic sentences are not always lenient, are they, Brother? Not to witches, murderers and adulterers!'

The franklin interjected again. 'Father Alban, please, contain yourself. This is a feast day to —'

'No more of your prattle about feasting and feast days and blessed St Julian!' returned the priest. He rose abruptly, and bowed to Master Hopwood and to Rowena. 'I thank you for your hospitality, but I can stomach no more.' Then he addressed the whole table: 'Can you not see the danger? The country is led by an adulterous couple who have imprisoned the King, put a puppet child on the throne in his stead and executed men without impunity. Now we have witchcraft threatening to sweep the land. Surely we see how the law is a sham, a powerless tool in the hands of witches and sorcerers and other evildoers.'

'Father Alban, perhaps you have said overmuch,' Brother Fergus protested.

'Nay! I see the evil about me, and it is my duty to speak out every time I climb my pulpit. From now on, sinners beware! I will reveal evil wherever and whenever I see it.'

Without further ado, he flounced from the hall, leaving everyone speechless.

Master Hopwood stood, smiling nervously. 'I crave your forgiveness. Father Alban can be overwrought in his opinions. I will talk with him tomorrow.'

'Father, it seems he suffers from an ill humour,' said Rowena, reaching up and clasping his wrist. 'Perhaps I could get you to take him a potion of bitterwort and valerian.'

The franklin patted her hand. 'My daughter knows so much about physic, she could almost be a physician or an apothecary.'

The guests politely agreed, but Richard noticed how very worried the franklin had suddenly become.

CHAPTER FOUR

Lady Wilhelmina was most interested to hear about her father's treatment by Doctor Flynn when Richard returned home that evening. She was also intrigued to hear that Rowena Hopwood had become skilled in herbs and potion-making.

'It does not seem long ago that she was just a young child being looked after by her mother.'

'Mistress Mary Wisley, the Kirkthorpe and Wragby reeve's aunt, told me that there was talk that her poor vision was the result of a curse on her father, by a witch that he had wronged.'

'That I had not heard, Richard,' Wilhelmina replied. 'Perhaps it was Kirkthorpe village gossip.'

'That was what I had thought,' he agreed. 'Her nephew, Gembert, seemed irritated that she had said anything, although I am not sure if he heard the full conversation. I had a long talk with him after the feast on Sir Thomas's behalf about the Manor of Wakefield affairs, and he does seem a very closed and guarded fellow.'

When he told her of Brother Fergus's posting to St Leonard's Priory because of Bishop Ledrede of Ossory's concern about the spread of witchcraft, she became quite concerned. 'But why should this part of the world attract such awful things, Richard? It is not long ago that Pontefract was blighted with it, and you know how dangerous that whole affair was for you. It is as well that my mother and I gave you—'

She stopped and tears welled up in her eyes. Richard put his arm about her shoulders. 'You gave me the medallion of St

Christopher, which proved very useful.' He patted his chest. 'And as you know, I wear it still for protection.'

I don't know whether I gain any protection from St Christopher by wearing his medallion, but it probably did save my life. Yet I have not the same devout belief in the talisman as Hubert has in his arrowhead.

He recalled how on the way back to Durkar after the feast Hubert had touched his arrowhead when he told him of the Dominican friar's talk of witchcraft. Like Wilhelmina, he had a horror of all things to do with the supernatural.

On the other hand, Hubert had enthused about the ale, the meat pies and the pastries that he had sampled at the franklin's fair.

'That fire-eater was a magician, my lord. I saw him catch one of the chickens that was running around and pull its head off. Then moments later he brought it back to life, its head restored after a snap of his fingers.'

He had told him of the people he had met and of how they felt about the service in the church. Almost everyone was unsettled by Father Alban's tale of St Julian and understood him to be directly critical of Queen Isabella and Roger Mortimer, whom virtually everyone in England seemed to know were living in sin and enjoying carnal relations. Yet they all wondered at his daring in actually saying it from the pulpit.

Hubert had also told Richard that he had noticed the glances and whispers between men and women as they chanced to pass each other, from which he'd inferred that they took Father Alban's railing against adulterers as being directed at them.

Richard had smiled at Hubert's homespun conclusion: 'There are many dogs, and bitches too, that are hard to keep chained up at home, if you get my meaning, my lord.'

At that point, Richard had asked about Brother Fergus's message when Hubert had reached for the reassuring feel of his arrowhead. 'That was different, sir. There are sinners everywhere, but witchcraft and sorcery are beyond pleasurable sinning. I drank a few mugs of ale with several fellows, good, strong, merry men, yet they all crossed themselves and looked scared to death at mention of witches. I doubt if there were any witches or sorcerers there.'

'Did you pick up any other useful information?' Richard had asked, having often found his man's chats with folk in taverns and markets revelatory about things happening in town.

'As a matter of fact, I did, my lord, and I was going to tell you anyway. I met the Widow Plowman. She had baskets to sell, and she was also selling her chewet pies that I enjoyed so much. A fine baker, she is.'

'Where is the interest there, Hubert?'

Hubert had chewed his lip for a moment. 'When she knew who I was, being your man, she gave me an extra chewet and said how grateful she was that you had been lenient in not hanging Peter as Cedric of Sharlston wanted.' He'd raised his eyebrows as he'd recalled the conversation he'd had with the widow. 'She spat when she mentioned the yeoman of Sharlston's name. I can't say I blame her either, my lord.'

Richard had reminded Hubert that he had not yet decided about the case.

'Oh, I know, sir, but it wasn't just that,' Hubert had replied. 'When we talked about the two priests, she went very shifty as I mentioned Father Alban talking about adultery. Then out of the blue she changes the subject and tells me what a good husband the franklin had been to his dead wife and how good he was to everyone.'

'Are you trying to say something, Hubert?' Richard had asked.

'She was blushing when she talked about him, sir. It was as if she had feelings for him.'

Wilhelmina brought Richard out of his reverie by opening a casket and taking out a locket. 'Can you give this to my father tomorrow? It has a snip of my mother's hair in it. I have prayed to St Dymphna, whom my mother revered. She can heal melancholy. Perhaps you could hang it over his bed or leave it close to him.'

'St Dymphna?'

'She was an Irish princess who was murdered by her insane father. Her mother had died, and in his madness Dymphna's father wanted to replace her as his wife. She fled from him but he tracked her down, and when she spurned him he killed her. Miracles occurred, and people afflicted with madness and fits were cured.'

The lives of saints are never easy, Richard thought.

Richard and Hubert arrived at Sandal Castle an hour after cockcrow, since Doctor Flynn had arranged to bleed Sir Thomas an hour later than the first day. They had gained entry via the drawbridge and had just dismounted on the bailey when they heard horses' hooves clattering across the drawbridge. A moment later, Doctor Flynn trotted towards them.

'Sir Richard, I think this morning you should not tarry for Sir Thomas's treatment,' he said as he quickly dismounted. 'Since you are the coroner, you are needed at Wakefield. I told the turnkey at the Tolbooth that as I was coming to the castle I would tell you. He and Ranald Brigg, the headman of the town watch, were preparing to send a messenger to fetch you. There has been a murder overnight. A body was found at first light, a hue and cry was raised and the murderer was caught and arrested. It will shock you, Sir Richard.'

'Who has been murdered, do you know?'

The doctor nodded. 'It was Father Alban, stabbed in the back before the altar in the Church of All Saints.'

Hubert and Richard stared at each other in disbelief for a moment. Then Richard asked, 'And who was the villain that murdered him?'

'It was the franklin, Master Geoffrey Hopwood. He was easily caught, I am told, and he now lies in a cell in the Tolbooth.'

'Have you seen either the body or the franklin?'

Doctor Flynn shook his head and pointed to the top of the barbican tower. 'As you know, I have a living patient in need of treatment this morning. In any case, I thought it would be for you to see and for you to seek my opinion if you wished it.'

Richard mounted his horse, as did Hubert. He nodded curtly. 'I think I most assuredly will wish it, Doctor Flynn. If you would treat my father-in-law and then meet me in Wakefield.'

A crowd had formed around the great doors to the Church of All Saints as people craned to see inside. Two constables of the town watch stood by the door, preventing any entry until they saw Richard and Hubert approach.

'Ah, Sir Richard,' the elder of the constables said as the crowd gave way to let them through. 'Ranald Brigg is inside with the body.'

Ranald Brigg was a capable fellow who had been in charge of the town watch for over ten years. From curfew at night when all four city gates were closed until cockcrow and the first bells, he and his constables were in charge, ensuring that no one was about except those who had good reason to be abroad.

Usually, that only meant the gong farmers who collected the waste from the town's latrines and cesspits and transported it in great wagons outside of the town. Otherwise, everyone who was out for any reason was required to carry a lantern and had to proclaim himself when challenged by Ranald or his constables.

Ranald Brigg was also a blacksmith. Almost as tall as Hubert, he had huge forearms built up over many years from hammering and working iron in his forge. He was sitting on a pew with his chin in his hands until he heard the door creak open and Richard and Hubert stepped inside. He jumped to his feet and turned to greet them.

'An evil business, Sir Richard,' he said, rubbing his hands as if trying to cast the unpleasant sight of violent death from his charge.

The body of the priest in his brown habit lay face down in front of the altar. The arms were outstretched and he was lying on his right cheek so his face was visible. A dagger was embedded in his back right up to the hilt, surrounded by many other stab wounds from whence a little blood had oozed to form small haloes on the back of his habit.

Richard bent down to look at the face. Father Alban's eyes were wide open, as if he'd been startled at the moment of his death. His tongue was protruding and a thin trickle of congealed blood had run from his mouth over his chin and dripped onto the floor to form a small puddle.

'Do you recognise the dagger, Hubert?' Richard asked, looking over his shoulder.

'I assuredly do, my lord. If you remember, I said when we first saw it in court that the bollocks were excessively large. This is the franklin's dagger, I am sure. If he killed this priest, then he certainly was taking no chances that he would survive.'

Richard nodded pensively. He was trying to imagine the priest praying before the altar and being suddenly assaulted in what looked like a frenzied attack and then pitching forward, possibly still being stabbed. 'We shall find out if it is his dagger soon enough, as he is this moment languishing in the Tolbooth.' He straightened and turned to Ranald Brigg. 'Who discovered the body?'

The headman jabbed his chest with his thumb. 'I did, Sir Richard. I was the one who found him after the hue and cry was raised.'

'You?' Richard asked in surprise. 'What time was this?'

'Not long after cockcrow, Sir Richard. My constables and I were on our way to open the town gates. I was heading towards the Kirkgate and was not far downhill from the church when I heard the first alert to start the hue and cry. I heard a man's voice shout out, "Murder! Murder! Murder! The priest is dead! Stop that franklin! Stop that franklin!" Then I saw a man running from the direction of the church towards the stables at Cheapside.'

'Who was it?'

'I didn't see clearly, but I beat my drum and started the hue and cry. I lost sight of him in the shadows, because it was still dark. "Stop him! A priest's murderer is making for the stables on Cheapside!" I yelled as I beat on doors and gave chase. Soon we had a real mob, and sure enough some folk had already caught him by the time I reached Cheapside. They had knocked him about, as is natural, and pinned him down.'

'And then you did what?' Hubert queried.

'When I and one of my constables arrived, I took command. We bound him and took him straightway to the Tolbooth, where Judd of Alverthorpe, the turnkey, was already up, roused by the commotion. We slung him in a cell.'

'And so when did you discover the body?' Richard asked.

'I went straight back to All Saints and found the door open. That's as I'd expect, because Father Alban was always there last thing at night and first thing the next day to say his prayers and worship alone. I found him just like you see him now.'

'And who was the person who actually discovered the body? The one who called out, starting the hue and cry?'

The headman scratched his stubbly cheek. 'That's what I was puzzling over, sir. Whoever he was has disappeared. I have no idea who it was.'

After instructing Ranald Brigg to remain with the body and stop anyone else from entering the church and disturbing it, Richard and Hubert left and made for the Tolbooth on the other side of the Bull Ring. It was a squat single-storey stone building with barred windows and a stout iron-studded wooden door.

Judd the turnkey slid the iron grille open in answer to the banging on the door from Hubert's sword pommel. 'Sir Richard, I was expecting you. I have the murdering dog in a cell.' He unlocked the door and swung it open.

Richard gave him a stern look. 'You mean you have someone suspected of murder in a cell,' he corrected. 'Only the court will decide if he is guilty of murder.'

The turnkey stared back, then bowed his head in acknowledgement of the admonishment. 'The prisoner is in a cell, Sir Richard, and I'll show you him,' he said, choosing his words carefully.

Bolting the door behind them, he led them down the short passage that was lit by oil lamps where there were three cells, and then down a flight of steps to a lower level where there was another row of cells. They then rounded a corner leading to another three cells. More oil lamps on protruding stone shelves illuminated this corridor and threw a meagre light into each chamber. In the first, Peter Plowman was grasping the bars and looking anxiously for Richard and Hubert.

'Sir Richard, why has Master Hopwood been put in here?' he asked. 'He won't talk to me.'

'You keep your mouth shut unless the judge speaks to you,' the turnkey snapped.

'But hear me. I heard the hue and cry going on and I heard what was being said when he was brought in here.'

'I told you to shut your mouth!' the turnkey said through gritted teeth.

'He called Master Hopwood a murdering bastard!' Peter Plowman continued, disregarding his jailor. 'That's not true, Sir Richard. He wouldn't harm a fly.'

'Shall I make him hold his tongue, Sir Richard?' Judd of Alverthorpe asked.

Richard stopped and looked at the youth with interest. 'Why are you so certain of this, Peter Plowman?'

'Because … because … he is a good man, Sir Richard.'

Very interesting, Richard thought. *Just as it was so interesting that the franklin went to pains to try to influence Peter Plowman's case.*

'I am still considering your case, Peter Plowman,' he said firmly. 'For now, just be silent.'

Judd of Alverthorpe grunted and led the way to the next cell, where he tapped a heavy key against one of the bars. 'Here is the prisoner, Sir Richard.'

As Richard stepped towards the door, Judd of Alverthorpe winked conspiratorially at Hubert, who frowned back to make it clear that he was there solely as Richard's assistant.

Geoffrey Hopwood was lying on a pallet bed. By the flickering flames of the torch, they could see the whites of his eyes. There were bruises on his face and he had a cut lip.

'Unlock the door,' Richard ordered. 'I wish to talk to the prisoner.'

The franklin did not look in their direction until Richard and Hubert were actually inside the cell. Even then, he turned his head slowly and stared as if he was in a daze.

'On your feet in front of the judge!' the turnkey bellowed.

Geoffrey Hopwood slowly swung his legs over the edge of the bed and rose. He stood for a moment, swaying unsteadily, and then he made the semblance of a bow, totally different from his usual vital self. 'Your pardon, Sir Richard,' he mumbled. 'I … I am shocked. I … I cannot talk.'

'I am told that a hue and cry was raised and that you were caught trying to get a horse from the stable on Cheapside.'

He stared back, as if trying to recollect what had happened. 'That may be true, Sir Richard. My … my memory is poor.'

Richard eyed him with interest and held up his hand as the turnkey was about to yell again. 'How poor is your memory, Master Hopwood? Do you remember attacking Father Alban, whose body was found in the Church of All Saints, with multiple wounds and a dagger in his back?'

The franklin hung his head.

'Your dagger!' Hubert exclaimed. 'That used to reside in a sheath hanging from your belt.' He pointed to the empty sheath and added, 'Next to where your fat silk purse hangs.'

The franklin looked down, then shook his head. 'I have nothing to say.'

'Did you kill Father Alban?' Richard asked.

The franklin blinked several times, as if finding it difficult to concentrate on what was happening. 'I cannot say anything, Sir Richard. I … I think I need to sleep. Perhaps my memory will return. Everything seems so … so unreal.'

'When you appear in my court, you will talk!' Richard said sternly.

The franklin continued to stare at his feet.

'Peter Plowman in the next cell is most anxious to tell me that you could not have committed murder. He says you would not harm a fly. Why does he say that? Is there something I should know, Master Hopwood?'

Once again the franklin shook his head. 'Perhaps when I am in court I shall find words.'

Richard stared at him for a moment then turned and walked out of the cell, followed by Hubert. As the turnkey was about to close the cell door, Richard instructed him, 'Take the franklin's belt, but leave him his purse.' *I have the image of one hanging man troubling my dreams. I do not wish another.*

Later, Hubert was despatched by Richard to find Doctor Flynn and duly found him riding up the street from the Kirkgate. 'Sir Richard wants you to look at the body of the priest, which we have moved down into the crypt,' he informed the physician.

A flight of stone steps led from the chancel of the church down to the crypt, a large chamber hewn out of the rock. Several guttering candles illuminated it, casting eerie shadows onto the walls and on several stone coffins containing the bodies of past incumbents. Father Alban's body had been laid on his stomach, just as he had been found in the church, on top of a large flat-topped tomb in the middle of the chamber.

'What do you make of this, Doctor Flynn?' Richard asked, as he and Hubert looked on.

'Undoubtedly death was caused by this dagger to the back,' the physician replied. 'From its position, it will have penetrated his heart. There also seem to be many other stab wounds.' He lifted an arm and hefted it in his hand. 'There is stiffness, so it has been some hours since he died.'

'As you know, he was found after cockcrow,' Richard replied.

The physician pointed to the dagger. 'Shall I remove it? I would like to see the other stab wounds.'

Richard nodded and the doctor grasped the handle of the dagger by the two oval swellings at the guard, which gave the weapon its suggestive name. A sickly sucking noise was emitted as he slowly pulled it free. Holding it up to examine the crimson-covered blade, he clicked his tongue and nodded.

'It is an unusual dagger, with large bollock guards. It undoubtedly pierced his heart, Sir Richard.' He laid it aside on one of the other stone coffins before beginning to raise the priest's habit off the body. Bending over the corpse, he examined each wound before straightening up. 'As you can see, there are ten wounds, all in the same area between his shoulder blades. They seem to have been angled slightly downwards, which I imagine would mean that they were delivered from above.'

'As if he had been knelt in prayer,' Richard said. 'That is precisely what I thought.'

Doctor Flynn nodded. 'It seems plain enough. Have you seen the franklin? Has he confessed?'

'He seems to be in shock and claims that he cannot remember anything. Does that make sense? Can someone commit murder and then forget that they have done so?'

Doctor Flynn stroked his beard and nodded. 'It is indeed possible, Sir Richard. The mind can play strange tricks on us, and if the person's humours are so upset that the mind stops working properly, then that is where madness occurs. It is all the more likely to happen around the time that the moon is full, as it was. As you know, I have been bleeding your father-in-law at the most propitious times according to the moon's position in the zodiac.'

'Yesterday at the feast of St Julian, which Master Hopwood hosted at his home, Father Alban became suddenly incensed, which upset the franklin.'

'Incensed about what, Sir Richard?'

'About things that he and Brother Fergus, a Dominican friar from Ireland, talked about at a service they held at St Peter's Church in Kirkthorpe. And also about infidelity and the current state of affairs with the throne. So my question now is whether a man could suddenly commit a brutal slaying without knowing what he was doing?'

'If he had enough provocation and his balance of humours was tipped so that madness occurred, then I would say, assuredly yes.'

'And if the moon is full?' Hubert asked.

'As it is,' said the physician, nodding.

John of Flanshaw was busy writing at the desk in the Rolls Office when Richard and Hubert came in. He immediately stood and vacated the chair for Richard.

'I have heard about the murder, Sir Richard. Can the franklin, Geoffrey Hopwood, really have killed Father Alban?'

'That will be for the inquest to decide. As I am the Wakefield coroner, I want you to issue the proclamation all over the town that there will be an inquest into the death of Father Alban tomorrow morning at the ninth hour.'

'May I ask where the body of the priest is, Sir Richard?'

'It is in the crypt at All Saints' Church. I have instructed Ranald Brigg, the headman of the town watch, to lock the church and have a guard posted there all night. He will also keep the key to the church on his person until I have need of it. As for Master Hopwood, he is safe under lock and key at the Tolbooth.'

'Along with Peter Plowman,' the bailiff added. 'Have you decided upon his case yet, Sir Richard?'

Richard shook his head. 'I am still deliberating. I think there will have to be some punishment.'

'Perhaps time in the pillory, my lord?' Hubert suggested. 'Mayhap even nailing his ears to the frame?'

Richard made a noncommittal noise as he sat down. *I will have to make some sort of example of the youth, but not until I have found out why the franklin was so keen to intercede for him. Yet now with the franklin himself facing a charge of murder, things have become infinitely more complicated. And if Geoffrey Hopwood has committed murder, he himself will assuredly hang.*

Once again, his mind floated the image of the hanged man, Quinn of Ryhill, before him.

Young Hal was feeding his sister with milk and sops when Hubert knocked on the door of the hovel where his family lived in Agbrigg. It was a crude dwelling with a turf roof and a smoke hole. Inside, the single room had a dirt floor covered in straw. The young girl was sitting on one of three stools at a trestle table and the mother was lying curled up in a bed which was clearly used by all of the family.

Hal pulled the door open and stood back in surprise to see Richard and Hubert.

'We have come to see how your mother is faring,' Richard said, as they bent low to come through the low door.

Hubert's own son was a strapping three-year-old, and Richard noted with a smile how good he was with children, despite his size and the fact that he very much a fighting man.

He kneeled down to talk to Hal and his sister while Richard addressed Hal's mother, who was struggling to sit up.

'Stay calm, Mistress,' Richard said. 'You don't know me, but I am Sir Richard Lee, the Judge of the Wakefield Manor Court. Hubert you already know. It was I who sent Doctor Flynn to see you.'

She was a woman in her late twenties who was clearly unwell. The family resemblance between all three was apparent, and like her son, she seemed to have a naturally smiling countenance. 'My name is Lorna, Sir Richard. My Hal told me all about you. I can't thank you enough for what you have done for us. I'd never be able to pay a doctor myself.'

'Doctor Flynn said he was going to try to shrink this wen of yours. And I know that Hal was going to get help from a local person.'

'Yes, sir, Doctor Flynn is going to apply hot irons to it,' she replied, grimacing a little. 'I can't say I'm looking forward to that. But I'm feeling a bit better with what the healer gave me, and I think it is a bit smaller.' She put a hand over her left breast. 'It was the size of a mouse, but now I think it is only like a shrew.'

'The healer is the local person Hal mentioned?'

She nodded noncommittally.

'I'm not allowed to say their name,' Hal chipped in. 'It won't work if I tell anyone. I promised.'

Richard smiled. 'Fear not, I don't need to know, Hal.' Then turning back to Lorna, he continued, 'But what has the healer given you? A medicine?'

Lorna nodded. 'It must be good, because it tastes horrible.'

'I watched it being made,' Hal volunteered. 'That toe was boiled in oil and all sorts of herbs and powders were added.' He beamed enthusiastically as he described the process.

'And is that what the potion was made from, a dead man's toe?' Hubert asked, his face contorted with revulsion.

'I would take any medicine, no matter what it is made of, if it would help,' Lorna Clegg said. 'But that wasn't all. The healer made a thick paste that I had to put on the wen and leave until it hardened, then I had to scrape it off and roll it into a ball along with some wax from this doll that was made using some of my hair.' She produced a small wax doll from under the blanket and held it up for them to see. 'The healer had made it with a little wen on it, so that was the bit I had to scrape off as well.'

'Then I had to stick the toe bones — because the boiling stripped the flesh from them — into it and take it back to the gibbet and bury it,' said Hal.

'Bury it?' Richard and Hubert both repeated in amazement.

'I did, too,' Hal said, pouring more milk from an earthenware jug into a tiny mug for his sister. 'Right underneath the hanged man.'

Hubert and Richard looked dubiously at each other.

'I would counsel you against telling Doctor Flynn about any of this. Keep that doll hidden also. Physicians are loath to treat someone when a healer is also treating them.'

Lorna nodded emphatically. 'The healer told Hal to make sure we said nothing to anyone.'

'And I was also told that it would be like the hanged man was taking away the wen,' Hal said.

Tears suddenly welled up in his mother's eyes and she stifled a sob. 'P-pardon me, sirs. I can't help it when I think of Quinn hanging there, but isn't it wonderful that in death he can still help me. That's what family is all about.'

'Family?' Richard echoed.

'Yes, Sir Richard,' Lorna replied, covering her mouth with her hands. 'Poor Quinn was my dead husband's cousin.'

The woman was anxiously waiting for him. It had been a long and difficult night. The danger had suddenly burst upon them, but there had been no immediate opportunity to talk or to plan. Death was the only option, the only way that they could be assured of safety.

When he did appear, she had felt some relief to see him looking so cheerful and confident.

He swept her in his arms and kissed her with the usual passion that followed the accomplishment of a task. Their tongues met and she felt the stirring of desire for him, a hunger that could only be satiated by violent love-making.

'I have been uneasy ever since the messenger did not return two weeks ago,' she confided.

'You worry too much. We have the perfect cover here.'

Somewhat convinced, she allowed her desire for him to bubble up. She pressed herself against him and sought his lips again.

'So, the priest is dead!' he murmured as his hands reached up under her skirts.

'And the other?' she whispered. 'He is dead, too?'

'No, not yet. It is better than that. We are totally safe.'

She pushed him back and slapped his face vehemently. 'You fool! I told you what needed to be done. You may have undone us. Now tell me exactly what you have done.'

CHAPTER FIVE

'I am feeling better, I tell you,' said Sir Thomas Deyville as he lay on his bed and glowered at Richard and Doctor Flynn. He pointed to the small wax image of himself that he had mischievously placed on the rim of the chamber pot. 'Look, that likeness of me that you made is feeling better, too. He has passed only clear piss overnight.'

Doctor Flynn forced a smile. 'That is good news, Sir Thomas, but you are by no means cured yet. I still need to remove blood from you, but this time I have brought my little helpers instead of opening a vein with my fleam.'

From his bag he drew out an earthenware jar and removed the lid. 'My leeches will drink their fill of blood and take about a drachm each, barely causing you more than a tickle in the process.'

With forceps he removed a wriggling black leech and encouraged it into a small metal tube. Then, pushing up Sir Thomas's nightshirt sleeve above his elbow, he placed the tube on the fleshy inside of the joint and slid it back to allow the creature to grab onto and bite into his skin.

'Ugly little brutes,' mused Sir Thomas as the physician applied them at various points all over his body. 'I can see them bloating up before my eyes.'

'How is your mood, though, father-in-law?' Richard ventured.

'I already told you, I feel better and will be better still once this bleeding treatment is over.' Then with a sarcastic nod at the wax doll, he added, 'And what about him? Is he escaping the kiss of these leeches?'

In answer, the physician produced a bodkin and prodded small holes in the parts of the doll's body corresponding to the places where the leeches had been placed.

Richard wondered what the physician would make of the unknown healer's hanged man's toe potion or of the advice to bury the toe bones underneath the dangling corpse.

He did not get the opportunity to ask, for there came the sound of footsteps running up the stairs and across the landing, followed by a hammering on the door. Richard darted across and threw it open to find an out of breath Wilfred and a step behind him Hubert.

'Sir Richard —' Wilfred began, but was quickly silenced by Hubert.

'My lord, Ranald Brigg the headman of the town watch has come himself to fetch you to Wakefield. It is most urgent. There have been more murders done overnight.'

Ranald Brigg was in animated conversation with two of the castle guards when Richard and Hubert descended from the barbican and crossed the castle's internal moat onto the bailey.

'Sir Richard, I cannot believe the devilry that has happened — and during my town watch! As usual, after we opened the town gates this morning, I went to check if Judd of Alverthorpe at the Tolbooth had any problems. The door was not bolted and he didn't answer my call. When I went in, the cell doors were open and inside his cell I found Peter Plowman in a pool of blood. His throat had been cut.'

'What of the franklin, Geoffrey Hopwood?' Richard demanded.

'He has gone, Sir Richard. Both him and Judd of Alverthorpe.'

'Did the hue and cry not find anything?' Hubert asked.

The headman stared at him with wide-eyed fear. 'N-No! I … did not call for one.'

'You didn't start a hue and cry!' Hubert exclaimed. 'You donkey!'

'I … I thought there would be panic in town and thought Sir Richard should know. I left my two constables on guard and came myself.'

Should I have foreseen this? Richard wondered to himself, then, 'Does anyone else know of this?'

'No one, Sir Richard,' the headman replied tremulously.

'You have made a foolish mistake, Master Brigg, but it may yet work to our advantage. We will view the body of the unfortunate Peter Plowman and then I will decide whether we have a hue and cry, late though it will be.'

'What of the inquest into the priest's death, my lord?' Hubert asked. 'It is set for this morning.'

'It will be delayed now. We will get John of Flanshaw to re-organise it.'

They all mounted up and one of the guards called for the portcullis to be raised. As they waited, Richard pointed to it. 'As soon as we get to the town, I want you to close the town gates.' *Yet I fear that the murderer and his accomplice will have fled the town already.*

The cloying, coppery smell of blood greeted them as they descended the steps to the cells, using an oil lamp from the corridor. As Ranald Brigg had said, the cells' doors were open. In the first, the body of Peter Plowman was lying across the pallet bed, an ugly gaping wound across his throat, which had bled profusely, soaking the bed and pooling on the floor. His eyes were open wide, and his hands were covered in blood about his throat, as if he had used his last dying moments trying to close the wound.

'Poor lad,' said Hubert. 'He was not over-large and he had already been beaten, it seems. His face is all bruised and his jaw is swollen.'

'He was badly beaten by Cedric of Sharlston and two of his men,' Richard replied, bending close to see the wound. He winced at the sight of the severed windpipe cartilage and stood up.

'The franklin's cell is empty, my lord. Just as this lummox of a night watchman said,' Hubert said gruffly, eyeing Ranald Brigg with undisguised contempt.

'Is there any sign of a weapon?' Richard asked, looking closely around Peter Plowman's cell, but he saw nothing in the blood-soaked straw.

'Nothing, my lord.'

Ranald Brigg was eager to regain some credibility. 'That is what I thought, Sir Richard. I looked for the keys, but I presume they are still on Judd of Alverthorpe's belt.'

Richard went into the franklin's cell to see for himself that nothing had been dropped that might give him a clue about what happened. Returning to the corridor, he asked the headman of the town watch, 'How long have you known Judd of Alverthorpe?'

Ranald Brigg thought for but a moment. 'For twelve years, Sir Richard. We were both constables of the town watch for two years before I was made headman and he was appointed as the Tolbooth jailor.'

'Is he an honest man?'

This time, the headman took longer to consider. 'As far as I know, Sir Richard. He was always complaining about money, especially when he was drunk in his cups, but in these days what working man does not wish he had more wealth? Meaning no offense, sir.'

'Would you be surprised to learn that he had been bribed to release the franklin?'

The headman's hesitation told Richard what he wanted to know.

'Would he have been able to cut a prisoner's throat?' he asked.

'He was a strong man, Sir Richard. He would have been able to deal with Peter Plowman.'

Hubert snorted impatiently. 'Would he have been capable of murder?'

'I ... I doubt it,' the headman replied, visibly sweating now.

Richard pointed to the body in the open cell. 'Which leaves us with the question, would he have been capable of standing by and watching Geoffrey Hopwood slit a youth's throat?'

The headman stared at the gaping wound in the throat of the prisoner and gulped. 'I would not have thought so, Sir Richard. But there doesn't seem to be any other explanation. The franklin must have bribed him to let him out, and then one of them must have killed Peter before they both let themselves out into the night.'

There was the sound of footsteps coming from above, and the elder of the two constables came down. 'The gates are closed, sir, and we have left instructions with the gatekeepers to let no one in or out, except for you and Hubert of Loxley or anyone under your authority until they are ordered otherwise.'

Richard pointed to the cell. 'Get one of the constables to bring the locksmith to make new keys for the cells and the main door. Meanwhile, start the hue and cry for Geoffrey Hopwood and for Judd of Alverthorpe. Say that murder has been done in the Tolbooth and they must both be found and caught. Look for blood, and if you find either of them, arrest anyone who may be harbouring them.'

Ranald Brigg looked doubtfully at his constable. 'If they are in the town, we may need help, Sir Richard.'

'You shall have it, since Hubert is going to return to Sandal Castle and bring back half a dozen of the castle guards to help. But you start making a noise now and begin the search. I will go with Hubert to the Kirkgate.'

'My lord, are you coming with me to Sandal Castle?' Hubert questioned.

Richard shook his head. 'No, I will begin my own search.'

The hue and cry had begun as Richard and Hubert parted company outside the Kirkgate. Crossing the bridge over the River Calder, Richard rode east for Kirkthorpe, looking for any sign of recent travel. From time to time, he saw droppings of dung, but they told him nothing, for he knew that the gong wagons travelled that way at night. He certainly did not find, nor expect to see, blood. He expected the two men to have wiped any from their hands and clothes.

He did not know the area around the village well, but he did know the beck that ran through it, a thin tributary of the river, and he knew the part that ran in a crescent that the locals called Half Moon Beck. It was there that Peter Plowman had lived, as he had told him in court. There were three dwellings built within the confines of the Half Moon Beck, and Richard had no difficulty finding the Plowmans' cottage, as it had great piles of willow branches stacked against a side wall and a work table and stool outside.

Dismounting a little distance away, he walked to the cottage, and with his hand on his sword and drawing his dagger to hold at his side, he called out, 'I am Sir Richard Lee. I come to see Master Geoffrey Hopwood.'

The door opened almost straightaway, and a working woman of about forty stood and stared at him in alarm. 'Sir Richard? Why would you think Master Hopwood would be here?' she asked suspiciously as she stood back to let Richard enter, which he did warily in case anyone within should attack him.

'I think you know Master Hopwood well,' he said. 'Very well indeed!'

She blushed and looked at her feet. 'You … you have my son Peter in the Tolbooth. Is he unwell? Has Master Hopwood done something foolish?'

Having assured himself that there was no one else in the cottage, Richard sheathed his dagger and released his sword handle. *She has not seen the franklin, that is clear. So he has not come to here for shelter.* 'There is no gentle way to tell you, Mistress: your son is dead. He was murdered in the night.'

She screamed, then covered her face with her hands and began to sob. 'But … but, he was in the Tolbooth. How —?'

'The franklin was arrested yesterday and imprisoned in the Tolbooth on suspicion of having murdered Father Alban in the Church of All Saints.'

Her face told him that she did not know this. Undoubtedly, her neighbours had tried to spare her or had not known what to tell her.

'Nell?' someone called from outside. An older woman tentatively pushed the door open.

'Come in,' said Richard. 'Your friend Nell has had a terrible shock. Her son has been murdered. She will need comfort. I must leave you now, but I or someone will return.'

The old woman nodded and ran to hug her neighbour.

'Have you seen Geoffrey Hopwood?' he asked as he let himself out. When the old woman shook her head, he nodded. 'If he should come, lock your doors. From now on, he must be considered an escaped felon. He is dangerous and must not be allowed shelter. Have you any menfolk?'

The old woman shook her head again. 'Peter Plowman was our only man in Half Moon Beck.'

Hubert had returned leading six of Sir Thomas Deyville's guards, and he quickly found Ranald Brigg. The hue and cry had not been successful, and no sign of either Judd of Alverthorpe or of Geoffrey Hopwood was found. It had been a shambolic hue and cry, for there was no one to chase, no one had been seen, so the result was that men had run about the streets banging pots, making lots of noise and generally alarming all of the women, children and older folk.

Taking charge, Hubert ordered his men and Ranald's constables to begin a search of all the taverns, middens and brothels where wanted men might try to conceal themselves.

'Could they be trying to claim sanctuary in church?' the headman asked Hubert.

'It is locked up, as you know, but let's make sure,' Hubert replied.

The headman looked nervous. 'Do you think the ghost of the priest could be there?'

Hubert had a strong belief in ghosts himself, but he did not want Ranald Brigg to think that he was scared of anything. 'The only ghost likely to be in the church is the Holy Ghost, and no one should be afraid of him. Come, I will accompany you.'

The guard on duty at the church looked relieved to see Hubert and Ranald Brigg approach, and he was emphatic that he had not fallen asleep at his post and that no one had either entered or left the church.

Daylight streamed in through the windows, and it was soon clear that there was no one in there. By the light of a candle, Hubert led the way down the steps to the crypt, his other hand touching the arrowhead through his tunic for comfort. The body of the priest lay upon the tomb covered by a blanket.

Ranald Brigg shivered. 'It is a good thing it is so cold down here, or the body would start to rot.'

Hubert nodded in agreement. 'Well, perhaps his presence will keep the living away, especially a murderer. Neither the franklin nor the turnkey have sought sanctuary in this church. Let's see how they are getting on with the search of the town.'

But he had a feeling that Sir Richard had not expected to find either man in town.

Judd of Alverthorpe thought he heard a noise outside the old sheepcote on the remote hill on the Heath.

Used to being the custodian, the one who made prisoners talk when he wanted them to and who shut them up when he wanted quiet, his natural instinct was to bark out a challenge. But now he did not dare, for he could not afford to have someone spying on him and then running off to alert others to where he was. Not now. Not after what they had done.

Sitting on the hard earth floor in the space he had cleared of sheep dung with his foot, out of sight of the entrance, for there was no door, he waited a few moments more, straining his ears to detect any further sound of movement.

Pah! Probably either a coney or one of the hundreds of sheep the franklin owned. Bastard, though! Why had he done that to the boy, Peter Plowman?

The moment the deed was done, he was finished. He could not go back but had to use the money he had been given along with the promise of far more.

Staring at the franklin's white silk purse stuffed with coins on the ground beside him, he shoved the murder from his mind and smiled. Money, lots of it, that would take him away from all this. The silver in the purse was just the advance payment. Soon there would be more, much more. He had hidden the pony and just had to wait until he came back with the money, and then he would be off, far away.

He felt a pang in his gut and the need for food. And more importantly, a drink. It was all in the basket, as the protector promised.

'A feast for a king, just like the franklin would expect,' he said to himself. He took out the food, wrapped in a cloth. 'Cheese, plovers' eggs, a partridge. Not bad.' He took out the two earthenware flasks, one of water and the other of mead. 'Here's to you. Hope you make it, Master Hopwood.' He pulled the stopper and drank copiously, relishing the satisfying warmth as it hit his stomach. He laughed. 'More importantly, here's to me, a rich man!'

Hubert and Ranald Brigg were summoned to one of the brothels behind the Shambles, the street of the butchers and sellers of offal, almost as soon as they had left and locked the church. It was one of the least salubrious of places, where the ale and whores were both cheap and few questions were asked of customers. Many men went to pains to conceal their identities and never removed hoods or gugels which covered head and shoulders and shielded most of the face, even during the height of their passions.

The hue and cry had not uncovered anything or given any lead to follow, but the search of brothels had uncovered several men who had no wish to be exposed as customers. They had their names taken in case Richard saw a need to interrogate them.

Osbert, the owner of this establishment, brooked no violence to his working women, being perfectly able to quell any drunkard or ruffian who lost their temper or felt in any way belittled by one of the women. This was not an uncommon situation, since the women had little recourse for complaint, and threatening to spread rumours about a customer's manhood was one way of boosting the meagre payments they received for their services.

It was Osbert himself who had called one of Sir Thomas Deyville's men as he came out from searching another brothel further up the street. 'You can take this drunken sot, who has been with two of my girls all night and took a belt to their bums,' he told Hubert. 'They showed me the bruises from his lashing.'

Hubert recognised the man as one Siward Trapp, one of the men from Ryhill. He was called that because he worked as a rat and mole-catcher, but folk poked fun at him, saying it was because of his rodent-like features. He was slumped on the ground outside the brothel where Osbert had deposited him.

'I cuffed him a bit, so take no notice of his bloody nose,' Osbert said contemptuously as the man snored.

'Why did you think we'd be interested in him?' Hubert asked.

'Because he's not long out of the Tolbooth, where your judge threw him for a week when he hanged Quinn of Ryhill. Ask at the Nag's Head, the Bucket Inn or any of the other taverns about, and you'll hear that he's been drinking since then. That and ploughing his furrows in honest places like mine. Well, I've had enough. Especially when we've had a hue and cry and now you've got men searching the town. Ask him what he said he was going to do to Judd of Alverthorpe.'

One of the whores appeared at the door behind Osbert. 'I've brought a bucket of water to wake him. Can I do it as payback for the thrashing he gave me and Sybil? He didn't offer to pay any extra. He just kept mumbling that he was going to do the same thing to the Tolbooth turnkey.'

Hubert frowned angrily. He had little time for any man who struck a woman. He nodded. And with a smirk, the girl tossed the bucket over the drunken Siward Trapp, who immediately roused, coughing, spluttering and cursing.

'Enough of that,' Hubert ordered. 'What were you saying about Judd of Alverthorpe?'

'Who wants to know?' the man returned, staring up blearily.

Ranald Brigg rewarded him with a toe in the ribs. 'This is Hubert of Loxley, you damned fool. He's —'

'I know who he is. I didn't say nothing except I'm going to settle with that swine for the flogging he gave me and for the way he treated me the week I was in there.'

'Where is he?' Hubert queried.

'How should I know?'

'Should we toss him in the Tolbooth until he sobers up?' Ranald asked.

'We'll toss him in one of the cells on the top level, away from you know what, and one of the constables can guard him,' Hubert replied. 'I reckon Sir Richard may want to question him.'

A crowd had gathered at all the commotion, and Sir Thomas Deyville's guard cleared a way through it as Hubert and Ranald Brigg frog-marched Siward Trapp towards the Tolbooth. He was unaware that among those watching were ones who were both angry and worried at the sight. So anxious that they needed to seek guidance from another. In guarded whispers, they agreed that death would probably be called for.

Richard had made his way to Kirkthorpe and to the Church of St Peter, but not with any real expectation of finding the men he pursued. Having searched the building, he mounted his horse again and headed for the franklin's manor house.

He was admitted to the mansion by a serving maid and shown into the kitchen where Rowena was pounding something using a pestle and mortar. As Richard entered, she laid them down and felt with nimble fingers on the table surface for a cloth to wipe her hands.

'Sir Richard, I ... I know not what to say. My father, I cannot believe he is imprisoned. You cannot believe that he would harm Father Alban.'

'Your father is no longer imprisoned, Rowena.'

Her face burst into a smile of joy. 'You have released him?'

'No, he has escaped. He has broken out of the Tolbooth with the aid of the town jailor, Judd of Alverthorpe. But there is worse, I am afraid.'

Rowena reached behind her for a stool and unsteadily sat down, her joyful expression replaced now by one of disbelief.

Richard was loath to cause her more pain, aware that he had already done so with Peter Plowman's mother. 'It looks very much as though either your father or Judd of Alverthorpe killed Peter Plowman.'

'No!' she shrieked. 'Peter cannot be dead! My father would not harm a hair on his head. You must be wrong.'

'Why do you say that, Rowena? Why would he not harm him?'

She looked amazed that he could ask such a question. 'Why, because my father is kindness itself. He cares for his family, his servants and all those who work for him or rent homes or land from him.'

Family? Rowena is his only living family, unless I am right and Peter Plowman was an illegitimate son. Yet I need to be careful what I say to her. 'I looked in the Church of St Peter on my way here, and also at Half Moon Beck where Peter Plowman lived with his mother.'

Rowena took a sharp intake of breath and then looked down at her lap. When she lifted her head after a few moments, Richard could see that she had bitten her lip. 'How did she take this terrible news?' she asked.

'She was distraught, as are you. She had lost a son. She did not know that your father had been arrested on suspicion of the murder of Father Alban. I suspect that her neighbours had been trying to spare her for some reason.'

Again, Rowena took a deep breath. 'Nell is a sensitive woman. My father was kind to her when her husband left her many years ago. He just disappeared, apparently. From then on, my father always took care of her and made sure that she had work.'

Richard nodded. 'It is important that I find him, Rowena. He has been foolish and by running away he makes matters worse for himself. Do you know anywhere that he would go, anywhere that he could be hiding?'

The young woman shook her head and was about to reply when a scream rang out from somewhere outside.

'Stay here, Rowena,' Richard said and ran out of the door and along the corridor in the direction of a screaming woman. Leaving the manor house, he saw a serving woman bent double and vomiting outside the great wooden door of a circular stone dovecote with a conical roof.

Menservants were running from the farmyard behind the manor house and Richard sprinted across the grass towards her.

'I … I came to collect plovers' eggs, sir,' the young woman said, her eyes wide with horror. She had a basket in her hand and pointed inside the dovecote.

Richard brushed past her and stepped inside. There were hundreds of nesting nooks for doves and pigeons, and in the centre of the building a huge timber potence pole had spars reaching out from it like the spokes of a wheel, each with a ladder attached.

Geoffrey Hopwood was hanging by the neck from one of the spokes. His tongue protruded and his face was purple. It looked as if he had fashioned a noose from his own breeches.

CHAPTER SIX

Richard and two of the menservants climbed the ladders and cut through the franklin's makeshift noose.

They lowered him to the ground and then Richard cursorily examined him. His face was bruised, as he had noted when he was alive in the Tolbooth, and his lip was cut. Otherwise, there did not appear to be any fresh bruising.

'Did your master often use the dovecote himself?' he asked one of the men, whom he recognised as George the pantler who had served them all bread at the feast in the manor house.

'That he did, Sir Richard. He was proud of these doves and pigeons and the eggs they gave him. He would spend time in here on his own, just as he did in the henhouses or the pigsties.'

Richard pensively stroked his cheek. *It looks as though he committed* felo de se — *self-murder, so the reason he chose the dovecote is evident with the ladders and those strong timbers. Perhaps he wanted to be near his daughter, but had not the courage to see her after what he had done in Wakefield. The murder of Father Alban, Peter Plowman and now himself.*

He placed the back of his hand against the franklin's brow and his cheeks. 'Still fairly warm, so it does not seem many hours since he did it,' he said aloud.

Picking up the franklin's right wrist, he noted dried blood on the palm of the hand. *This could be from his cut lip, but it did not look to have bled much when I saw him in the Tolbooth.*

He let the hand down and looked around the floor of the dovecote, which was virtually carpeted in pigeon and dove droppings. But almost against the wall, as if tossed there, he saw a short quillon dagger. He stooped and picked it up, raising it to the light to look at the bloodstained blade and handle. *This is not the franklin's own blade, for that was buried in the back of the priest, yet it must be the weapon that was used to slay Peter Plowman.*

Looking then at the top of the breeches, he noted a smear of blood. *It looks as if he shoved it there as his belt and sheath were taken from him in the Tolbooth. So whose blade is this?* He lay it beside the body.

'None of us saw him come, Sir Richard,' said the pantler. 'Otherwise we would have talked to him. Certainly, we would not have let him do this terrible thing.'

'Will he go to hell, Sir Richard?' asked one of the other men. 'It's a mortal sin, after all. He won't be able to be buried in St Peter's cemetery alongside his wife, God rest her soul. Nor rest for eternity with his parents.'

Richard stood up. 'I will be holding an inquest and that will be when decisions are made. But now, I need to have his body taken back to the Tolbooth in Wakefield.' He pointed at the two younger servants. 'One of you must go and comfort the maid who found him and the other must ride to Wakefield and seek my assistant Hubert of Loxley. The town gates will be closed, but say that you are there with my authority. Tell him to bring a wagon to carry your master's body along with this dagger back to the Tolbooth. Also, tell him to alert Doctor Flynn, for I will want to speak to him as soon as I return.' Turning then to George the pantler, 'You must stay here and let no one else into this dovecote.'

He sighed. 'I will tell his daughter Rowena the bad news.'

Two hours later, Richard, Hubert and Doctor Flynn were standing in one of the middle cells downstairs in the Tolbooth looking down at the body of Geoffrey Hopwood. The flickering oil lamps cast an eerie light upon the cadaver.

'This I would never have expected, Sir Richard,' said Doctor Flynn. 'I did not know Master Hopwood well, but from all that I heard he was not the type to commit violence.'

'Yet he certainly seems to have done so. His dagger was found embedded in Father Alban's back, as you know.'

'And another —' Hubert began, but was silenced by a slight shake of the head from Richard. 'And another odd thing,' Hubert continued, quickly correcting what he was going to say, 'is that he strung himself up.'

'Which he undoubtedly did,' said Richard. 'I found him. And that is why I would like you to look at him, Doctor Flynn. Can you tell if he died by hanging?'

'I think so. But the first thing to note are these bruises and this cut lip. He had been struck several times in the face.'

'Those are injuries he received during the first hue and cry,' Richard explained. 'There are no new bruises that I can tell.'

The physician nodded and leaned over the body. He pointed with a long finger at the face. 'You see his tongue protruding like that, his bluish discolouration and those tiny red spots around his eyes and in his eyeballs? They are all signs of being throttled.'

Richard described the dovecote architecture to him. 'And he was hanging from one of those timbers. The timber was about twelve feet from the ground and the ladder was attached to it, so it would have been a simple matter to climb, tie the breeches securely to the timber and put his head in that makeshift noose. Then all he had to do was step into mid-air and hang himself.'

'Could he have jumped, my lord?' Hubert asked.

'Possibly, yes. I had been thinking about this. Would he have broken his neck if he had jumped?'

Doctor Flynn frowned. 'I think not. The length of the noose he made would not be long enough for him to drop. But I will look.' And he bent again and examined the neck with his fingers. After a few moments, he shook his head. 'I cannot feel any gaps between his neck bones, but there would be only one way to be sure. I saw it done in Oxford University and I have operated on the necks of soldiers wounded in battle.'

'You need to open his neck?' Richard asked. When the physician nodded, he said, 'Then please proceed.'

Opening his satchel, the physician asked Hubert to turn the body over and pull the clothes down away from the neck. This done, he used his fingers to feel the spinous processes of the cervical vertebrae, and then with a scalpel he made an incision all the way down from the base of the skull to the root of his neck. Turning the scalpel over, he used its bone handle to push the skin and fascia tissues aside to get a view of the vertebrae. Pushing his fingers into the incision, he felt down along each vertebrae.

'There are no gaps, no fractures, so I think this is clear. He died by hanging, and was throttled to death.'

'I will be holding an inquest into the death of Father Alban and also of the franklin. We will exhibit both bodies for the court to see. I take it you are familiar with the phenomenon of cruentation?'

Doctor Flynn looked surprised. 'I am indeed, Sir Richard, and I have seen it occur at least three times in my life. The body of the victim of murder bleeds in the presence of their killer. It must happen by God's will.'

From the corner of his eye, Richard saw Hubert touch his concealed arrowhead.

'Do you plan to keep the bodies apart, Sir Richard?' the physician asked.

'I do. The priest will stay in the crypt and the franklin will remain in this cell, as will the other body.'

Doctor Flynn turned his head and looked askance at Richard. 'The other body?'

Hubert stepped forward. 'That is my fault, my lord. I did not tell Doctor Flynn about the murder. I presumed he had heard about the hue and cry.'

'Peter Plowman was in the cell adjoining the franklin. He was murdered when the franklin and Judd of Alverthorpe made their escape.'

'Do you wish me to examine his body?' the doctor asked.

Richard shook his head. 'That will not be necessary at this stage. We shall see him at the inquest as well.' He gestured to the door. 'Ranald Brigg, the headman of the town watch, will be waiting upstairs and will let you out. I thank you for your examination of the franklin's body. The inquest on Father Alban was due today, but now it will be tomorrow or the day after, and a proclamation will go out. Your expertise will be needed.'

Once the physician had departed, Hubert closed the cell and locked it with the new key that the locksmith had provided. He turned and told Richard all about the arrest of Siward Trapp during the search of the town. 'I had Ranald Brigg put him in one of the cells upstairs on the ground level with a constable to guard him, so that he was not exposed to the dead body of Peter Plowman. I thought you would want to interrogate him because he was saying what he was going to do to Judd of

Alverthorpe for flogging him and treating him badly while he was in the Tolbooth.'

Richard recalled the man only too well — he had been one of the three men who had taken part in the hue and cry in the hamlet near Ryhill. Believing them to have unsuccessfully tried to restrain Quinn of Ryhill, he had sentenced them to be flogged in public, which they were at the pillory on Cheapside, before they were imprisoned for a week.

Siward Trapp seemed to have sobered up and was looking fearful as the constable on guard opened the cell to let Richard and Hubert in.

'So, Master Siward, you are back in the Tolbooth again,' Richard said in his sternest tone.

'Your pardon, Sir Richard. I have paid for my part in Bryce-a-Green's death. The skin on my back will take a long time to heal, even though the salve that I got from the physician helped.'

'And how did you obtain a salve from the physician while you were in the Tolbooth?'

The mole-catcher's jaw fell open in puzzlement. 'Why, I thought that you had allowed and arranged it, Sir Richard. All three of us did. Me, Emmet Waller and Jay Groff. That blasted turnkey said it was for us from the physic.'

'Did he mean Doctor Flynn?'

'I ... I assumed he did, sir,' he replied. He shook his head and blinked, as if trying to clear his jumbled mind.

'Did he actually say physic or physician? Think hard, man.'

Siward closed his eyes and concentrated. 'Healer! He said healer, and I just thought he meant the physician.'

'Did he want payment?'

'No, Sir Richard. That's why we all thought it was from you. I mean, from the court.'

I do not like this. Who would send men who have been flogged a salve? Who would take pity on all three? 'I heard that you had been drinking in several of the taverns in town since you were released. Where did you get the money?'

The Adam's apple in his scrawny neck bobbed slowly up and down, as if his mouth had suddenly gone dry from fear. 'I … I was given it. Someone paid me for some rats I got rid of for him.'

'His name?'

Looking like a cornered animal, Siward Trapp shook his head. 'I can't remember, sir. I only did the job for him.'

Hubert interlocked his own fingers and cracked his knuckles. 'Shall I help him to remember, my lord?'

Richard shook his head. 'He will remember on his own, or face me in court when I may not be as lenient as I was last time.' *But perhaps I should have been more lenient toward Quinn of Ryhill,* he thought as his mind conjured up the image of the decaying corpse hanging from the gibbet.

John of Flanshaw was not in a good mood. The perfect clerk, he liked order in all things. He kept the court rolls with meticulous precision, arranged the court proceedings and maintained communication with all the guildmasters in Wakefield. He had sent out the proclamation the day before for the inquest into the murder of Father Alban only to have it postponed by the hue and cry for the franklin and the turnkey.

'Do this! Do that! Send this proclamation and then cancel everything, he says,' he grumbled to himself as he opened the door to the Rolls Office, only to find Richard at his desk, writing on a piece of vellum, and Hubert of Loxley sitting on a stool, carving a small doll.

Both looked up at his entry and he stopped short, unsure whether they had heard his muttered complaint.

'Sir Richard, I did not hear you come in,' he flustered. 'I have sent out the notice that the inquest has been cancelled.'

Richard held his stare for a few seconds, then said, 'Clearly! But yet there will have to be another tomorrow or the day after, for now we have the case of the franklin who has committed self-murder and also Peter Plowman, who was murdered when the franklin and the turnkey made their escape.'

The court bailiff listened in horror as Richard recounted the finding of the franklin in his dovecote at Kirkthorpe. He visibly paled as Richard went into the details of his examination of Peter Plowman and then of Doctor Flynn's assessment of the corpse of the franklin.

'I have written my account of all this, which you will please transcribe into the official documents once I have completed my investigations and held the inquest.'

Hubert held up the small doll that he was carving for his son. It was one of many, for the boy was now of an age where he liked to make stories with them. He blew some shavings from it. 'Apart from arresting Siward Trapp, the search we made has not yielded any clue as to where Judd of Alverthorpe has gone.'

'Siward Trapp was released just a couple of days ago,' said John of Flanshaw.

'And now he is back in the Tolbooth until I see him in court,' Richard said. 'I need him to remember who recently paid him for catching some rats.'

'Do you think he knows and is conveniently forgetting, my lord?' Hubert asked.

'Possibly. Under normal circumstances, I would not have thought it of great import, but since he made threats against

Judd of Alverthorpe who carried out the flogging and who is now missing and wanted by us in our investigation of the murder of Peter Plowman, it could be a vital piece of information.'

Hubert placed the doll on the edge of the desk and touched the tip of his blade. 'If it is really important, I am sure I could coax his memory, my lord.'

'No, Hubert, I want the information voluntarily when he has had time to reflect on it. I do not think that Siward Trapp is endowed with great wit, but I will give him the opportunity to work out for himself what he needs to do. If he is concealing something, then it will be obvious to me if he tries to make up a story.'

Hubert picked up the doll again. 'Perhaps my three-year-old son could give him a lesson in story-making, my lord. Once I add this doll to his collection.'

And I hope that it will not be long before Wilhelmina and I are able to dote on an infant and make dolls like that. Richard thought of Hubert's son making a story up with lots of wooden dolls that Hubert had carved. And then, forcing his mind back to the important matters in hand, he said, 'I think it is time that I found out more about what was in the franklin's mind that made him suddenly murder Father Alban.'

'And how will you do this, my lord? The man committed self-murder. Surely that is because of guilt?'

'That is what I mean to find out. I shall interview the guests who were at his St Julian's Day feast, beginning with those he was sitting near to, Sir Basil de Roxford and Lady Katherine. I want to know what their perspective was on the interactions at that feast.'

'What shall I do, my lord?' Hubert asked.

'Continue the search. We need to find Judd of Alverthorpe.'

John of Flanshaw coughed. 'And is there a task for me, Sir Richard?'

Richard looked at his notes on the vellum, then sprinkled ground cuttlefish bone onto it from the pounce pot to dry the ink. 'There is one matter I would like information about,' he said as he tapped the vellum to spread the powder before blowing it away. 'How many folk are there in Wakefield who could call themselves a healer? Apart from a proper physician like Doctor Flynn.'

The court bailiff chewed his lower lip for a moment, making his square black beard fan out like a hedgehog rolling up. 'There is an old woman who gathers herbs and sells potions in the market, and an apothecary near the Westgate, but that is it as far as I know. The apothecary is old and has not got a good name. Too many of his patients have died, and there are those who say he is more poisoner than apothecary.'

'It would help me if you went to them and found out if either made up salves for the prisoners in the Tolbooth. Siward Trapp says that a healer sent them such a remedy after they had been flogged.'

Sir Basil de Roxford and Lady Katherine lived on an estate near the village of Stanley. To reach it, Richard rode through the great forest of the Outwood, leaving Wakefield by the Northgate. Stanley Manor itself was a rambling mansion surrounded by stables, outhouses and Sir Basil's own windmill, as he was one of the few landowners possessing the right to grind his own flour. The latter stood off to the side on a slight crest, where it would be exposed to the winds.

As he rode through the open gates into the courtyard, a male servant immediately appeared from the mansion. Richard recognised him as the servant who had stood at the rear of the church and who had helped first Sir Basil onto his horse and then Lady Katherine into her covered coach upon leaving the Church of St Peter for Kirkthorpe Hall. He was a good-looking, clean-shaven fellow with long curly black hair.

'Good day, Sir Richard,' the man said, meeting Richard in the courtyard. He bowed and then quickly whistled. A moment later, a youngster came running from the stables. 'Allow me to take your horse. I am Aiken, Sir Basil and Lady Katherine's butler. Shall I announce your arrival?'

Richard nodded as he dismounted and handed the reins to the young servant and followed Aiken into the hall. Moments later, he was shown into a large hall bedecked with tapestries and fan-shaped arrangements of hunting weapons on the walls.

Sir Basil de Roxford pushed himself up from a settle and leaned heavily on a stout stick. He bowed his head as Richard was announced. Lady Katherine curtsied before coming forward for Richard to kiss her hand.

'This is an unexpected pleasure, Sir Richard,' she said with a smile, revealing perfect, even white teeth.

'Yet I think it is not simply a social visit,' Sir Basil said, gesturing Aiken to come and take an arm to assist him nearer the window, where there were more formal chairs. 'We heard there has been a hue and cry in Wakefield and Hopwood lost his senses and killed that mad priest, Father Alban.'

They all sat and Aiken was despatched to bring wine.

'There was another hue and cry this morning and the franklin and the town jailor fled, but not before killing a prisoner.' Richard waited for them to absorb this, then told them that the franklin's body had been found on his estate and that it looked as if he had committed self-murder.

Sir Basil and his younger wife stared at him in astonishment, before expressing their disbelief in various ways. Lady Katherine did so demurely and her husband gruffly.

Richard leaned forward. 'Why did you say that Father Alban was a mad priest, Sir Basil?'

Lady Katherine interjected quickly. 'My husband can be tetchy when his ague is on him, Sir Richard. He does not mean to speak unkindly of the dead.'

'I mean what I say, Kate,' the old man said irritably. His expression of disdain added to the grizzled impression that Richard had formed of him. 'The priest was impertinent! He was utterly rude about our Queen, and he cast aspersions about Her Majesty and the noble Lord Mortimer.'

'My husband is strong in his likes, Sir Richard,' Lady Katherine said, reaching out and touching her husband's hand. 'Which is one of his great virtues.'

Sir Basil squeezed his wife's hand and went on. 'I never liked the way Edward of Caernarvon behaved. Those young men he surrounded himself with when he had the love of a true queen. It was a great day for England when Lord Mortimer and Queen Isabella took matters into their own hands.'

'You are a supporter of our new monarch, King Edward the Third of his name?' Richard asked.

Aiken returned with a tray of wine and some small delicacies to eat and then departed like the skilled and dutiful servant he clearly was.

Sir Basil raised his goblet. 'His Majesty, King Edward.' He took a sip then added, 'I am indeed loyal to him, young though he is. And I am loyal to Queen Isabella his mother, and I admire Lord Roger Mortimer.'

'Father Alban rather incensed my husband at the feast,' Lady Katherine explained. 'I have to admit that I also found his conversation overbearing.'

'I saw that there were words spoken between you. Master Hopwood seemed to be trying to placate him.'

'Pah! That is the franklin all over. He always tried to please everyone. As a landowner, an employer and as a knight of the shire. To be honest, I think he tended to go along with anyone if it meant a quieter life. He served as a knight of the shire for this county for five years. In that time, he professed himself to be a devoted follower of King Edward the Second all the way up to him being captured by Lord Mortimer's army. Then he actually voted in favour of deposing King Edward the Second at the parliament in January. And he attended and was ecstatic about being invited to King Edward the Third's coronation as a knight of the shire on the first day of this month.'

Richard swirled his wine in his goblet for a moment. 'But what I cannot quite understand is why he should suddenly become angered enough to go to Wakefield, presumably in the evening before the gates closed for the curfew, and commit a brutal slaying.'

'Perhaps you need to talk to his daughter, Rowena,' Lady Katherine suggested. 'We stayed for a while after the feast was over and after you had gone. She and he had some sort of quiet discussion. They both seemed rather upset by something, or by someone.'

'By Father Alban?'

Lady Katherine daintily shrugged her shoulders. 'I think it was someone else. She told me that she had heard her father talking with one of the guests and he had been frightfully upset from then on.'

'I will ask her,' Richard replied, tasting the wine and nodding appreciatively. 'This is an excellent wine, Sir Basil.'

The old knight nodded. 'It is Burgundy, my first wife's favourite wine. She died four years ago, may the Lord keep her and protect her.'

'Ah, so have you and Lady Katherine been married long?' Richard asked politely.

'Only two years,' Lady Katherine returned. 'That is something that we had to thank Master Hopwood for. I had lost my husband to a sweating fever in London. Master Hopwood was at parliament at the time and had known him.'

'I needed a wife,' Sir Basil said in his brusque manner. 'I need an heir.'

Lady Katherine looked pained, as if on the verge of tears. 'Dear Geoffrey Hopwood arranged our marriage. Sadly, we have not yet been blessed with a child.'

From the mansion at Stanley Richard rode to Kirkthorpe Hall, where he found Rowena being comforted by several of her female servants, including the maid who had found Geoffrey Hopwood hanging in the dovecote.

'Has the sun stopped shining, Sir Richard?' she asked him when they were alone. 'Has the moon fallen from the sky? It seems as if it must have, for my life is meaningless without my dearest father.'

'I cannot plumb the depths of your despair, Rowena, but I know something of grief. My own father-in-law, Sir Thomas Deyville, is suffering from melancholia after his wife, Lady Alecia, was taken from us. The physician Doctor Brandon Flynn is treating him every day by trying to restore his humours.'

The ghost of a smile hovered across her mouth. 'Would you have a doctor bleed me to death, too, Sir Richard?'

'It seems to be helping him. He also uses purgatives and a wax image of him that he also bleeds, and he is now taking a potion called *aurum potabile.*'

'Your pardon, Sir Richard, but I have used herbs, flowers and roots from the fields and woodlands since my mother taught me as a child. I will if I feel the need take some of my own.'

Ah yes, Mistress Wisley told me that she was skilled in this. 'I am going to be holding an inquest into Father Alban's death and into that of your father and Peter Plowman.'

She looked horrified. 'M-must I attend?'

I intend to exhibit the bodies, which would be unpleasant for anyone. But for her, barely a woman, unable to see properly yet knowing that her father's body is visible to the whole court, it will be terrible. There is no telling how the crowd in the court will react to the franklin's felonies. He harrumphed. 'I am afraid that the law demands it, Rowena. It will be an ordeal, I know, which is why I must now ask various questions of you. If I ask you again during the inquest, it will not be such a trauma.'

She hung her head for a few moments then asked in a quavering voice, 'Can you prove he was innocent, Sir Richard?'

'I must find the truth, whatever that is, Rowena. I am a judge and I must not start with my mind swayed one way or the other.'

She nodded and wrung her hands in her lap. 'I understand. I just hoped it would be otherwise. I will answer your questions as best that I can.'

'It is a mystery to me that your father suddenly seemed to decide to end not one person's life, but two. I need to discover why that was. So firstly, tell me, did your father leave for Wakefield on the evening of the feast?'

'Yes, in the late afternoon he told me he had business in town and would see me on the morrow.'

'Was he angry then?'

'My father rarely showed anger. He was not an angry man.'

'Yet Lady Katherine, who was sitting near you at the feast, said that Father Alban was saying provocative things. He irritated Sir Basil and your father tried to calm the situation.'

'As he always did.'

'She also said that both you and he seemed upset later, after he had talked with someone. She did not know who it was.'

Rowena sighed. 'Nor do I, Sir Richard. I did not see the person. They were in his counting room, where he sees people in private. I was passing the door and I think it was a man's voice that I heard.'

'Did you hear anything of the conversation?'

'Only one sentence was clear, and that was from my father. He said, "We are betrayed and I must warn him." That was it, as far as I can remember.'

Richard repeated it verbatim, then asked, 'Are you sure he said "betrayed" and "must warn him"?'

Rowena nodded, then as if she had been holding back the floodwaters, she sobbed uncontrollably. Richard called one of the servants, bid her farewell and left.

As he rode to Wragby to see Gembert Cooper the reeve, Richard went over the things he had learned from his talks with Sir Basil, Lady Katherine and Rowena Hopwood.

I know that someone had said something to the franklin that upset him, but I do not know who that person was. Also, the franklin said that 'we are betrayed,' so was he involved in some plot or other? He also said he 'must warn him.' That sounds as if he had to warn a fellow plotter. Yet he ends up murdering Father Alban by a frenzied attack, stabbing him some ten times. It makes little sense.

He found the reeve's house with little difficulty. It was not a mansion or a manor house, yet it was the most substantial house in Wragby, as it had clearly recently been extended as the reeve had told him it had at the franklin's feast. A well-tended garden and rose bushes on either side of the front door indicated a female touch.

'Sir Richard, I wondered if you might need to talk to me about Master Hopwood and this whole unfortunate business,' said Gembert Cooper after he and his aunt, Mary Wisley, had exchanged formal pleasantries and made him comfortable in the room that Gembert used as an office. Here, he explained to Richard, he kept tallies of the cattle, sheep, pigs and horses within the graveships of which he was the reeve, as well as the work and accounts on behalf of the franklin. 'Master Hopwood owned extensive lands between Kirkthorpe and Wragby, and I am reeve to both villages. I also keep a record of the crops of each tenant, and I keep a running diary about the weather. Everything that happens in my little patch, I know about.'

Richard listened politely, and affirmed his impression that Gembert Cooper was quite a pedantic fellow, undoubtedly good qualities for a reeve. 'There have been further developments in Wakefield that you may not be aware of,' he told them. He watched them carefully as he recounted the main details about the franklin's death and Judd of Alverthorpe's disappearance. Like the old knight and his wife, they were horrified, but they did not react the same way. They unconsciously reached for each other's hands, but not in the way that Richard would have expected an aunt and nephew to react. He made a mental note of it.

'I cannot believe that Master Hopwood would twice commit murder, Sir Richard,' said Gembert Cooper.

'He was a gentle man, and he would surely never do anything that would leave his daughter Rowena on her own,' said Mistress Wisley, nodding in agreement with her nephew.

'Can either of you help me to understand how he could change so much and do something that runs contrary to the impression that people have of him? I have heard that he had discussion with someone after the feast in his counting room.'

Gembert Cooper sat back in surprise. 'Why, I had a talk with him there, Sir Richard. It was after you and I had our talk and after you left. I had to talk to him about some of the levies, for payment to the Manor of Wakefield, which you and I had just discussed.'

'Did you talk about having to warn someone about something?'

The reeve stroked his neatly groomed beard and shook his head. 'It was simply a short talk about finance, Sir Richard.'

'Which I knew that my nephew was going to talk to him about.'

Richard asked some more questions about their relationship with the franklin and with his daughter Rowena, but he did not feel that he learned anything new from them. Once or twice during their conversation, however, he thought that he picked up looks of consternation from the reeve, as if concerned that his aunt should say too much. He also noted the reverse and had the impression that each sought the opinion and approval of the other.

He then changed the subject. 'As the reeve of Kirkthorpe and Wragby, how well do you know the people and events in the surrounding villages?'

'I know most of the other reeves, Sir Richard. And I know many of the people in the surrounding areas, but I do not interfere with the other villages, just as I would not expect others to interfere with me and my work.'

'Did you know Bryce-a-Green and Quinn of Ryhill?'

'I knew them, Sir Richard. Bryce-a-Green and his family were long enemies of Quinn of Ryhill and his family. Wherever one could do the other family a disservice, they would do so. Sheep stealing, cattle robbing, they did it to each other.'

'You know about the case? Bryce-a-Green had his head cut off by Quinn of Ryhill and the three men of a hue and cry.'

'I know about it, Sir Richard. You had Quinn hanged and those three men were flogged and sent to the Tolbooth.'

'Do you know the three men?'

Gembert looked at his aunt, as if seeking approval, Richard thought. From the corner of his eye, he thought he saw her nod. 'I know them, yes. They are common folk, labourers and scoundrels.'

'Men who would do things for money without asking questions?'

'Possibly, yes.'

'Were any related to Bryce-a-Green?'

This time, he was sure he saw the aunt give a slight shake of the head.

One thing is clear from this meeting. Aunt and nephew they may be, but there is more than that. I feel they are more like two people whom ecclesiastic law forbids that they become lovers.

It was afternoon by the time Richard reached the Priory of St Leonard's. Typical of the Dominican order, it was not ostentatious but rather simply built. It nestled in a small valley on Ackworth Moor a mere hundred yards from the main road from Wragby. A low wall surrounded it. Inside that, it had a central bell tower with wings on either side, one being the chapel and the other the kitchens. A chapter house with a quadrangle and cloister stood in front of it, and to the side of that was another square building with its own fenced garden. As he entered the wide-open gates, he saw several friars working around the priory, stacking wood, pushing wheelbarrows of dung or coaxing errant hens into wooden henhouses.

On seeing him, a portly friar put down the handles of his barrow and trotted over to meet him on sandaled feet. Richard recognised him, as indeed he thought he would know all of the friars, since theirs was a mendicant order and they were often seen in and around Wakefield, preaching and receiving offerings from passers-by.

'Sir Richard Lee, is it not?' the friar asked. 'I am Brother Caspar. Have you come to see Prior Norbert?'

Richard dismounted. 'Actually, I have come to see your manciple, Master Drewitt, and also his sister, Mistress Myrtle Drewitt.'

Brother Caspar first nodded and then gave a weary sigh. 'We have heard such dreadful news from Wakefield. Such evil things to happen.' He made the sign of the cross. 'Some demon must have entered the franklin's head and told him to kill. We have prayed for Father Alban's soul and also for Master Hopwood.'

'I am afraid that there have been further developments and another murder. Master Hopwood is dead, by his own hand.'

Brother Caspar muttered something in Latin that Richard assumed to be a quotation from some obscure part of the Bible and again made the sign of the cross. Then he launched into a diatribe about eternal damnation.

Richard did not wish to get into a discussion about spiritual matters and was relieved when he heard Matthew Drewitt call his name from the direction of the square building. He excused himself and walked his horse over to the fence, where he tethered the reins.

'Please, come and take a cup of mead,' said the manciple. 'Brother Fergus and Prior Norbert are with us.'

Richard followed him into the building.

'This is the priory's hospital,' the manciple explained. 'My sister has her own physic garden here and prepares her remedies and simples in the dispensary and helps Brother Norman, our hospitaller with some of our patients. And here,' he said, pointing to a door at the end of a short corridor, 'is our private quarters, where I and my sister live and I work on the priory's business.'

Richard was a tall man, but the manciple was at least a hand's breadth taller and had to stoop to get under the door lintel. The room they entered was clearly a dining room in which Myrtle Drewitt, Brother Fergus and an older man with a grey tonsured head were sitting with small cups of mead.

For the third time that day, after pleasantries Richard was seated with a drink on the table in front of him.

'This is mead of the highest quality,' said Prior Norbert. 'We make it here ourselves.'

Richard sipped it politely, wishing that instead of drink he had been offered food, for he had begun to feel his stomach rumble. Once again, he watched them all closely as he told them of the day's gory events.

Myrtle Drewitt reacted throughout it with a look of increasing disgust, all the while sitting perfectly still, just as she had at the feast. She gave the impression of one able to keep perfect control of her emotions.

Prior Norbert and Brother Fergus both repeatedly made the sign of the cross and closed their hands as if silently saying prayers.

'Wickedness!' was the prior's assessment.

'Indeed,' Brother Fergus agreed. 'It shows, I believe, that Bishop Ledrede was correct in sending myself and my fellow brothers around the country to try to stem this tide of evil.'

'I cannot believe that Master Hopwood could do such a thing and then commit a further mortal sin by killing himself,' Matthew Drewitt said, his pinched nose twitching as if the whole story was like a bad smell to him.

'This is exactly why I have travelled here,' Richard explained. 'Not one person that I have interviewed has had an ill thing to say about the franklin. I wanted to know if any of you had noticed anything at the feast on St Julian's Day that could account for him becoming violent and committing such felonies as these two murders.' He paused then added, 'or anything after the feast?'

No one was able to offer any explanation until Brother Fergus drained his mead and pushed the cup away from him. 'I would be surprised if this does not prove to be the result of witchcraft!'

This time, Myrtle Drewitt gasped and reached out to clutch her brother's hand. Richard saw the look that the manciple gave her in return.

Like the reeve and his aunt, that was not the interaction I would expect from a brother and sister. 'Can you enlighten us, Brother Fergus?' Richard asked.

'I told you at the feast that Bishop Ledrede had sent us abroad because of his concerns about the rise in witchcraft around the country. His Holiness Pope John has himself been the target of witchcraft. I talked about this from the very pulpit that my briefly encountered friend, Father Alban, had preached from. He issued a papal bull, *Super Illius Specula*, which makes the practice of witchcraft a heresy, punishable by excommunication and then by death. Bishop Ledrede has made it his mission to carry out His Holiness's charge to rid the world of this scourge. When he uncovered the coven in Kilkenny, he rooted all of the heinous creatures out and put them on trial and had them executed by being hanged, strangled or burned. Except their leader, Alice Kyteler, who disappeared along with her familiar, a demon called Robin Artisson or Robin, son of Art.'

Richard had heard him tell this at the feast, and just like previously, the friar's voice rose and a patina of perspiration formed on his brow. It was clear that he was passionate in his hatred of witches.

'But are there witches here, where we live?' Myrtle asked, her voice trembling a little.

'I think it is likely,' the friar replied. 'Bishop Ledrede sent many of us to holy institutions that he believes are in the heartland of witchcraft.'

'How do you think witchcraft could be involved here?' Richard asked.

Brother Fergus raised his hands, palms upwards. 'How else can you account for a man doing such things? It sounds as if a spell was cast and a demon entered his head. Father Alban had spoken out about evil and may have incensed witches, so they sent a demon to enter the franklin's head, where it forced him to do murder, once, twice, perhaps more times.'

Prior Norbert nodded sagely. 'It is so. And a powerful demon raised by witchcraft could tell him to send his soul to Satan. Which he assuredly has by committing self-murder.'

'And how will sending you and your brother friars stop such outbreaks?' Matthew Drewitt asked. 'By prayer?'

'Through preaching,' Brother Fergus returned. 'Prior Norbert has agreed that myself and the other brothers shall go forth from now and preach against witchcraft. By doing so, by educating the common people, they will recognise when spells are being cast against them and evil is being done. They will tell us and we will root them all out.'

'We begin our work tomorrow,' Prior Norbert announced. 'Our brothers will be travelling to Wakefield, Pontefract and Castleford and spreading the message in villages and hamlets along the way.'

'You look concerned about this, Master Drewitt,' Richard said, noting the manciple's even more pinched nose.

'To be honest, I am, Sir Richard,' he replied. 'As you know, the Dominican order is a mendicant one. We depend upon gifts and donations. It is my experience that when our friars preach about things that people do not want to hear about, like witchcraft and sorcery, our donations are reduced. The coffers swell far more when the message is that one should pay for sins. Guilt, in my view, is a more powerful emotion than simple fear.'

Richard noticed the glimmer of a smile on Myrtle Drewitt's face, as if she was pleased that he had deflected a tricky question.

As Richard rode back towards Wakefield, he reflected that he had learned something from every one of his visits, yet nothing that gave him any real clue about why Geoffrey Hopwood should have become a triple murderer, if he included the taking of his own life.

He saw a cloud of dust rising from the trail some distance away, thrown up by a rider travelling at speed towards him. He was surprised to recognise the horse and the rider as they crested a rise.

'My lord,' cried Hubert of Loxley as he approached, then drew to a halt with a strong pull on the reins. 'We have found Judd of Alverthorpe.'

'Was he hiding in the town after all?'

'No, my lord, he was hiding in an old sheepcote on a hill on the Heath. A yeoman from Sharlston sent a boy to Wakefield with urgent news for you. The gatekeepers sent for me and the lad told me that he and his master had found him when they were taking their flock up to the high pasture on the Heath. It's common land shared by the yeoman and other local landowners.'

'Was this yeoman's name Cedric, by any chance?'

Hubert looked puzzled, but nodded. 'It was, Sir Richard. They were surprised to find a pony hobbled in a thicket not far from the hut and went to check on the sheepcote. As we know, there are folk around here who will risk stealing cattle and sheep.'

And who know they risk death for such a felony!

'When they approached it, they heard a slight tinkling and thought either a stray cow or a sheep must be in there with a cowbell or sheepbell dangling from its collar. Apparently, the shepherds use them on the leading sheep in their flocks. Not surprisingly, when they went inside they were shocked witless to find a body hanging from the roof. They knew who he was, but since they didn't know about what had happened in Wakefield today, they couldn't understand why he would be there. He had hanged himself with his belt, and the tinkling was from the rattling of the keys that still hung from it.'

CHAPTER SEVEN

Cedric of Sharlston and one of the young lads who worked for him had tied up the pony to a gorse bush outside the sheepcote and stayed to guard the body while Hubert had sought Richard. They were both relieved when the judge permitted them to go home after he had interrogated them about the finding of the Tolbooth jailor.

The body of Judd of Alverthorpe lay on the hardened mud inside the sheepcote. Cedric and the boy had managed to untie the belt from a timber in the crude purlin roof and eased the body to the ground in case he might still be alive.

Richard bent down to inspect the body first. His leather skullcap was still on his head. The thickly bearded face was slightly discoloured, but curiously it was not contorted with agony as the franklin's had been. The eyes were closed and there were flecks of saliva on the lips, but there were none of the tiny red spots around the eyes that Doctor Flynn had drawn his attention to on the body of Geoffrey Hopwood.

'He looks as if he had made peace with himself, my lord,' Hubert said, almost echoing Richard's own thoughts.

'He has no signs of injury, as Geoffrey Hopwood had,' Richard mused. Then he clicked his tongue. 'But there is no reason that he should, is there? There was no hue and cry, and he was not beaten.' He looked at the hands, which were calloused, as most working people's were, yet they were not blistered, bruised or cut. 'He has done hard work in the past, but that is all I can tell. He has not been in a fight.' He stood up and looked about the sheepcote, which was empty apart from dried sheep dung scattered all over the earth floor, and the body. The belt was still tied about his throat, and with some difficulty Richard untied it and held it up to examine. 'The keys for the Tolbooth are here, just as you said. But his sheath is empty. Can you tell anything by it, Hubert?'

'I would say it was meant to hold a quillon dagger. Does that mean —?'

Richard nodded. 'It looks as if the franklin used Judd of Alverthorpe's dagger to kill Peter Plowman.' He looked back at the body and frowned. 'Now what is this bulge?' Bending again he reached inside the jailor's tunic and drew out the franklin's hefty silk purse. 'Well now, this may make the puzzle simpler. If he took the bribe to set the franklin free, this was probably at least a first payment. Perhaps they separated and the franklin went home with the promise that he'd bring more money while Judd of Alverthorpe lay low. Probably this was an agreed place to meet. It is out of the way.'

Hubert nodded in agreement. 'That seems likely, my lord. Both men probably knew Wakefield like the backs of their hands, or well enough at least to evade the town watch and make good their escape.'

Richard stroked his beard. 'What happened then, we have yet to find out, but it seems that the franklin went home and committed *felo de se*, that is, self-murder. Judd seems to have ridden here, hobbled his pony overnight, then realised the enormity of his felony and also committed self-killing.'

'So what shall we do now, my lord?'

'We'll take the body back to Wakefield on the pony and put it in the Tolbooth in his own quarters. Tomorrow we shall consider this further. But since we now have the franklin and the jailor, we can permit the town gates to be opened as usual in the morning.'

That evening, as they were talking about Sir Thomas's condition and his treatment by Doctor Flynn, Richard and Wilhelmina drifted into a conversation about the nature of grief.

'I am sure that if I was not with child I would be feeling my mother's death a great deal more, Richard. I almost feel as if she is looking after me and has not gone completely.'

'She was a great lady, my love. Even when she was in great pain she smiled, and she could always soften your father's moods.'

'I am not sure that I understand these humours that you say Doctor Flynn is trying to correct by bleeding him.' She shuddered. 'And as for that doll that you say he has made and treats by pricking with a bodkin, it sounds like ... like witchcraft.'

Richard laughed. 'That is exactly what your father said. Yet I have to admit that it seems to work.' He had not told her of his doubts about the hanging of Quinn of Ryhill, partly because he had no wish to upset her by talking about felons and their punishment. Although Wilhelmina was a strong-willed lady, she had a softness about her, and talk of executions could well move her to tears. Worse, it could affect the baby she carried, which would be a risk he was unwilling to take.

'These humours that affect us are indeed strange,' Wilhelmina said. 'It seems they can make us melancholic, angry, jealous — fearful, even. It is as if things that happen in our lives must alter the levels of these fluids in our bodies. Are they contained in us like water and wine in flasks?'

Again, Richard laughed at the thought. 'The physicians call them organs. The heart is full of blood, the lungs of phlegm, the liver and spleen of the two types of bile. They all must connect and mix and then unmix again.'

Once more, Wilhelmina shuddered. 'And that mixing of humours can turn a person mad? Like the franklin, Geoffrey Hopwood? It amazes me that he could murder anyone. He always seemed such a gentle fellow.'

'Hubert was not of that opinion, Wilhelmina. He thought there was something off about him that did not sit well in his mind. He thought that there was a potentially deceitful side to him. It may be that he acted out of fear.'

'Whyfor would he be fearful of the priest, or yet of Peter Plowman?'

Richard had not yet told her of the *felo de se* of the franklin or of the Wakefield jailor, again lest it upset her in her condition. 'I do not know yet, Wilhelmina. But I am concerned about people making people fearful about witches and witchcraft.'

She listened as he told her about his conversation with Brother Fergus and Prior Norbert and of how the Dominican friars were planning to go preaching about the evil of witchcraft and sorcery. 'I am concerned that it will lead to many people being denounced as witches or sorcerers.'

'Just as happened some years ago in Pontefract?'

'Exactly, my love. And as you will recall, it caused mobs to form. And when mobs get angry, they do not listen to the order of the law. They can take things into their own hands.' *Perhaps I was thinking of this when I sentenced Quinn of Ryhill to death for making himself a judge in the case of Bryce-a-Green.*

Wilhelmina yawned. 'I think I must retire to bed soon, husband. I am sorry that you feel you cannot lie with me; it makes me feel guilty to think of you sleeping in a chamber on your own.'

Guilt! Ah, there is an emotion even more powerful than fear. I know of this emotion myself and how it gnaws away at you. I must be careful of it and not allow it to grow, for it seems a most destructive emotion. One that can drive men to take their own lives.

He stood as his wife rose to her feet, and he hugged her and kissed her gently. 'Have no guilt, Wilhelmina. Such an emotion can make you ill. Sleep well, my love.'

Later, on his own he pondered further on these deep, dark emotions and what they could do to a person. Indeed, what they may even drive people to do.

Lust is another such emotion which could drive seemingly normal people to do evil acts. And who knows what carnal desires lurk in people's hearts?

The man and the woman had celebrated by making passionate love as the moonlight shone into the chamber.

When they finally fell apart to lie side by side on the bed, breathless and damp with perspiration from their exertions, they laughed.

'At least now we will have convinced that buffoon of a judge,' he said.

'Was it very difficult?' she asked.

He guffawed. 'You have to ask me that! You knew it was going to be, but I managed them both.'

'Which was the hardest?'

He shrugged. 'Both had their challenges. They had to be coaxed, convinced that I was their protector and that I was going to find a way out for them.'

'And you arranged everything as we planned, to cover our tracks?'

'Exactly as planned. No one will ever know. We should be safe forever now.'

She giggled, that silvery sound that so excited him. 'The fools!'

'They all are,' he agreed.

As their passion renewed with the excitement of the deeds and the relief that they had brought, they made love again.

Richard paid a visit to Sandal Castle the next morning to see again how Sir Thomas was progressing. He was relieved to find that he seemed in better spirits than he had been ever since Lady Alecia had died.

'I am reducing the amount of blood that is to be removed, so I am using fewer leeches this day,' Doctor Flynn told the patient as he examined Sir Thomas's urine in his matula.

'My friend the doll will be relieved,' Sir Thomas said, his expression still that of a surly child. 'You will note that I have allowed him to lie abed rather than sit on the chamber pot.'

The physician allowed himself a rare smile. 'Another jest! This is the progress that I expected. The bleeding and the *aurum potabile* that you are taking each day are working well.'

Sir Thomas was silent while leeches were this time applied to his legs. Then he said, 'I think that this night I will return to my own bedchamber. I feel I would be more comfortable.'

My Lord! Progress indeed.

Hubert was waiting on the bailey with the saddled horses. He waited until the doctor and Richard finished the discussion they'd been having all the way down the barbican stairs.

'The improvement in him is remarkable, Doctor Flynn. But what part do you think the wax image of him plays in the process?'

'A great one. The image is fashioned as I see him and it has his hair, which forms a link with his body. I treat the body and the doll, and the malign influences will drain from both. This is part of the art of physic.'

'I have heard that healers who are not as educated as yourself also use such images to take disease away, perhaps by rubbing something on the body of both the person and then on the image.'

Doctor Flynn nodded. 'They are both techniques used in the art of physic. The bleeding that I have done with Sir Thomas is an example of *principium sympathiae*, the sympathetic principle. It means using the link to facilitate or increase the strength of a treatment. The other you mentioned is the *principium transfero*, which means to transfer a disease to a creature. Depending on which element is at the base of the problem, and all the humours are based on the elements, you could give it to a creature of that element.'

'Interesting. Can you give me some examples?'

The physician thought for a moment. 'A problem of the waters, a bladder disease, could be given to a fish or a water creature. A disorder of the lungs would be of the air, so you could use a bird, and a problem of the bowels could be of the earth and given to a worm, or a mole. Both principles are valid and were written about by the great Gilbertinus, or as he is better known Gilbertus Anglicus, the author of *The Compendium of Medicine*. He learned his craft at the Schola Medica Salernitana at Salerno in Italy. I studied all seven volumes of it myself.'

'And can a disease be transferred by the *principium transfero* to a dead creature? To a dead man, perhaps?'

The physician eyed Richard suspiciously. 'Now you are getting into darker waters, Sir Richard. Such practices exist, but are performed by common folk with little learning. You are talking about sorcery or witchcraft, which I will have nothing to do with.'

That is what I suspected you would say. It was as well that I told young Hal's mother Lorna to say nothing of this. The fact that she was related to the hanged man, Quinn of Ryhill, was another matter that worried him and which seemed to be feeding into the guilt he felt when he allowed himself to dwell too much upon it. *But I have other important matters that need my immediate attention this day.*

John of Flanshaw was awaiting Richard and Hubert in the Rolls Office of the Moot Hall. 'I have the information that you instructed me to get, Sir Richard,' he said once Richard had taken a seat at his desk. 'The old woman who sells her wares in the market is known by all as Mother Oulton. She seems a good woman of almost sixty or so years. She makes potions from herbs and sells cheap cures. Poor folk swear by her. The apothecary's name is Oliver Mopp, and he seems even older. A drinker of mead and a man who looks as if he is either in need of his remedies or has taken too many. He looks like a poisoned man, Sir Richard. Neither of them has made up a salve for anyone at the Tolbooth, either knowingly or unwittingly.'

'There are no others?'

'Not in the town walls, Sir Richard.' He stood with his thumbs hooked in his belt, then with an attempt at diffidence he went on, 'The whole town is growing restless, Sir Richard. You and Hubert were seen last night bringing the body of Judd of Alverthorpe back on a pony and taking him to the Tolbooth. I would not say that he was a popular man, especially not among those who had spent time in the Tolbooth or who had been on the receiving end of a flogging, but there has been talk of little else since then. Everywhere, in taverns, the market, and in the streets, people are aware that murders have been done and now with the jailor brought back dead, well, they want answers, Sir Richard.'

Hubert snorted. 'The impertinent rabble!'

Richard raised a restraining hand. 'The people have a right to know, Hubert. But it will be done in the correct manner. With an inquest, or a series of inquests.'

'There is more that you should know about, Sir Richard. It may or may not be important.'

'Speak, John.'

'These were found this morning.' He went over to a corner and picked up a sack. Placing it on the floor in front of them, he delved inside and took out by its tail the body of a rat. A number of nails had been driven into its back.

'Where was it found?' Richard asked.

'At the side of the Church of All Saints. An urchin said a drunkard pointed it out to him. It may have been there a day or two.'

'You mean it may have been there before Father Alban was murdered?' Richard queried.

The bailiff reached into the sack again and pulled out two more dead rats. One with its throat cut, so that the head was almost severed from its body. Another had a rope made from straw tied tight about its neck, like a noose. 'One was found on top of a waste heap outside the Tolbooth by one of the gong farmers in the night, and the other was left hanging by the pillory on Cheapside.'

'Could all three have been there a while?' Hubert asked. 'Even the one that was hanging? Ratcatchers often leave them thus to frighten off other vermin, but also as a sign to show that they have done their job.'

Richard looked unconvinced. 'The one hanging from the pillory is more likely to be one that was put there and meant to be found. Yet they were not newly killed, you think?'

John of Flanshaw nodded. 'They are all as stiff as if they were made of wood, so they have been dead some time.'

'And they stink as if they have started to rot, too,' said Hubert.

'News about them has also spread around the town, Sir Richard. I think that has made people even more fearful.'

This is what I was talking with Wilhelmina about yesterday evening, and is exactly what I did not want to happen. When a town gets riled up, then mobs can form.

'But surely it is all becoming clearer, my lord,' Hubert said. 'When you hold the inquest, it will be clear that all the deaths are linked and can be explained. Then it will be over.'

'Except for these!' Richard replied, pointing to the dead rats.

'Shall I throw them away, Sir Richard?' John of Flanshaw asked, as he gingerly picked one up and held the sack open with his other hand to receive it.

'No! Just leave them in the sack and put it in the corner again. They may be more important than they seem.'

'Do you not think they are just a stupid jest by someone, my lord?' Hubert asked.

Richard shrugged his shoulders. 'I am not sure, Hubert. We have another rat to consider.'

Hubert and John looked at each other in puzzlement.

'Another rat, Sir Richard?' the court bailiff queried.

'Siward Trapp, who is in the Tolbooth at this very time.'

Some men are natural orators. The Church seemed to attract such men. Brother Fergus and his fellow friar Brother Caspar had been despatched to Wakefield after Vigils, the first service of the day when the silence of the night was broken. Others were sent to the other towns within the district to begin the Lord's work to warn people to be on their guard against the forces of evil and the practitioners of sorcery and witchcraft. They had separated upon entering the town and arranged to meet at the end of the day at the Kirkgate before trudging homeward to St Leonard's Priory.

Brother Fergus made his way to the market cross at the Bull Ring, where he began to preach. 'Brothers and sisters, come, I prithee, listen to the words that the Lord says to you through the mouth of this miserable creature that I am. Aye, I said that I was a miserable creature, friar though I am. I am miserable because I see and hear evil wherever I go.'

Whether from his accent or from the way he delivered his words, he quickly garnered a crowd from the market around him.

'You're not from round here!' someone cried out.

'No, my friend, I am not from here. I am from across the water in Ireland.'

'You'll get no money here; be off with you,' shouted another observer.

'I do not seek money, brother. Instead, I bring you salvation if you would have it. Aye, and I bring you the chance to save lives. Perhaps even your own.'

Their interest whetted, the crowd gathered closer and grew in size.

'As you can see from my humble habit, I am a Black Friar. I have been sent by my bishop from the Black Abbey at Kilkenny in Ireland with a message from His Holiness Pope

John himself. I come to warn you about the plague of witches that is spreading across the land and which could soon drown good people in a sea of evil.'

'There be no witches here,' someone cried.

'Did you hear that man, brothers and sisters? He says there are no witches, but there are witches everywhere. They work their damnable art in darkness, so you can't see them. They whisper behind closed doors, so you can't hear them. And they fornicate in moonlight on heaths and in forests while you sleep. They fornicate with each other and with demons who let them ride on poles through the air, they steal babes, they blight crops, make cows go dry of milk and they spread disease.'

What started as murmurs and mumbles grew into gasps and squeals of horror and revulsion.

'Who among you knows of people that have suddenly fallen ill and died? Or who have had accidents for no reason? Or good mothers who have bled while carrying and lost children?'

The mood of the crowd grew agitated as many called out or simply nodded eagerly.

'Have there not been murders in Wakefield? I am just a wandering friar, but I have heard of these. Father Alban, who you all must know, lies dead in his own church. I preached with him myself in the Church of St Peter in Kirkthorpe on St Julian's Day.'

Some women screamed.

'I enjoyed the hospitality of a franklin, Master Geoffrey Hopwood of Kirkthorpe, who I heard was found after this murder and put in the Tolbooth.'

'Aye, and he escaped and killed again!' someone called out.

'Brothers and sisters, good men do not just do things like this. Witchcraft is at work. Witches are among you. Perhaps even now, standing beside you, plotting and planning to bring their evil upon you through their devilish spells and incantations.'

'The rats! Have you heard about the rats?' A call went up.

'Yes, a rat with a slit throat.'

'Another stabbed with nails!'

Brother Fergus pounced on these utterances from the crowd and made an emphatic sign of the cross in front of him. 'Witchcraft, brothers and sisters,' he said, almost spitting the words out. 'Well, do you know what you must do, brothers and sisters?'

'Tell us!'

'You must do as His Holiness says and root them out. Put them in a church court and try them. If they are guilty — as the Bible says — do not suffer a witch to live.'

'Burn them! Burn them! Burn them!' went the cries until a chorus of anger spread around the whole market.

In the Rolls Office, Richard, Hubert and John of Flanshaw heard the shouting.

It has begun, thought Richard. *Just as I feared it might.*

Hubert and John of Flanshaw made their way to the marketplace as Richard instructed them to in order to see exactly what had roused the people to such a clamour. But by the time they'd arrived, the furore had died down and the crowd had dispersed.

'What was all that noise about, Mistress?' Hubert asked a woman making her way from the market with a basket of eggs.

'A friar was preaching and warning us about witches,' she said, her voice trembling and her eyes full of alarm. 'He said we must all be on guard because they might be your neighbour or your friend.'

As the two men entered the market and separated to ask others what had transpired, they were answered in similar manner.

'You can't trust anyone,' an old man selling liquorice roots said, proffering his meagre bundle in the hope of earning a coin. Hubert delved in his purse and bought a handful to take home for his son to chew to keep his bowels open.

'Brother Fergus, his name was,' a youth told John of Flanshaw. 'An Irish friar from Kilkenny, where they burn witches all the time.'

'He said the Pope orders us to root out anyone who casts spells and fornicates with demons at night,' another wild-eyed lad told them enthusiastically.

Having heard enough, they returned to the Moot Hall where they found Richard in the Rolls Office. He had taken the dead rats from the sack again and laid them in a row on the floor.

Hubert and John of Flanshaw informed him of the things they had been told.

'So there was no sign of a mob?'

'No, my lord. Yet all of the people we talked to seemed stirred up.'

'Many were fearful, Sir Richard,' the bailiff agreed. 'I would also say they looked suspicious, as if they should not trust anyone.'

'That is the danger of such talk,' Richard replied. 'It is like tossing a cinder into a roof of thatch. It may smoulder away without anyone being aware of it, then a strong wind will suddenly make the whole thing catch fire before there is time to stop it.'

'What should we do, my lord?'

Richard shook his head. 'We will alert Ranald Brigg of the town watch now and also Sir Thomas at Sandal Castle when we return later today. We need to be able to respond if things get out of hand, and having half a dozen of the castle guards again would be a sensible precaution. Apart from that, there is little we can do, for the friar is doing what friars are permitted to do. And in this instance, Brother Fergus and his fellow friars are doing what has been sanctioned by a bishop and by the Pope himself.' He pointed at the three dead rats. 'The question I find myself asking is whether these rats have been where they were found for some days, which is possible, for who notices a dead rat lying in a gutter or on a dung heap? It is strange that all three have come to light today. And all three killed in the same way as three people in Wakefield. A stabbing, a slit throat and a hanging.'

Hubert frowned. 'There is one thing wrong with that, my lord. Father Alban was stabbed in the church, Peter Plowman had his throat slit in the Tolbooth, but the franklin, Geoffrey Hopwood, hanged himself at his manor in Kirkthorpe.'

'That assumes that this rat that was throttled represents the franklin. It could be another hanged man.'

'But Judd of Alverthorpe hanged himself in that sheepcote on the Heath,' said John of Flanshaw.

'If these three rats had been there for a while, unnoticed as I just suggested, then it may be that this third rat represents the recent hanging of Quinn of Ryhill.'

Once again, Richard experienced that hollow, nagging sense of self-doubt and guilt. And his mind went over the conversation that he'd had with Doctor Flynn that very morning about the use of what he called images to represent the patient in physic. He recalled how the doctor had looked suspiciously at him when he had asked about using *principium transfero*, as he termed it, to transfer a disease to a dead creature or man. He had said these were dark waters to get into.

Richard picked up the rat with the cord about its neck. The body was stiff as wood, the mouth open to reveal its ugly, sharp teeth, its eyes also open, but shrunken in their grey furry sockets like dark seeds.

It has been dead for many days, methinks. And if it was made for Quinn, an image of him with a witch's spell upon it to bring about his death by hanging, then does that mean that I unwittingly fell victim to that spell? That my judgement was forced on me by witchcraft?

'Return them to the sack, please, John. I think that I need to have another word with Siward Trapp!'

CHAPTER EIGHT

The scream of agony was unmistakeable.

Then there was the noise of running feet as people either ran to investigate, or ran for cover.

'Murder!' a voice cried.

'There's an archer on the loose!'

'Start the hue and cry!'

'Help! Help! Help!'

'There's a bowman abroad!'

Richard and Hubert rushed along the corridor to the entrance to the Moot Hall and paused as they opened the door. Both battle-hardened, they instinctively knew better than to dash into an area where an archer could pick them off. They cast an eye into the street then ran across to the buildings opposite, flattening themselves against the wall while they plotted their next move. The screaming was coming from the direction of the Tolbooth.

'Keep close to the walls!' Richard hissed at a crowd of people rushing towards them. Grasping a man who was half dragging a lad with him, he queried, 'What has happened? Who has been shot?'

'I don't know, Master. Except a man is lying in the street outside the Tolbooth with an arrow through his back or his shoulder. He's wriggling like a stuck pig; you can hear him.'

John of Flanshaw joined them, similarly flattening his back against the wall. 'I thought you might need assistance, Sir Richard,' he gasped.

Richard signalled for the man and lad to move on, still seeking the cover of the walls. Hubert gestured authoritatively at other runners to do likewise.

There was general noise and much shouting as they made their way towards Cheapside and the Tolbooth. Those who had answered the hue and cry had armed themselves with whatever weapons they could, improvising shields with baskets, stools or pieces of wood. Making as much noise as they could — crying out 'Archer!' 'Bowman!' 'Murderer!' 'Get him!' — they ran in clusters of three or four, not knowing which way to go, but searching warily in alleyways and glancing at open windows as they tried to catch sight of anyone with a bow.

Hubert tapped his chest. 'Better let me go first, my lord. I have my arrowhead to protect me.'

Richard knew that Hubert was as skilled a man as there ever was in all manner of combat and he had the eyes of a hawk, so he nodded, watched him run while keeping close to the buildings, then followed.

Hubert was first to reach the wounded man writhing in agony as he tried to grasp the shaft of an arrow that was sticking out of his shoulder.

'Let go, my friend,' he commanded. 'The worst thing you can do is to move the arrowhead. Lie still and try to keep quiet lest your attacker is still nigh.' He pulled the wooden doll from his tunic and with a momentary reluctance proffered it to the man's mouth. 'Bite on this; it will help the pain and quieten your screams.'

'Who is he?' Richard asked, bending over the man. 'He looks familiar to me.'

John of Flanshaw reached them a moment later, and after also casting a look round in case an archer was lurking, he squinted at the wounded man. 'Why, it is Emmet Waller, Sir Richard. He's —'

'One of the three men that were flogged for their part in Bryce-a-Green's murder!' Richard said. He nodded to the bailiff. 'Run straight to Ranald Brigg's home and if he is still abed, which is unlikely with this din, get him to call out the watch and take charge of this hue and cry. They need to look for an archer. And once you've done that, go and get Simon the Fletcher and bring him to Doctor Flynn's house. I will have need of his advice.'

Crouching down and running bent almost in two, the bailiff went off on his errands. Hubert had already hefted the wounded man onto one of his broad shoulders. 'Chew on that doll, but not too much,' he said, turning his head to Emmet Waller. Then to Richard, 'Keep behind me, my lord.'

Doctor Flynn was riding up the hill from the Kirkgate and had just turned towards his house on the Warrengate when he was hailed by Richard, approaching on foot with Hubert, who was carrying the wounded Emmet Waller. The physician immediately dismounted and listened as Richard explained.

'I have just come back from seeing the Widow Clegg at Agbrigg, who I must say is responding remarkably well to treatment. I heard the commotion coming from the centre of Wakefield. Is this man the cause of it all?'

'He is the victim of a felony and his name is Emmet Waller,' Richard said. 'He has need of your services as soon as possible.'

The doctor made a cursory inspection of the arrow then nodded and remounted. 'I will ride to my house and get ready for surgery. Come as swiftly as you can.'

Doctor Flynn's house was a grand two-storey building with several rooms. A servant showed them into his chirurgia and treatment room, where he did his operating. This ranged from lancing boils and carbuncles to removing toenails, cauterising piles, splinting broken bones or cutting for bladder stone. Accordingly, it had a large wooden table in the centre of the room, buckets for sluicing blood away onto the reed floor, and a fire with a hanging cauldron for melting wax, pitch or other substances, as well as for heating his cautery irons. Upon shelves fixed to the walls were numerous pots and jars, painted in ochre and green, each labelled in Latin with the contents.

'Lay him down on his front and let me see the wound,' the doctor said, taking command of the situation.

Emmet Waller was a well-built man in his early thirties, with unkempt straw-coloured hair. He was biting hard on Hubert's doll with strong but yellowed teeth.

'What is your name, fellow?' Flynn asked, prising the wood from his mouth.

'Em-Emmet Waller, Master. Please … please, pluck it out. I am dying.'

'You will not die from this wound. The arrow is in your shoulder, not your chest,' the physician assured him. 'I must remove it to stop the blood from flowing, but it is in God's hands how much it will fester.'

Hubert stood to the side with his arms crossed. 'He was trying to pluck it out, but I knew if he did that then the arrowhead would remain buried deep inside.'

Without further ado, Doctor Flynn replaced the doll in Emmet Waller's mouth and with large scissors cut through his blood-soaked clothes to expose the wound fully. Blood had oozed out of a wound in the shoulder.

'You are quite right,' Doctor Flynn replied. 'Arrowheads are tied to the shaft with catgut, and when it is inside a wound, the body's fluids swell the catgut so that any attempt to pull it out will detach the shaft and leave the arrowhead inside. The body dislikes that, and if the person survives long enough then too much pus will form as it tries to heal.' He pointed to the patient. 'Sir Richard, it would help if you would hold his arms down and lean on his back. And you, Hubert of Loxley, kindly do the same with his legs. Try to keep him as still as you can.'

Dipping his fingers in a bucket of water placed by the table, he grasped the shaft of the arrow with his other hand and then slid the moistened finger into the wound, along the shaft. Emmet Waller's body immediately bucked and he screeched in pain despite the doll gripped betwixt his teeth. Doctor Flynn ignored the reaction and delved deeper.

'I need to picture the arrowhead exactly and feel where it is,' he explained, drawing his finger out. 'He is fortunate, as it missed the bone and the major blood vessels and is imbedded in the muscles.'

Hubert was idly touching his arrowhead through his tunic. 'On the battlefield I saw surgeons push an arrow right through an arm or leg and break the arrowhead off, then pull the shaft back through.'

Doctor Flynn nodded in agreement. 'If it had been in the arm, I would have done that, but if I tried to shove this arrow through I fear I would puncture his blood vessels, and that could be fatal. At the very least I would have to amputate his arm, and few survive amputation at the shoulder. No, in this instance I must do an extraction.' He went to a cupboard and opened it to reveal countless surgical instruments. He selected one and returned to the table.

'An arrow extractor,' said Richard. 'I benefitted from one of these after the Battle of Boroughbridge. And I lay several days as the doctor treating me kept opening the wound to let out the pus that formed.'

The physician nodded. 'Indeed, *ubi pus, ibi evacua*. Where there is pus, let it out. It is our maxim, handed down by the great Galen himself.'

'Sir Richard kept His Majesty waiting all that time, Doctor,' added Hubert with a grin.

'King Edward the Second?' Doctor Flynn asked as he nodded for them to again hold the patient down. He gradually insinuated the arrow extractor down the shaft, again causing the patient to curse and howl and buck and sway. Richard and Hubert pinioned him to the table.

'Yes, I told you the other day,' Richard reminded him.

'Ah, so you did. Mayhap the number of King Edwards is confusing me,' the physician said lightly. He probed deeper with his instrument and then with a grunt of satisfaction wiped his brow with the back of his hand. 'I have ensnared the actual tip with a ringlet. Now all I have to do is keep turning this screw that lies alongside the shaft and the whole arrow will be extracted.'

Holding the squealing patient down, Richard and Hubert watched as the doctor skilfully screwed his arrow extractor until he was able to grasp the ringlet that encircled the arrow tip and pull it out of the wound to bring the arrow with it.

He laid it aside and then washed his hands in the bucket before going over to the workbench, where he took a pestle and mortar and began to pulverise various ingredients from four different jars. 'We need now to staunch the bleeding and slow the initial pus production,' he explained to Richard. 'I favour *Apostolicon cirurgicum*, otherwise known as the ointment of the Apostles. It is made from the four elements, each blessed accordingly.' He tossed the contents of the mortar into the cauldron and stoked the flames beneath it. Soon the mixture melted, filling the room with the disagreeable odour of pitch.

When he applied it to the wound some minutes later, Emmet Waller gave a single loud scream and then passed out.

Simon the Fletcher was a large fellow with a cauliflower ear. He was short of temper, but had a prodigious knowledge of his craft, Richard knew, as he had called him as a witness in his court on several occasions. Richard questioned him in Doctor Flynn's hall while the physician finished treating Emmet Waller.

John of Flanshaw, who had brought the fletcher, told Richard that the hue and cry had been scaled down to a search for a bowman by Ranald Brigg, so the noise had considerably reduced. 'But folks are scared and angry at the same time, Sir Richard,' he said in finishing.

Richard nodded then turned to the fletcher and held up the arrow taken from Emmet Waller's shoulder. 'What do you make of this arrow?'

The fletcher took it from Richard, despite the gory arrowhead and still sticky blood extending down the shaft. He hefted it and then held it up to look down its length. He nodded. 'It is a good enough arrow, Sir Richard. It has a shaft made of poplar, which is light, and it has goose feather flights that are well trimmed.' He held the arrow up and pointed to the arrowhead. 'It is a narrow broadhead arrowhead, well weighted and as good an arrow as you could find.'

'Is it one that you made?' Hubert asked.

'No, Master. I use ash for my shafts. It's a bit more sophisticated than my fletching. Folks round here want simple hunting arrows, while this is made for accuracy. This could be a noble's arrow, not a simple man's.'

'So, a good archer's arrow?' Richard asked.

'I would say so, Sir Richard, yes.'

'Do you know anyone in Wakefield who uses arrows that match these?'

Simon shook his head. 'I am at the archery butts on the Ings every Thursday afternoon, as are all the menfolk as we are obliged under the law, and I have not seen anyone shoot these. I notice these things, Sir Richard. It could belong to someone not of Wakefield.'

Turning to John of Flanshaw, Richard said, 'Go back and find Ranald Brigg. Tell him to instruct the constables that the arrows we seek are made of poplar, not ash. Take Simon the Fletcher and this arrow so he can explain exactly what we are looking for. Then take the arrow back to the Rolls Office.'

After they had gone, Richard and Hubert returned to the doctor's chirurgia and treatment room where Emmet Waller was sitting propped up, his shoulder heavily bandaged and supported in a sling made of rope. His face was ashen pale and beads of sweat hung from his brow. His hair was also lank from excessive perspiration. He was breathing fast and looked in pain.

Hubert picked up the doll he had been fashioning for his young son and noted with a wistful smile that it was now marred by Emmet Waller's toothmarks. He dunked it in the bucket of water, shook it and then stowed it in his tunic.

'What were you doing at the Tolbooth, Master Waller?' Richard queried.

'I … I was wanting to see if I could get news of my friend, Siward Trapp. The guard wouldn't let me in. He shut that grille in my face and then *thud*! I was knocked over and all I felt was pain. Someone tried to murder me!'

'What did you want to see Siward Trapp about?' Richard asked.

Emmet Waller looked scared. 'I … I told you, Sir Richard. He's my friend.'

'You live in the same hamlet, yet you are both in Wakefield.'

'W-we were both released from the Tolbooth, my lord.'

Richard pointed to his pouch and tapped it. 'You have much money in there. As does Siward Trapp. How comes this, after a stay in the Tolbooth?'

Emmet Waller suddenly clutched his shoulder. 'Sir Richard, for pity's sake, I … I am in agony after the attempt on my life.'

Doctor Flynn was concocting a liquid at his workbench. He turned, stirring a goblet. 'He will be in great pain and will not be thinking clearly, Sir Richard. With your permission, I will give him this nostrum I have made up of henbane, hemlock, valerian and skullcap. It will ease his pain and help him to sleep.'

Richard considered for a moment. 'Very well, but I will want to question him further later.' He turned to Emmet Waller. 'You must stay in Wakefield. For your safety, it will be best to stay in the Tolbooth.'

The wounded man stared at Richard in horror. 'Not there again, Sir Richard, please!'

Richard shook his head. 'Someone shot at you, and if they realise that you are not dead, as they assuredly will, then they may try again. No, the Tolbooth will be the safest place for you.'

Emmet Waller reached for the goblet with his good hand, but the doctor held it back.

'This nostrum will work quickly, so it will be best to take it once you have a bed to lie on.'

The patient groaned.

Hubert patted his leg. 'Don't worry, I will fetch a bier and two men to carry you to the Tolbooth, and I will carry this remedy and give it to you myself.'

'And so you will be able to see your friend Siward Trapp after all,' added Richard.

Back in the Rolls Office, Richard asked John of Flanshaw about the search.

'As you can imagine, Sir Richard, just about every house has a bow and arrows, but we did not find any like the poplar arrow. As Simon the Fletcher said, virtually everyone uses cheaper ash arrows.'

'Why do you think he was shot, Sir Richard?' the court bailiff asked. 'Could it just have been a personal matter?'

Richard sat back and stroked his moustache with a finger. 'That is probably the case. I will know more when I question him further once he wakes. Hubert should be back soon.'

Footsteps outside were followed by a tap on the door, and Hubert came in.

'Ah, I was just saying that I expected you back soon. Did you give Emmet Waller his nostrum from Doctor Flynn?'

'I did, my lord. And I watched him fall asleep like a baby within minutes. It seems to be powerful medicine.'

'Powerful indeed, Hubert. All of those ingredients Doctor Flynn used are poisons if you take enough of them. That is the skill of physic, to give just the right amounts. Did you put him in the cell next to Siward Trapp?'

'I did, my lord. Siward Trapp is sober now, and he looked like a frightened coney. He had heard the hue and cry and all the noise. The guard had told him that a man had been shot outside, but he did not expect it to be his friend.'

'Did they talk?'

'Barely, my lord. Strange, after Waller had tried to visit him, and with them supposedly being friends. Anyway, Emmet Waller was in so much pain he practically snatched the flask that Doctor Flynn had put the medicine in out of my hand. I had to hold it back and pour him the exact amount Doctor Flynn said he could have in a small mug. But Siward Trapp said he would watch over him as he slept.'

'Then I will question them both later, when he wakes,' Richard said. He looked down at the arrow on his desk. 'Did you also see where the bowman could have shot from?'

Hubert had taken the wooden doll from his tunic and was idly feeling the teeth marks that Emmet Waller had made on it. 'I tried, my lord. To tell the truth, there are so many possible places. There are many alleyways round there, and without knowing exactly where he was standing I couldn't tell. What I could say, though, is that he wasn't much of a shot, because he would not have been firing from far away. A man's back should make an easy target.'

Richard ran his fingers over the goose feather of the arrow's flight and then handed it to John of Flanshaw. 'Keep this safe for now, along with the two daggers and the other items from these deaths that we retained. We will need it to match against if we find other poplar arrows.' He picked up a quill and dipped it in the inkpot and spent several minutes writing on a piece of vellum. He dusted and blew powder off it and laid it flat on the desk. 'What of Jay Groff? He was released from the Tolbooth the same day as Siward Trapp and Emmet Waller.'

'I don't know, Sir Richard. I had not seen him, but the town watch and the searchers were not looking for anyone in particular, just for a bowman.'

'In that case, Hubert, go and find Ranald Brigg and see if he has seen him. If so, find him and bring him here in an hour. I will be back.'

Then, pursing his lips, 'What of the friar, Brother Fergus?'

John of Flanshaw shook his head. 'I cannot say, Sir Richard.'

'Ask about him, too. And any other friars who may have come to Wakefield with him.'

Hubert stowed his doll away again. 'Are you going far, my lord?'

'I am going to Agbrigg. Doctor Flynn said that Widow Clegg was responding to his treatment. I am intrigued and wonder what treatment exactly she is responding to. The doctor's or the healer's?' He stood and walked to the door, turning as he opened it to address John of Flanshaw. 'It is important that we hold this inquest on these four sudden deaths tomorrow. Have a proclamation sent out. Select a jury of twelve men, making sure that none have recently been jurors. And also organise a *villatae* jury of three others from the surrounding villages to ensure we have no bias.'

'For the *villatae*, shall I get the reeves of Kirkthorpe and Wragby, Stanley and Thornes?'

'No, not Kirkthorpe, for I do not want Master Gembert Cooper to sit on the jury, but I do want him to be in court. Indeed, I want everyone who attended the feast at Geoffrey Hopwood's home to be there. Choose the reeve of Featherstone instead of Kirkthorpe and Wragby.'

John of Flanshaw bowed. 'I will arrange it, Sir Richard. Does this include the franklin's daughter, Rowena?'

'Everyone who was there.' Richard pointed to the vellum he had written on. 'I have made a list of the people I want you to summon and also the arrangements that I want made for the inquest. It will be held at the ninth hour.'

Hal was shooting crude flightless arrows at a sapling tree with a rudimentary bow that he had made when Richard arrived at his simple home. His young sister was sitting on the ground watching him, giggling with delight as his arrows struck the sapling again and again.

'You have the makings of an archer, young Hal,' Richard said as he leaned forward to rest his hands on the pommel of his saddle.

Seeing Richard, Hal leaned his bow against the sapling and bowed, deferentially tugging his hair. 'My father taught me a little before he died, my lord.'

'It looks as if he did a good job. It will not be long before you train with a real bow and arrows.' He dismounted and tied the reins to a tree. 'I have come to see your mother, Hal.'

'She is resting, as Doctor Flynn told her to when he came earlier, my lord,' Hal replied, running to push open their primitive door.

Inside, Widow Clegg was dozing on her bed, propped against a sack of straw. She was about to stand when Richard gestured for her to stay. 'I am much improved, I thank you, Sir Richard,' she said in answer to his question about how she fared. 'The wen hurts where Doctor Flynn has burned it, but he has given me a medicine to take, which helps. It makes me sleepy.' She suppressed a yawn.

'It was already getting better,' Hal interrupted. 'The healer's paste, medicine and the magic doll are healing it.'

Hal's mother nodded enthusiastically. 'I do believe Hal is right, Sir Richard. It gets smaller with the paste, and each time I scrape it off as well as the tiny lump on the doll, it looks smaller. I feel stronger, too.'

The little girl, Emily, came in and ran to hug Hal's waist.

'Emily would be at Hal's side all the time if she could,' the widow explained.

Richard smiled at the two children. 'Hal, show your sister some more of your archery skills while I talk with your mother.' After Hal took his sister's hand and led her out, Richard turned to Mistress Clegg. 'The other day when we were talking about the toe that Hal cut from the hanged man, you became tearful and said that it was wonderful that Quinn could help you.' *And I did not ask further because I was shocked to hear it, for I had been the judge that sentenced him to be hanged and to rot until his bones dropped. I felt too guilty to tarry longer.*

She averted her eyes. 'Yes, Sir Richard, I was upset because he was my husband's cousin. He … he was a good man.'

'You do know that I had him hanged for the murder of Bryce-a-Green?'

She grasped the blanket and wrung the edge in her hands. 'Y-yes, Sir Richard. As I heard it, he … he cut off Bryce-a-Green's head. They were enemies for years. Quinn had a hot temper even as a boy, that's what my husband used to say. If … if he did such a terrible thing, then he deserved to be hanged.'

She would not dare to be critical of me, of course, but I sense that she is sincere. I do not think that she hates me for it. 'My memory may play a trick upon me, but I think you said that in death Quinn could still help you. In what way had he helped you while he was alive?'

Tears welled up in her eyes. 'After my Aston died, he was very good and brought us food and he got work for me to do. He always said that families had to stick together.'

'Was he a popular fellow?'

'He was, Sir Richard. That was part of the reason that Bryce-a-Green hated him so. My Aston told me that. Bryce-a-Green and Quinn had been friends as lads, but Quinn was more liked by girls and the older women, too. They say that Quinn lay with Bryce's widowed mother and put her with child. Neither of them admitted it, of course, him being a lad and her his friend's mother. But she died in childbirth, and Bryce never forgave him. Any opportunity to steal from him or do him an injury, he took it. I don't doubt that there was a hue and cry and a fight, but Bryce was not a weakling. It would have taken more than just Quinn to kill him. And that's why I could hardly believe it when those men said that he did the killing himself.'

Is this why I have had such an uneasy feeling about this hanging? Something has not felt right. 'Did Bryce-a-Green have any other family?'

She nodded. 'Quinn told me that he had an uncle, but he had never seen him before.'

'Did you know any of the three men who were with Quinn in the hue and cry? Their names were Jay Groff, Emmet Waller and Siward Trapp.'

'No, Sir Richard. They were all from Ryhill, that's as much as I know.'

Richard nodded. 'I thank you and I trust that you will continue to improve in health. I just have one final question. What is the name of the healer that is treating you?'

Mistress Clegg covered her face with her hands and gasped. 'Oh please, Sir Richard, do not press me, I beg you. Hal said he was told that if he or I revealed the name, the treatment would stop working. I … I dare not, my lord.'

It would be unkind of me to press her further. 'Very well, it will stay that way for as long as necessary. I bid you good day, for now I must return to Wakefield.'

Ranald Brigg let Richard into the Tolbooth and locked the door with the new key. He had volunteered for himself and the guards of the town watch to take over the Tolbooth until another jailor was appointed.

'We have not found the archer, Sir Richard, or any poplar arrows. Nor did any of us find the friars. Plenty of people had seen the Irish one in the marketplace, of course. The other one was preaching on the Northgate and then on the Westgate areas, but they both must have left. In all the commotion, the men on the gates had run to see if they were needed. They could have left unnoticed during that time.'

'What about Jay Groff, the third man who was in the Tolbooth?'

The head of the town watch shook his head. 'If he is in Wakefield, he is keeping his head low.'

'Where is Hubert now?'

'He has gone in search of food, Sir Richard. He said his stomach was wondering if his throat had been cut.'

Richard frowned. 'Not the most appropriate turn of phrase, considering the murder in this very Tolbooth. Have the two men been talking?'

Ranald Brigg blew air through his lips. 'That's the strange thing, sir. Siward Trapp asked Emmet Waller what happened before Hubert gave him that potion from the physic. Waller just made a sign over his throat with his good hand and then he took the draught and was asleep almost straight away.

Siward Trapp said he'd look after him, but how he could do that when they are locked in separate cells, I don't know. Waller is awake now, but they haven't spoken since, according to Gimlet, my constable.'

Richard went to the cells and questioned Siward Trapp about how he had obtained money and from whom.

'I don't know his name, Sir Richard. He just wanted me to kill some rats for him. I met him in the Bucket Inn, I think, and he paid me then and there.'

'Describe him.'

'He was average, Sir Richard. I don't rightly recall, as I was drinking to celebrate getting free.' He cast an eye around the cell. 'Though not for long.'

Emmet Waller was equally uninformative about his purse, claiming that his pain was stopping him from thinking clearly.

Richard was tempted to refuse his request for more of the nostrum from the flask that Hubert had left with Gimlet the constable. However, he gestured to the guard to pour a small measure. *But someone has paid them. And it seems as if that payment has also bought their silence.* Then he asked both men, 'Where is your companion Jay Groff?'

Neither man answered at first. Then they both professed ignorance and denied having seen him since their release.

Richard noted that the mole-catcher had grown pale suddenly and his hands shook.

'When can I get out, Sir Richard?' Siward asked, his voice quavering slightly. 'I am anxious to get home.'

'When your memory clears,' Richard replied sternly. 'Certainly not before the inquest on all of the deaths in Wakefield that will be held tomorrow. Even then, I want clear answers to my questions.'

Emmet Waller drained the mug and handed it back through the bars of the cell door to the constable. 'I'm happy to stay as long as you like, Sir Richard. It isn't safe out there for the likes of simple honest men like us.'

The two friars rode their donkeys side by side along the trail, sharing a skin of ale as they went.

'I don't know about you, Brother Caspar, but preaching always works up a powerful thirst in me,' said Brother Fergus.

'It does indeed with me, too, Brother Fergus,' Brother Caspar replied. He patted his considerable girth. 'And it also makes me hungry. I was fortunate to be preaching near a pie booth, and the good woman looked kindly on me and let me have a small pigeon pie.' He took a swig from the skin and handed it over.

'There was a fair commotion going on somewhere,' the Irish friar said. 'Do you know what it was about?'

'I heard that someone was shot. Did you not hear about it?'

'No. To tell you the truth, I went to Father Alban's home to pray for him. The Church of All Saints is still locked, so I thought his home would be the best place. I stayed with him the night before I came to St Leonard's. The manciple, Matthew Drewitt, had arranged it, and the good priest was very hospitable.'

'Why did you not wait until we got back to the priory? We could all pray for him.'

'I worry that there might have been malevolent forces involved, and the prayers that Bishop Ledrede has taught me could banish them from his house and help free his soul.'

Brother Caspar shivered. 'I do not like to hear about such wickedness, Brother. Let us get back to the safety of St Leonard's.'

Sir Basil de Roxford had drunk more wine than usual. Normally a goblet or two would ease the pains in his hips and back and calm his mood, but not on this evening. He had been unsettled ever since the judge's visit, and he was a worried man.

'Do you think there is any danger, Kate?' he asked his wife as she contemplated her next move. They played chess every evening before retiring to bed. He had taught her to play shortly after they had wed, and she had become a good player. Although he always won, he fancied that she often declined to make a move that could be to her advantage and often made a series of moves, anticipating his so that the game could be prolonged until he moved to checkmate.

Lady Katherine looked up at him with questioning eyes. 'Danger, Basil?'

'From that judge. Danger that he could find out.'

She smiled and reached for his hand. She kissed it and then shook her head. 'Of course not, my love. How could he? Not now that the franklin is dead.' She moved her queen's knight into the middle of the board.

He smiled. 'You are so sensible, Kate. I think I am just becoming overcautious these days.'

'There is never any harm in that, my love,' she replied.

He gave a short laugh and then drained his goblet. 'But perhaps you should be a little more cautious. I may have distracted you when you were thinking.' He moved his queen. 'Checkmate.'

'Oh! Foolish me,' she said, raising her hands and shaking them petulantly.

'It is only a game, Kate.'

She reached for his hand again. 'You are so good to me, Basil. Shall we to bed?'

CHAPTER NINE

The next morning, Richard paid his usual visit to Sandal Castle to meet with Doctor Flynn while he treated Sir Thomas. While Sir Thomas was having his urine examined and then leeches attached by the physician, Richard updated him on the recent developments in Wakefield.

'I think that the inquest will be bound to repulse people, as by law I need to have the bodies exhibited to the jurors.'

'The people of Wakefield are already mumbling about witchcraft,' Doctor Flynn volunteered. 'I hear about it from my patients, and it is common knowledge that rats with nails and cut throats have been found in the town.'

'Rats?' repeated Sir Thomas.

Richard nodded. 'One with a cut throat, another with nails driven into its back and another that was found hanging from the pillory on Cheapside.'

'Why this talk of witchcraft?' Sir Thomas asked.

'The Dominican friars have been in town preaching about witchcraft. It could not have been at a worse time. And just after that, a man was shot outside the Tolbooth.'

'Killed?' Sir Thomas grunted.

'No, Doctor Flynn removed the arrow from his shoulder. I have had him moved to the Tolbooth for his own safety. He is joined there by Siward Trapp, another man who was involved in the killing of Bryce-a-Green. They are both hiding something and I mean to get to the bottom of it, but first I must hold this inquest into the four deaths of Father Alban, the franklin Geoffrey Hopwood, Peter Plowman and Judd of Alverthorpe, the Tolbooth jailor. In case there is further unrest and a mob gets incited, I would like to take at least half a dozen of the castle guards again.'

Sir Thomas sucked air through his teeth. 'That killing was a bad business. That Quinn fellow deserved to be hanged. You did good work there, Richard.'

Did I? I am even less sure after my talk with the Widow Clegg.

Sir Thomas waved a hand. 'Take a dozen men if you like, and you had best sort these deaths out quickly, Richard. Be sure to stamp out any talk of witchcraft.' He pointed at the doll in his image that Doctor Flynn was stroking against the mouthparts of one of his leeches. 'We are good Christian folk here, and such mad and evil ideas must be rooted out.'

Brother Fergus said something like that when I was at St Leonard's Priory. But rooting out as they did in Kilkenny is bound to mean more death.

John of Flanshaw had arranged everything according to the list that Richard had given him. He had despatched runners throughout the town to announce the inquest for that morning at nine hours. He had also sent messengers to all of the people who had attended the feast of St Julian's Day at Geoffrey Hopwood's manor in Kirkthorpe. So that there could be no excuse for non-attendance even by those of exalted positions, he had written official summonses and sealed them with the official Manor of Wakefield Court seal.

'You have done a fine job, John,' Richard said as he sat in the Rolls Office going over the notes that he had personally made the night before so that he could conduct the inquest in what he considered the most logical manner. 'Have you selected the jury?'

'Yes, Sir Richard. I double-checked my ledgers to ensure that none of the jurors have sat on cases recently. Nor have the three members of the *villatae* jury.'

'And all of the people on the list?'

'They were all contacted, and most of them have already arrived and are seated awaiting the start. Others still have time before the nine bells.'

'Are the coffins ready?'

'They are, Sir Richard. And all of the bodies have been placed in them as you required.'

'What of the exhibits?'

'They are in a chest under my desk in the courtroom, ready to be produced at your word or your signal according to the list you gave me and which I have here,' John said, raising a parchment roll.

'Good, then go and prepare the court. I shall come in once the bell is rung.'

The court bailiff bowed and picked up his staff, which was his badge of office, and let himself out.

Hubert had been sitting quietly on his usual stool, having arranged already for the guardsmen from Sandal Castle to be positioned both inside the courtroom and also at the Tolbooth, the Church of All Saints and in the marketplace according to Richard's instructions. 'Do you expect any trouble, my lord?'

'I trust not, Hubert, but since emotions are high in Wakefield, I think it is best to be prepared.'

Hubert nodded. 'With four violent deaths, the people will expect justice and retribution. Yet the murderer of two is dead and the fourth is dead by his own hand. The people may feel cheated of executions.'

'It is not just that which concerns me, Hubert.'

'How so, my lord?'

The nine bells rang out.

Richard put on his coif, picked up his gavel and stood up. 'We will see soon enough.'

As Richard and Hubert made their way down the corridor to the court chamber, they heard John of Flanshaw's sonorous voice within calling for silence. When Hubert opened the door for Richard, the bailiff rapped his staff on the floor and called out, 'Silence! All rise for Sir Richard Lee, Circuit Judge of the King's Northern Realm and of the Wakefield Manor Court and Coroner for the Wakefield District.'

Richard mounted the dais and surveyed the court chamber, which as expected was full to capacity, all adults being expected to attend. He noted those who had seats were all in front of the standing masses. He mentally ticked off all of the attendees at the franklin's feast. He bowed to the chamber and sat down.

'Those who may, can now be seated,' boomed out John of Flanshaw. 'This session is an inquest into the sudden deaths of four men, all of whom resided within the Manor of Wakefield. Their names are, first, Father Alban, priest of the Church of All Saints. The second, Peter Plowman, a common labourer of Half Moon Beck. Third, Geoffrey Hopwood, franklin of Kirkthorpe and a knight of this shire of Yorkshire. Fourth and finally, Judd of Alverthorpe, jailor of the Wakefield Tolbooth.'

Richard waited for the bailiff to take his seat at his desk and then rapped his gavel to draw the court's attention. 'People of Wakefield and of the surrounding district, this inquest is one of the most unusual we have ever held in Wakefield, for it concerns four men. We are dealing with it in one single session for one good reason. The deaths of all four men have occurred within two days of each other, and there is a strong sense that they are all linked. There are two definite murders that have been committed and two cases of self-killing, which in the Latin of the law we call *felo de se*. There is undoubted tragedy here, but —'

'There be evil!' a voice called out from somewhere in the crowd. Immediately, Hubert stepped forward and John of Flanshaw rose from his seat and rapped his staff.

'Witchcraft!' a voice from another part of the crowd called.

'Silence!' Richard said sharply, rapping his gavel. 'Guards, watch this court and if you see anyone making another outburst, seize them. The Tolbooth has yet room for overnight residence, and the pillory on Cheapside can accommodate a miscreant during the day.'

He looked around the court with a steely and forbidding regard, sparing none, not even those sitting at the front of the proceedings. He noted that Brother Fergus and Prior Norbert were sitting on the end of the seated row of dignitaries.

'As I was about to say, there are elements about these deaths which are alarming and which need to be examined in order to understand how they came about.'

He signalled to John of Flanshaw. 'We have twelve men of the jury and three *villatae* jurors, who are here to ensure representation from outside the town. Swear them all in please, bailiff of the court.'

Once all fifteen jurymen had been sworn in, Richard proceeded.

'I am going to go through these deaths in the sequence they occurred, calling and questioning witnesses as we progress. The first murder was that of Father Alban, whose body was discovered on the morning of the thirteenth of February, the day after St Julian's Day. A feast was hosted by the franklin, Geoffrey Hopwood, at his manor house in Kirkthorpe on the twelfth of that month. Call the first witness, Ranald Brigg, the headman of the town watch.'

The headman took his place in the witness pen and swore an oath on the Bible that the bailiff presented to him. He replied to Richard's direction to tell the court about his discovery.

'My constables and I were on our ways to order the opening of the town gates. We tend to rotate which gates we go to as it keeps the gatekeepers on their toes. I was heading towards the Kirkgate when I heard the first call for a hue and cry. I heard a man's voice shout out, "Murder! Murder! Murder! The priest is dead! Stop that franklin! Stop that franklin!" Then I saw a man running towards Cheapside, where the stables are.'

'Did you recognise him?'

'No, Sir Richard, but I gave chase, knocking on folks' doors on my way. People were already up, of course, and a sizeable crowd gave chase. They had caught him by the time I got to the stables, and they'd punched and kicked him a bit.'

'Who was this person?'

'It was the franklin, Geoffrey Hopwood. We marched him to the Tolbooth and Judd of Alverthorpe the turnkey put him in a cell.'

'And then you found the priest?'

'Yes, Sir Richard. I went back to the Church of All Saints. The door was open and his body was lying in front of the altar. He had been stabbed many times and a dagger was sticking out of his back.'

'Do you know who began the hue and cry?'

'No, Sir Richard. I just reacted to it, as is the duty of every man.'

Richard dismissed the headman and signalled to John of Flanshaw, who in turn gestured to his constables. They went out the side door of the court chamber and returned after a few moments, carrying a coffin between them. Horrified gasps rang out from the court as they propped it in front of the dais and removed the lid to reveal Father Alban's body lying inside. A strip of cloth had been wound round his eyes. His face was mottled blue-purple and his tongue hung from his mouth. Dried blood covered his chin.

'Turn the body and show the jury his back,' Richard ordered.

To further exclamations of shock from the assembly, the constables part-lifted the corpse and turned it before replacing it so that the back could be seen clearly. The brown habit was riddled with ten holes, each surrounded by a small halo of dried blood.

'Call Doctor Flynn,' Richard said, prompting the physician, sitting on the front row next to Mistress Mary Wisley, to take to the witness pen.

'Can you confirm the cause of death?'

'Multiple stabbing to his back, Sir Richard.'

'Was this the weapon that killed him?' he asked, snapping his fingers at John of Flanshaw, who opened the chest under his desk and produced the bollock dagger, its blade crusted with old blood. He crossed the space to the pen for the physician to inspect.

'I believe it is, Sir Richard. I removed it when you asked me to examine the body. I remember saying the handle protuberances were unusually large.'

One or two men in the crowd smirked, but were silenced by a rap of Richard's gavel.

Richard thanked him and dismissed him back to the bench. 'I can confirm that this dagger belonged to the franklin, Geoffrey Hopwood.'

Rowena Hopwood, sitting between Sir Basil de Roxford and his wife Lady Katherine, let out a sob and clutched her staff with both hands. Lady Katherine immediately put a consoling arm about her shoulders.

Richard shuffled vellum sheets before him. 'So, Geoffrey Hopwood was being held in the Tolbooth, where I tried to interview him soon after his arrest. He seemed dazed and drowsy, too much indeed to remember anything. He said that he would only speak in court. Since he is no longer on this earth, we are not able to question him further. Yet we can go back to the feast at his home. Call Sir Basil de Roxford.'

In some surprise, the old knight tried to raise himself from the bench, but tottered and almost fell back. Lady Katherine reached across Rowena and put a concerned hand on her husband's arm.

'Sir Richard, may I call Aiken, our butler?'

Richard nodded and saw Aiken, their servant with long curly black hair beneath a simple red skullcap, make his way through the crowd from the rear of the chamber. Reaching the seated row, he slid a strong arm under his master's arm and round his back and effortlessly helped him stand and then walk to the witness pen. He stood there with Sir Basil for support.

'Tell us, Sir Basil, what transpired at the feast. You were sitting next to Father Alban and close to Geoffrey Hopwood.'

'There was argument, Sir Richard. I admit I was involved in it myself.'

'Specifically, when the argument was about the law, what did Master Hopwood say?'

Sir Basil opened his mouth and nodded. 'Ah! Yes, he said that Father Alban need have no worry about the law, because he could always claim the Benefit of Clergy. He said he always had some Latin at his command in case he was ever tried in a court. He said he'd be able to be tried in a Church court. Then he babbled some Latin or other to show off.' He suddenly turned towards Rowena in embarrassment and bowed. 'I beg your pardon, Rowena.'

'Thank you, Sir Basil, you may return to your seat,' said Richard. He waited until Aiken had helped his master back to his seat and then departed for his place at the back of the chamber.

'When someone claims Benefit of Clergy by being able to quote from the Bible in Latin, it means that they choose to be tried in an Ecclesiastic Court instead of one such as this. The benefit is that felonies, which are major crimes that ordinarily receive corporal punishment or a sentence of death, do not get such severe outcomes. What the franklin said was "*Amen dico vobis quia unus vestrum me traditurus est*," which means, "Truly I say to you that one of you shall betray me."'

He looked around the court, watching for reactions. 'I believe that when I questioned him in the Tolbooth, he intended to say nothing until he could claim Benefit of Clergy. Enough of that for the moment.'

He signalled to John of Flanshaw, who again indicated for his constables to bring in another coffin. They placed this next to the first coffin but this time, instead of opening it, they stood to attention by it.

'The following morning there was another hue and cry, although it was not called as soon as it should have been. Some hours elapsed, which may have been crucial.'

Hubert of Loxley coughed noisily, attracting Ranald Brigg's attention, as he intended. The headman of the town watch withered under his glare.

'What had been discovered was that the Tolbooth was unlocked and Judd of Alverthorpe and the franklin, Geoffrey Hopwood, had both gone. The franklin's cell was empty. Yet in another cell, there had been a most brutal slaying of a prisoner. A prisoner that had been tried in this court just a day before St Julian's feast. His throat had been cut.'

He snapped his fingers and John of Flanshaw gestured to the constables, who removed the lid to reveal the body of Peter Plowman. The great gash in his throat had been covered in a winding cloth, as had his eyes. His jaw hung open and there was extensive bruising on his face, much purpler than when he had first been discovered.

The crowd sent up a cacophony of noise; a mix of disgust, sympathy and anger. Yet beyond that, none dared to cry out as the presence of the Sandal Castle guards and Richard's warning at the start of proceedings had made their impression.

'Call Cedric of Sharlston,' Richard ordered.

Looking shocked at being called to the witness pen, the yeoman was sworn in on the Bible. 'Sir ... Sir Richard,' he flustered, 'I had nothing to do with his death.'

Richard noticed that several of the members of the jury and most of the people in the front row were covering their noses as best they could with hands, kerchiefs or sleeves. With the opening of Peter Plowman's coffin there was a greater smell of the grave. He silenced Cedric of Sharlston with a raised hand and took a moment to tell John of Flanshaw to have candles brought in and lavender to strew about the coffins. Then he said, 'No one has said that you did, yet it is pertinent to point out that you pleaded for the death penalty the other day in court when he was accused of stealing your sheep. I left the case open, hence why he was being held in the Tolbooth. And the franklin offered to pay you for that sheep.'

The yeoman's face grew red. 'That was then. I … I had no wish to see him die by having his throat cut.'

'That is the method, but perhaps you still wished his death, for inflicting that flesh wound on you.'

'I am not a vindictive man, your honour.'

'Did Geoffrey Hopwood pay you for the sheep?'

Cedric of Sharlston hesitated. 'Yes, Sir Richard. He paid me directly from that silk purse of his that he was so proud of flashing about and which always seemed to be full.'

'Did you like the franklin?'

'Like him? Of course, Sir Richard. Everyone liked him. He could — arrange things. He was a man of influence. A knight of the shire. I daresay there are many folk sitting and standing close by that he arranged things for.'

Richard picked up a fresh quill that had been newly cut and dipped it in the inkpot on the desk and made some notes. 'You may sit again,' he said, dismissing the yeoman. 'Another hue and cry was called for Judd of Alverthorpe and for Geoffrey Hopwood. While the hue and cry was going on in town behind closed town gates, I went to Kirkthorpe and discovered the franklin hanging in his own dovecote.'

Rowena Hopwood again began to sob at this and once more was comforted by Lady Katherine.

Richard signed for John of Flanshaw to bring in a third coffin, which again was propped up beside the other two against the dais. The constables removed the lid and stood back.

The reactions in court were once again mixed. But this time, even the presence of the Sandal Castle guards did not prevent people from showing their feelings. Some whistled, others brayed, and still others called out.

'Murdering bastard!'

'Hang him though he be dead and let his corpse rot.'

Rowena screamed and covered her ears with her hands. Lady Katherine tried to comfort her and was aided by both Mistresses Mary Wisley and Myrtle Drewitt, who rose and went to kneel in front of her, to shield her as best they could from the sight of her father's body, even though they knew her vision was so poor she would not see.

As with the other two bodies, the franklin's eyes had been covered, as had the neck to conceal the examination that Doctor Flynn had made. The tongue, swollen and purple, protruded from between his lips.

'I understand the distress that seeing Master Hopwood's body will cause, but by law the jurors at an inquest must see the bodies of those whose deaths are under investigation. I will tell you that Doctor Flynn examined the body after death and confirmed that his death is consistent with the franklin having hanged himself.'

He snapped his fingers again, the prearranged signal for John of Flanshaw to act on the actions that he had written down. John opened the chest and produced another dagger, holding it aloft for all to see.

'This is the bloodstained quillon dagger that was found on the floor of the dovecote close to Geoffrey Hopwood's hanging body. It looks as if he tossed it aside before he hanged himself. The blood on it does not seem to be the franklin's own as he had no bleeding injury, but it looks as if he had carried it on his person, as there are bloodstains on his clothes and on his hand. Yet note — it is not his dagger.'

Richard signalled again to the court bailiff and a fourth coffin was brought in and placed beside the other three, propped at an angle against the dais. At his nod, the lid was removed to reveal the body of Judd of Alverthorpe. His face looked calm, and if it was not for the discolouration of his flesh in death, he might have been sleeping.

'Judd of Alverthorpe was found hanging by his own leather belt from a sheepcote on the Heath.' He looked straight at the yeoman sitting uncomfortably in the front row. 'He was discovered by Cedric of Sharlston and one of his lads.'

There were sighs and expressions of incredulity from around the courtroom, people now less reticent despite the threat of the Tolbooth and pillory, so heated were emotions becoming after all of the revelations. It was not clear how Judd of Alverthorpe was generally regarded in the town.

Richard gestured to John of Flanshaw, who opened the chest and took out the jailor's belt and the franklin's white silk purse. The bailiff held them both aloft and shook them to demonstrate that the Tolbooth keys still hung from the jailor's belt and that the franklin's purse was full of coin.

'Here is Judd of Alverthorpe's belt, which you see has an empty sheath. And here is the franklin's purse, which was found on the floor of the sheepcote.'

Richard had been looking at the jury throughout the inquest to gauge their reactions. He deduced from the way eyes kept being drawn to the coffins and various facial expressions when the sequence of events were unfolded before them, that many of them were already drawing conclusions.

'Thus far, it looks as if the franklin, Geoffrey Hopwood, followed Father Alban to Wakefield after the feast at Kirkthorpe on St Julian's Day, then in the morning while the priest was at prayer he stabbed him ten times in the back before fleeing. He was captured and put in the Tolbooth in a cell beside Peter Plowman —' he pointed at the coffins — 'just as they are now side by side in death.'

Looking at the front row, Richard noted that Rowena, Mary Wisley and Myrtle Drewitt were all visibly weeping, as were many of the women in court. The men were either nodding in agreement with his assessment or were showing pent-up anger.

As I expected, this day will see much emotional reaction.

'The franklin seemed to have a soft spot for Peter Plowman and stood up for him in court, even paying for the sheep that he stole from Cedric of Sharlston. Yet he had committed a felony, as bad a felony as it is possible to commit. He murdered a priest, possibly in a fit of madness, so what is he to do? He bribes the jailor, Judd of Alverthorpe, and that morning the jailor sets him free. Perhaps he had also bribed him to set Peter Plowman free, too, for his case was still under my consideration. The death penalty was still a possibility for Peter Plowman, so the jailor may have been promised much money, starting with the purse. He would expect them to simply slip away, but instead the franklin grabs Judd of Alverthorpe's dagger and slits Peter Plowman's throat to silence him.'

Richard glanced around the court and saw many nods of agreement.

'So then, in horror Judd decides that he too must flee, otherwise how could he explain the death of Peter Plowman? The two men know Wakefield well and can evade Ranald Brigg and the town watch. They escape and go their separate ways, probably intending to meet up later so the franklin can pay the rest of his bribe and then leave forever. But how can Geoffrey Hopwood leave his daughter? Guilt overcomes him, and he goes to his dovecote and hangs himself. Meanwhile, Judd of Alverthorpe is also overcome with remorse and hangs himself. One in a dovecote and the other in a sheepcote.' Richard looked at the jurors. 'What say you, foreman of the jury, does that sound plausible?'

After mere moments of discussion, the elected foreman stood and nodded. 'Aye, Sir Richard, that sounds likely.'

Richard picked up his gavel and rapped it. 'But why? That is the question. There was an argument at the feast.' He suddenly looked at John of Flanshaw and said, 'Call Brother Fergus of St Leonard's Priory.'

Surprised, the Irish friar rose and took his place in the witness pen, where he was sworn in. In response to Richard's direction to identify himself to the court, he stated, 'I am Brother Fergus, a Dominican friar from the Black Abbey in Kilkenny in Ireland.'

'And you come on a mission?'

'I do, from Bishop Richard Ledrede of Ossory in Ireland. He has been working on a papal bull called *Super Illius Specula*, from His Holiness Pope John, the twenty-second of that name. It proclaims all witchcraft and sorcery to be heresy. I and several fellow friars have been sent around the country to friaries and priories to preach about the wickedness and evil of witchcraft and to root out any witches.' As Richard had noted twice before, his voice rose in passion as he railed.

'You preached about this yesterday in Wakefield?'

'I did, Sir Richard. I did so with the blessing of Prior Norbert, who sits on that row in front of the court.'

'And you did in the Church of St Peter in Kirkthorpe and again at the feast on St Julian's Day in the franklin's home?'

'I did indeed. I do the Lord's work.'

'At the feast was there an argument, as we heard from Sir Basil de Roxford?'

'There was, between Father Alban and Master Hopwood. It came about after I had talked about the murders that had occurred as a result of witchcraft and sorcerer's spells. Father Alban was angered. He talked about some case when a man had been recently hanged, but another had not been. I believe the one who was not hanged was this young man here —' he turned and pointed to the open coffin containing Peter Plowman. 'I had the impression that he was in some way critical of your judgement, Sir Richard,' he added.

Silence fell across the court, and Richard was aware that all eyes suddenly fell upon himself. He felt that hollow, nagging guilt again. 'But was the franklin angry at that point?' he asked.

The friar shook his head. 'No, Sir Richard.'

Richard nodded and made more notes. 'And what do you make of these?' he asked, signalling to John of Flanshaw.

The bailiff again opened his chest and drew out a sack, from which he took out the three dead rats. He dangled the one with nails in its back and the one with the cut throat by their tails from one hand and the one with the cord round its neck from his other hand.

The crowd reacted strongly. There were collective cries of horror, curses, and blessings, and many made the sign of the cross.

'Witchcraft, Sir Richard. I have little doubt. Those are rats that have been used in the casting of spells. A cut throat, a stabbing and a hanging.' Again he turned and pointed at the coffins. 'I would say there are certainly witches at work here.'

'Could witchcraft account for the sudden change in character of a man, such as seems to have occurred with the franklin, Geoffrey Hopwood?'

Brother Fergus pursed his lips and then nodded emphatically. 'I would say so, yes.'

Thanking the friar, Richard dismissed him. 'There is yet another strange thing that has occurred during all of this. A man was shot in front of the Tolbooth by an unidentified archer. He happened to have been a prisoner in the Tolbooth along with two others who were involved in the case of Bryce-a-Green, which Brother Fergus just referred to. For their safety, they are both being held in the Tolbooth.'

He looked over the court, to see if anyone reacted, but none seemed to.

Turning again to the jurors, he said, 'Well now, what say you all to this, so far? Do you think that supernatural forces or witchcraft could have been at work?'

Once again, after momentary discussion among themselves, the foreman of the main jury rose and said that they all agreed.

Richard turned to the three members of the *villatae* jury. 'And what is your opinion?'

They too nodded at each other, then the reeve of Stanley stood. 'We agree, Sir Richard.'

Richard frowned. 'Call Doctor Flynn again.'

The physician clicked his tongue and walked to the witness pen.

'Doctor Flynn, we talked at one stage about cruentation. Please explain what this is to the members of the jury and to the court.'

'Cruentation is a divine phenomenon. If someone has been murdered, the body of the victim will bleed in the presence of their killer. It happens by God's will.'

'You have seen this happen, Doctor Flynn?'

'I have, Sir Richard, on at least three occasions.'

'Would it also happen in cases of self-murder, when someone has taken their own life?'

The physician considered for a few moments and then nodded. 'I believe that is possible.'

Richard pointed to the four coffins. 'Then why, especially if supernatural forces have been involved, which must be an abomination to God, are none of these bodies bleeding now?' He rapped his gavel. 'It is my conclusion that none of these conjectures is yet proven. At least one felony has been committed, but I am not sure by whom. Until I am, these cases are all still open and under investigation. I declare this inquest is closed.'

An eerie silence fell across the court as Richard stood and left. It was broken only by the weeping of Rowena Hopwood.

CHAPTER TEN

John of Flanshaw sat at the side of the desk transcribing the notes Richard had made during the inquest. As usual he worked methodically, only occasionally asking Richard for clarification.

'I am afraid that I do not understand this line, Sir Richard,' he said, getting up and carrying the vellum round for Richard to see. 'It looks like a question. "Why only three rats?" Is that correct, sir?'

'It is, but do not add that to the court roll. I was thinking and it was a reminder to myself. Indeed, there are several points I made that I need to consider further, so just leave these notes for now.'

'Would you like me to leave you to consider these points in peace, Sir Richard?'

Hubert had been toying with his son's wooden doll and also looked up. 'And shall I leave you, too, my lord?'

Richard shook his head. He leaned back in his chair and removed his coif, placing it on the desk beside his gavel. 'No, both of you stay. Let me tell you of the things that have bothered me about the inquest and let me have your thoughts.'

John of Flanshaw took his seat again and Hubert laid his doll on the desk, both pleased that the judge was prepared to consider their opinions.

'Firstly, the exhibits. Let us have them all set before us on the floor.'

The court bailiff went to the chest and took out the sack of rats and the daggers, belt and purse. He laid them all out in a row in the middle of the office.

Richard looked at the vellum before him and hummed. 'So, let us begin with the rats. If they were indeed part of some witchcraft spells, why are there only three of them?'

'I do not follow, Sir Richard,' said John of Flanshaw.

'There were four deaths when they were discovered, so why are there not four rats?'

'Perhaps one rat, the hanged one, was meant for two. For both the franklin and the turnkey?' Hubert suggested.

'Mayhap there is still a fourth, but it has not yet been found,' the court bailiff pondered. 'I could make a search for it, Sir Richard.'

Richard tapped his fingers on the desk. 'That is possible, of course, yet I think there are at least two alternative explanations. The rats may have been part of malevolent spells, but when they were cast and the rats put in place, there were only three deaths intended.'

John of Flanshaw leaned forward and brushed some pulverised cuttlefish bone powder from the desk. 'Yet self-murder must be something that can happen without much warning, if a person is so distraught after either committing a murder or having seen one and been powerless to prevent it. The narrative that you gave in your summing up of the inquest was quite compelling, Sir Richard. Perhaps only three rats were needed by the witch or the sorcerer.'

Hubert touched his arrowhead through his tunic. 'I dislike the thought of such evil being practised in this town.'

'That brings me to the second alternative explanation,' Richard said, picking up a goose quill and stroking the barbs of the feather. 'There are no witches or sorcerers involved at all. Those rats were planted where they would be found in order to make us all believe that witchcraft was involved.' He pointed to Hubert's son's doll upon the desk. 'We have taken those rats as

192

being images used by witches. I have been thinking a lot about this lately, since Doctor Flynn made a waxen image and used some hair cut from my father-in-law's head in order to treat him. He bleeds Sir Thomas and then symbolically bleeds the image. Sir Thomas himself called it witchcraft, but, of course, we can all accept it from a doctor skilled in the art of physic. I asked him whether a disease can be transferred to a dead object and he was reluctant to discuss it, saying that was indeed witchcraft.'

Seeing John of Flanshaw's bemused expression, he explained about Hal Clegg's mother and her growth that both the doctor and a healer were treating. The court bailiff grimaced at the description of using a hanged man's toe to make a potion and a paste.

'And this boy Hal buried the toe under the hanging corpse of Quinn of Ryhill?' John of Flanshaw queried, and Richard nodded.

Hubert picked up the wooden doll and idly ran his fingers over the toothmarks. 'But why plant these rats, my lord? What would be the purpose of that?'

'To cover murder committed in cold blood rather than in the frenzy of madness, as it looks.'

'You mean the murder of Father Alban?' John of Flanshaw asked. 'But why would the franklin Geoffrey Hopwood —?'

'But surely that is not possible,' Hubert interrupted. 'Why would the franklin plant rats that foretold his and the other deaths?'

'Indeed,' Richard replied. 'It makes no sense. But what if the franklin did not commit the murder?'

'But he was seen running from the church and caught trying to escape at the stables on Cheapside,' said the court bailiff.

'He was caught, yes, but he refused to say anything. Indeed, if you remember, he seemed dazed, not just from having been beaten by his pursuers, but almost as if he was drunk or had been drugged. But in any case, I think I was right about him intending to claim Benefit of Clergy.'

'Who else could have killed the priest, my lord? And why? The franklin had an argument with him, after all, that much we all know.'

Richard shrugged his shoulders. 'This I do not know. But consider Ranald Brigg's testimony.' He picked up his notes and read out: 'He saw someone run from the church and he heard someone cry out, "Murder! Murder! Murder! The priest is dead! Stop that franklin! Stop that franklin!" When I asked who that person was, he did not know. It was after the franklin was taken and cast into the Tolbooth that he went back and found the body.'

'I will have to carve over these toothmarks,' Hubert said distractedly, as he looked at his doll. 'It looks like it has lots of stab marks all over it. Poor thing, it would have bled like a stuck pig if it had had any blood in it.'

Richard stared in amazement at him for a moment. 'Hubert of Loxley, you have a mighty wit. Tell me, how often have you seen a stuck pig?'

Hubert looked stunned. 'Many times, my lord. Both when hunting and when a pig is slaughtered ready to be butchered; its throat is slit.'

'And how much blood is in a pig?'

'Why, several buckets, my lord.'

Richard abruptly stood up. 'John, where are the four coffins?'

'Two are in the crypt in the Church of All Saints and two are back in the Tolbooth. They are all safely locked so none can get at them. And both places are cool, which is needed as they are becoming ripe and starting to offend the nose.'

'Where is the key to the church?'

'Ranald Brigg gave it to me and I have kept it in my chest, Sir Richard.'

'Why put them apart?' Hubert asked the bailiff.

'Father Alban and Peter Plowman will surely be buried in consecrated earth, while the franklin and the jailor cannot be, since they committed self-murder, and must be buried in unmarked graves outside the town.'

'Come, bring the key. We must go first to the crypt,' said Richard.

By the light of several candles, Hubert and John of Flanshaw opened Father Alban's coffin.

'If you don't object, Sir Richard, I would rather not touch the corpse,' the court bailiff said, his voice quaking slightly.

'Of course. Hubert and I will lift the body out and lay him on the tomb there.'

Neither Richard nor Hubert were strangers to dead bodies, having fought in battles during the conflict with the Scots and then with Sir Andrew Harclay's army against that of Thomas, Earl of Lancaster at Boroughbridge. They lifted the body of the priest between them and set it down on the flat tomb.

In the flickering candlelight, the mottled face seemed an even deeper shade of purple. Richard pointed to the swollen tongue and the dried blood that covered the chin. 'When we first saw his dead body, there was a small puddle of blood under his face. You can see where it trickled from his mouth. Why was there blood coming from his mouth if he was stabbed in the back? Surely the blade could not have reached his gullet.'

Bending over the body, he grasped the lower jaw and pushed it hard to overcome the stiffness in the muscles. John of Flanshaw lifted a candle and held it high so that Richard could look inside the mouth.

'There is a bite mark on the tongue, as if his teeth had clamped down on it,' he declared. 'But again, I wonder why does his tongue protrude so much?' Richard bent again and closely examined the skin of the priest's throat. Looking over his shoulder, he said, 'There is definite bruising around the neck.' Lifting the head, he unwound the cloth that covered the eyes, revealing them to be still open in death, and sunken like those of a dead fish. Leaning close to the face, he searched around the eyes. 'See there,' he pointed, 'there are tiny bruises around the eyes, and the eyeballs are bloodshot from broken blood vessels. When Doctor Flynn examined the body of Geoffrey Hopwood, he showed me similar ones. He said they were a sign that the franklin had been throttled and were consistent with death by hanging.'

'But the priest was stabbed, not hanged, my lord,' Hubert said, puzzled.

Richard did not immediately reply. 'Let us turn him over.' Together, they gingerly rolled the corpse over on top of the tomb. Richard pointed to the ten holes in the priest's back where he had been stabbed. Each of them was surrounded by a small halo of dried blood. 'Back in the Rolls Office, I asked you how much blood a stuck pig would bleed, and you said several buckets. A man probably contains some similar amount of blood. If Father Alban was stabbed ten times as he prayed, why is there so little blood loss?'

The court bailiff gasped, and Hubert slapped his forehead with his hand.

'So this means he was strangled and then stabbed after he was dead?' Hubert said incredulously.

'That is almost certain. And I think we can say more than that. He was strangled several hours before he was stabbed. I would imagine he was murdered in the evening and then his dead body was stabbed several times in the morning with the franklin's bollock dagger, which was left to incriminate him.'

'So Geoffrey Hopwood did not murder Father Alban!' John of Flanshaw said.

'I think that he was present when he was murdered, but that he was drugged with something to silence him overnight, and then in the morning he was cast out in a confused state after seeing how the priest's murder had been staged and the hue and cry was started. He would have run for his life.'

'So what do we do now, my lord?'

'We look at the other body.'

'At Peter Plowman?' Hubert asked, looking at the other coffin.

Richard nodded. 'Yes, but not for the cause of death, because there is no doubt that he died from having his throat slit. It is to look at his face before we go to the Tolbooth to see the others.'

The woman was furious. 'I knew you would not obey my instructions.'

'Obey? I obey no one and you presume too —'

'Be silent. We have no time for arguments. That judge may not be quite as stupid as we thought, and he may know something that we do not about the messenger. He has not closed the cases, which means something troubles him.'

'As it should. Those rats!'

'Yes, the rats. There is only one thing for it. There must be more death, and only then will we be safe.' She looked down at the small flask on the table before them. 'We both know what must be done now.'

He nodded and, leaning close, brushed her lips with his. 'Then there will be more death.'

Ranald Brigg recognised Jay Groff as he slid open the grille in the Tolbooth door in answer to the knock upon it. He had not slept for a long time, but took his position as headman of the town watch seriously and had accepted that he was the natural man to act as the temporary jailor of the Tolbooth after Judd of Alverthorpe's death. Accordingly, he had sent his constables home to sleep, arranging that Gimlet, the oldest of the constables, would relieve him later.

'Hello, friend,' said Jay Groff. 'I have come to visit my friends Siward Trapp and Emmet Waller. I have brought them mead to raise their spirits.' He raised a flask and shook it. 'It will do poor Emmet good, what with someone trying to murder him.'

'Prisoners should not be given drink other than water,' Ranald returned, doubtfully.

'But they are not actual prisoners, are they? Just as you are not a proper turnkey. Go on, friend. I will make it up to you later.'

After a moment's thought, Ranald opened the door and let him in. 'I don't suppose it can hurt, but not for long.'

Jay Groff was a wiry fellow with hawk-like eyes and a crooked mouth. Ranald Brigg had drunk with him and his two friends at times, although he was loath to call them friends. He liked Siward least of all, but Jay had a wit about him and could make a tavern full of men laugh with his ribald tales.

'You lucky dogs!' Ranald said as he led Jay Groff to the cells. 'Your friend has brought you some mead. It may help your pain, Emmet Waller.'

Siward Trapp stood up and grasped the bars of his cell, and Emmet Waller swung his legs over the side of his pallet bed and sat up. Both looked at their friend with suspicion.

'Let's see you drink first,' said Siward.

'I'm not taking poison for anyone,' agreed Emmet Waller.

Jay Groff grinned and took a noisy swig, then tossed his head back and gargled so they could see the liquid in his mouth. He swallowed with relish. 'See, lovely mead.'

Ranald Brigg stayed his hand before he could pass the flask through the bars to Siward Trapp. 'I'll just taste it myself.' He put it to his lips and drank. Wiping his mouth with the back of his brawny hand, he nodded. 'It is good. Go ahead.'

Pulling up his belt from which hung the new keys, he sauntered off to his room, sat down and put his feet up. Within moments, he was asleep.

The flask was passed between the bars to first Siward Trapp and then back to Jay Groff before finally being handed to the wounded Emmet Waller. Not a word was passed between them.

None of the three were too keen on actual work and preferred those ways that were unlawful and decidedly risky if they were caught. They had generally been lucky, and although they had been individually caught, none had sustained punishment more than a birching or time in the stocks or pillory. The floggings had been their worst punishment yet.

None of them had intended getting embroiled with Quinn of Ryhill, but when they were offered money to get rid of Bryce-a-Green, a fellow scoundrel that they all felt they had a score to settle with, they took the money and the offer of much more to follow.

Jay Groff was the brains of the bunch and had it all planned. They enticed Bryce-a-Green with their idea to steal a cow from Quinn of Ryhill. It had gone well and Bryce had gone ahead with the cow, allowing them to alert Quinn and start the hue and cry in the hamlet. The four of them soon caught Bryce-a-Green. Quinn had just wanted to rough him up before getting him locked up, but all three of them had been paid and so, using Quinn's scythe, which they had brought along, they chopped his head off.

They felt no guilt, because Bryce was a cutthroat himself. As for Quinn, it was their word against his. Their boss, the one who had paid them, had said that they might have to take a flogging or some such, but he'd take care of them and make it worth their while. Which he had. After they were flogged and shoved in the Tolbooth, he had arranged for a salve to be given to them, and when they were released he had paid each of them another pouch of coins and the promise of more.

'You bloody fool, Siward,' Jay whispered at last. 'Why did you thrash that whore and get yourself so drunk that you ended up in here?'

'I didn't say nothing,' the mole-catcher returned, swigging more mead. 'Not even when that judge asked me. What the hell were you playing at, shooting Emmet? Scared the life out of me.'

Emmet Waller groaned as he took the flask again. 'We couldn't take a chance! A careless word and you could get us all hanged! How do you think *I* felt, having to let Jay shoot me?'

Jay Groff smirked, his crooked mouth taking on an evil leer. 'You couldn't have had a safer pair of hands on a bow. I could knock the wings off a fly.'

'You near crippled me for life.'

'But at least you got put in here and Siward got the message anyway. Remember, any careless word and we are all dead men. Our boss would see to that.'

'I thought he'd given the word to kill Emmet,' grumbled Siward. 'Like I said, I wouldn't say anything anyway.'

'It will be worth our while,' said Jay Groff. 'Now remember, both of you, say only what I told you to say.' He shook the flask to show it was empty. 'Now I'll get Brigg to let me out, and I'll tell the boss that everything is safe. Do as I say and you'll be well paid, both of you.'

Hubert's banging on the Tolbooth door roused Ranald Brigg from his slumber and he came running. Sliding the grille back to check who it was, he let Richard and Hubert in and raised his eyebrows in surprise to see that John of Flanshaw was with them.

'We are going down to look at the bodies in the coffins,' Richard said. 'Let us have the keys.'

'I will get oil lamps and put them down for you, Sir Richard.'

'And while you do, we shall see Siward Trapp and Emmet Waller. Have they been more communicative?'

'Barely, Sir Richard; they both sleep most of the time.'

Hubert preceded them and banged unceremoniously on the bars of the cells. 'You two, Sir Richard Lee has come to question you further.'

The two men were lying on their beds. At the sound, Emmet Waller clutched his shoulder and moaned. 'Pain! I am in great pain. May I have more physic?'

'Perhaps,' said Richard. 'Two simple questions for each of you. Who paid you when you were released from the Tolbooth?'

201

'Tell his honour the judge the truth, Siward,' urged Emmet Waller.

'It was a friar. He paid me for getting rid of the rats at the priory.'

'And I helped him, Sir Richard,' said Emmet Waller.

Richard nodded, careful not to display any emotion, although he had to admit to himself that he was surprised. 'My second question to you both is, who brought the salve that you were given after your flogging?'

'No idea, Sir Richard,' said Waller.

'It was just a boy, I think that swine Judd said,' Siward Trapp replied.

'Can we be released now, Sir Richard?'

Richard thought for a moment. 'Not yet. For your safety, this is the best place for now. And I want to check your story first.'

Ranald Brigg had placed oil lamps on ledges down the steps and along the lower corridor. He had unlocked the two cells that each contained a coffin and retreated to his room as Richard had instructed him.

'First the franklin, Geoffrey Hopwood,' Richard said as he and Hubert removed the lid. John of Flanshaw held the oil lamp above so that they could see inside.

'My lord, what are we looking for? I see the protruding tongue like that of Father Alban.'

'The face. Remember I said to look at Peter Plowman's face? Well, what do you see here in the franklin's visage?'

'Now that you say it, he looks like an older version of Peter Plowman.'

'Are they related, Sir Richard?' asked the court bailiff.

'They are almost certainly father and son,' Richard replied. 'The resemblance between Rowena and Peter Plowman is also apparent.'

'So this would explain Master Hopwood's eagerness to have leniency for Peter Plowman,' said Hubert.

'Now, let us go to the next cell and see the body of Judd of Alverthorpe.' With the coffin lid removed, Richard pointed to the face of the Tolbooth jailor. 'It struck me that he looked so composed, almost as if asleep. This is totally unlike the facial expression of the priest and the franklin. Both of them had been throttled to death and their tongues had stuck out, but although this man has similar red spots about his eyes and discoloured flesh, his tongue is not out. I think the franklin and the priest were strangled while they were awake, but Judd was drugged and poisoned. He was hanged after death.'

John of Flanshaw gasped incredulously. 'So Father Alban was strangled in the evening and then stabbed in the morning to make it look like that was the cause of his death.'

'And the franklin was strangled in the dovecote and then hanged,' added Hubert.

Richard nodded. 'And Judd of Alverthorpe was drugged and poisoned, then hanged in the sheepcote.'

'So we are looking for how many murderers?'

'Just one, I think,' replied Richard. 'For now, this must remain secret between the three of us.'

The court bailiff's face looked paler than usual in the candlelight. 'I understand, Sir Richard. I will remain silent until you say otherwise.'

Mary Wisley slapped Gembert Cooper's hands away as he attempted to circle her waist. 'Stop, Gembert. Not here and not now. There is not time.'

The reeve laughed and sat down on his chair. 'There is always time, and after that inquest I think we need some diversion. Some celebration.'

She turned and kissed him lightly before stepping back adroitly away from his questing hands. 'We must still be careful, Gembert. The cases are not yet completed by Sir Richard Lee. I will not be happy until all is finished and Geoffrey Hopwood is in his grave.'

'Yet we won't know where the grave is, Mary. Since he killed himself, it will not be in consecrated soil and it will be unmarked. Now come.'

'No! You have work to do. You will have to wait until night.'

He grinned. 'At night when the witches are abroad?'

She adopted a mock look of disapproval. 'Enough of such talk, nephew. You know I dislike talk of witches and witchcraft. You heard that Brother Fergus say that they had to be rooted out and brought before an Ecclesiastic Court and that you must not suffer a witch to live.'

'I am never quite sure when you are jesting — aunt!'

'Gembert Cooper, you know that I never jest about Ecclesiastic Courts. They would not deal kindly with the likes of us.'

CHAPTER ELEVEN

Jay Groff had gone straight from the Tolbooth to the stables on Cheapside, where he had left the pony. He knew that the boss would be anxious to know that there was no danger from Siward Trapp or Emmet Waller. The boss had wanted him to kill Waller outright, but he had convinced him that a stronger and more convincing message would get through to Siward if he simply wounded Waller. He had argued that since Waller trusted both his wits and his bowmanship, he would agree to take an arrow in the shoulder for the right price. Siward would of course be scared witless, but once Waller was put in the Tolbooth, he would be reassured that he was actually safe.

He had been sure that Waller would be put in the Tolbooth for his own protection. And he was confident that when he visited with the mead, he'd be able to persuade both of them to definitely keep their mouths closed. Ranald Brigg had been easy enough to bribe with that purse of coin. No skin off his nose, after all.

When they were ultimately released, he would be ready and it would be simple to take care of them both. As a reward, he'd take their shares.

And then, who knows? he thought as he rode through the town gates with his bundle of cloth before him. *Maybe I'll take care of the boss as well, once I've taken his wealth. I still have three of those fancy arrows he gave me hidden in Wakefield at the whorehouse and three more in the quiver hidden in this bundle of cloth that I carry before me. I could easily silence that tongue once and for all with one straight in the gizzard.*

Richard had given Hubert instructions, sure that he would

carry them out and discover what he wanted to know. He would have gone himself, but time was of the essence and his own task was important.

He could not completely cast aside the feeling of guilt and self-doubt that he had been carrying with him ever since the hanging of Quinn of Ryhill, but he had a gut feeling that he was getting closer to an answer. It had something to do with the two men in the Tolbooth, which was why he was reluctant to release them. That plus the fact that whoever had shot Waller could be waiting to finish him off.

Hubert's task might lead them further along that line of investigation. But more importantly, he needed to talk to the Widow Plowman again.

He forded the Half Moon Beck and approached the simple house with the willow stacks outside and the shelter with the baskets that she had made.

Nell Plowman had heard the approach and the neigh of his horse and appeared at the door. Her face was drawn and she looked miserable. Tear streaks down both cheeks were in evidence.

'Good day, Mistress Plowman,' Richard greeted as she curtsied to him. 'I come to tell you good news amid this awful tragedy that surrounds you.'

'I fear that there is little that could give me good cheer these days, Sir Richard,' she replied.

'You know that I held an inquest this day?'

She nodded. 'I could not bring myself to go, sir. Whatever punishment you inflict on me for it, I care little.'

'Did you hear that I have not closed the cases?'

She hung her head and shrugged. 'I hardly listen to anything my neighbours tell me. My heart is numb and my mind will not take anything in. All I can do is weep.'

Richard dismounted and pointed to the stools by the workbench under the shelter. 'I am giving no punishment or any fine, Mistress Plowman. You have suffered greatly. I have come to tell you that I do not think that the franklin, Geoffrey Hopwood, killed your son.'

'No, sir, he never would.'

'Of course not, for what father would murder his son?'

She looked up abruptly, a gasp of disbelief escaping from her lips. 'I … I have never told —'

'You never told anyone, but surely your neighbours knew? There was a resemblance between the two.'

She wrung her hands. 'I … I never even told Peter. How could I? Geoffrey Hopwood was a gentleman and I but a poor woman who makes baskets and chewet pies. But … but he loved me, despite him being married to a good wife, Sir Richard.'

'And what of your husband?'

'He never knew while he lived, but another did. One that I spurned when I accepted my good husband's hand. He … he threatened to take everything from me, sir. And … and now he has.'

Hubert found Hal and his little sister playing outside their simple home. 'How now, Hal and Emily,' he called. 'I have come to see your mother.'

'I am here, Master,' came a voice from the side of the hovel. 'I have been collecting milk from my neighbour's cow.' She placed an earthenware jug of milk on the ground and stood with her hands clasped together.

Hubert beamed as he climbed down from his horse. 'Are you well, Mistress Lorna?'

'Aye, I am, Master. Whether by chirurgerie, physic or my healer's treatments, my wen has almost gone, and I have more life in me than I have had for weeks.'

'I know what did it, Mother,' Hal said, kneeling in front of his sister Emily so that she could climb upon his back. 'It is the healer and her magic.'

'Magic?' Hubert repeated with a smile. 'Do you think it was magic, Hal? Do you think so, Mistress Lorna?'

Lorna shrugged her shoulders. 'I care not, Master Hubert. If I am getting well when I thought from the size of that wen that I was dying, then I bless the one that has saved me.'

'So you could be blessing Doctor Flynn?'

'Aye, Master, I could.'

Hubert smiled at her. 'Or you could be praising — who?'

'Mother, we must not say —' began Hal.

But Hubert put a finger to his lips. 'Hold, Hal. And hold, Mistress Lorna. Have no fear, I am not asking about magic — or witchcraft.'

'Forgive me, Master, but I hear so much talk about witches and witchcraft and sorcery in Wakefield, I … I do not wish to get anyone in trouble.'

'There is no trouble from me, nor yet from my master, Sir Richard Lee. He has sent me to try to find out your healer. He wants to know for good reasons, not to find a witch. All I need to know is where this healer may be found. I need no name.'

'And there will be no trouble? I fear that in saying the name the treatment will stop working.'

'My master Sir Richard is only interested in the good. No harm will befall you, and he is sure that no harm will come from telling me the place.'

Lorna sighed. 'Very well, Master. But would you like to sup some milk with us?'

'I would be pleased to, Mistress.' He grinned at Hal with his sister still on his back. 'I have a boy about the same age as Emily. He likes me to carve him dolls from wood. Perhaps I could carve one for Emily.'

'Could you make me a bow, a proper bow, Master Hubert?' Hal asked.

'Of course I can, Hal. Sir Richard told me that you have the makings of a bowman. And perhaps if your mother will allow it, you could show my boy Jack how to shoot it.'

He did not want to press Lorna any further for the information.

Prior Norbert was praying in the sacristy of St Leonard's Priory when Matthew Drewitt the manciple sought him out. At the sound of footsteps, he finished his prayer, made the sign of the cross and opened his eyes.

'Ah, Matthew, were you looking for me?' he asked over his shoulder before pushing himself to his feet.

'Actually, no, Prior Norbert. It was Brother Fergus that I was looking for. I thought he had returned from Wakefield with you.'

'He did. We came back in the wagon, but as we came through Kirkthorpe he said that he felt the need to pray for Father Alban's soul at St Peter's Church, where he had preached with him on St Julian's Day. So I left him there.' He gave a short laugh. 'He is a young man still and well used to travelling on foot. He will be back before nightfall.'

The manciple smiled. 'It is of no great importance. I will speak with him when he returns.'

The smile faded as soon as he turned to leave. The moment he left the chapel, he picked up his pace. He needed an urgent talk with his sister.

Jay Groff had stopped at his home to pick up his bow, which he secreted in the bundle along with the quiver and then continued on his way.

He was proud of his skill with the bow. There were not many that could place an arrow into a man with such precision. The more he thought about it, though, the more he realised how much he had enjoyed it. The boss was wealthy and no mistaking, but he was a mean and vindictive bastard. He'd learned that in this whole bloody business, and even though he'd been paid well, he had still taken a flogging for his trouble.

'Well, no more beatings for me,' he said to himself through gritted teeth. 'You're going to pay dearly for that.'

He made for the copse of trees and dismounted. Unwrapping the cloth, he shouldered his quiver, and with his bow at the ready he proceeded on foot. As he neared the building, he nocked an arrow. He had no intention of letting the boss know that he was coming for him, and he intended to be ready.

Hubert rode from Agbrigg to St Leonard's Priory and entered the courtyard just as several friars were walking through the gates.

'You look as if you have walked far, Brothers,' he remarked as he dismounted and handed the reins to an obliging novice.

'Our feet are sore, perhaps, but our hearts are beating with joy, for we have been doing the Lord's work,' one replied.

'Preaching about witchcraft?'

'Indeed. I have been to Castleford, and my fellows have been to villages around the surrounding countryside.' He pointed to another friar who was sitting on a barrel, rubbing his feet. 'Brother Joshua there has been to our brother friary of St

Richard's in Pontefract. He carried a letter from Prior Norbert about our mission.'

Hubert clicked his tongue. 'So that is how the word spreads. Should we now expect that soon many people will be denounced as witches?'

'If they have fallen into Satan's hands, then they must be found and punished,' the friar replied, the fervour showing in his eyes.

Prior Norbert came out of the chapter house and immediately came over to greet Hubert. 'Ah, Master Hubert of Loxley. Have you come on some errand from Sir Richard? Is there something he wanted after the inquest?'

'No, it is Master Drewitt and his sister Mistress Myrtle Drewitt that I have come to see.'

Prior Norbert gave an amiable laugh. 'Why, they are very popular these days.' He pointed to the square building with the fenced garden. 'They live in the hospital building. You may find Matthew Drewitt in his office, and Mistress Myrtle is likely to be in the dispensary.'

Hubert followed the prior's directions and found that Myrtle Drewitt was indeed compounding medicines in the dispensary. She was startled to see Hubert.

'Is it my brother you wish to see, Master Hubert? I am afraid that he has had to go on urgent business, although I know not in which direction he has gone.'

Hubert held up a hand and smiled. 'No, Mistress, it is you that I have come to see. I am on a commission from Sir Richard Lee. It is information that he needs.'

'I will help however I can,' she replied, wiping her hands on her apron.

'Good, then can you tell me how you knew how to treat the Widow Clegg's wen?'

Myrtle Drewitt stared at him in alarm. Her eyes opened wide and worry lines suddenly appeared on her brow. 'I … I am not sure I know what you —'

Once again, Hubert held up a hand to halt her. 'Fear not, Sir Richard knows about the method you used and about the hanged man's toe that young Hal brought you and then buried under the hanging corpse. He is not concerned about it.'

'But … but what of Brother Fergus? What if he summons us to the Ecclesiastic Court?'

'For what, Mistress?'

'For … for witchcraft!'

Hubert laughed. 'It seems to Sir Richard that physic and witchcraft are not so different. Doctor Flynn, he tells me, uses a small effigy of Sir Thomas to treat him when he bleeds him. No, there is no harm in that, and nothing will be said to Brother Fergus. As I said, Sir Richard has no concerns, as he is just grateful that Mistress Clegg is much improved.' He again raised a reassuring hand. 'And rest assured that neither young Hal nor his mother told me your name. They told me only that this was the place that the healer could be found. From what Sir Richard had told me, I knew that it must be you.'

Looking obviously relieved, she said, 'I do whatever I can to help the poor people, and I make them promise not to reveal who their healer is. I am thankful that she is doing well. Her son Hal is a good boy.'

Hubert grinned. 'He is indeed. But now I come to my main errand, Mistress. Sir Richard wants to know if you made a salve for three prisoners in the Wakefield Tolbooth a little over a week since?'

She shook her head. 'I have treated no prisoners, Master Hubert.'

He clicked his tongue in disappointment. 'But have you made a salve in that time? For anyone who had been flogged or beaten?'

'I made a salve, but not for a person. I was asked to make it for a wounded animal that had sores that the owner said seemed to be festering.'

'Was it a large animal, Mistress?'

She nodded. 'It was a horse.'

'Perhaps it was not a horse but enough for three men. Can you give me the owner's name?'

She bit her lip. 'I was asked not to if anyone asked, Master Hubert. The owner did not want anyone to think that they would mistreat a horse.'

Some minutes later, when Hubert left the dispensary and stepped out into the garden, he was surprised to see the novice who had taken his horse was now leading Sir Richard's horse to a trough to drink. He whistled to him, and when he turned Hubert ran and vaulted over the fence towards him.

'Has Sir Richard come to the priory, too?'

'Yes, Master Hubert. He saw your horse and is now with Prior Norbert in his private office.'

Hubert nodded. 'Then I will wait.'

Inside Prior Norbert's office, Richard refused the offer of refreshments. 'My time is short, thank you. Had I known that my assistant was coming here, I could have given him my question for you. It is a fairly simple one.'

'The simplest of things are often the most complex, Sir Richard. Please ask me.'

'I have a mole- and rat-catcher in a cell in the Tolbooth. His liberty depends on this question: did he come here and rid you of rats?'

Prior Norbert smiled. 'It is not as simple an answer, as I said. He did indeed come at Matthew Drewitt's request to rid us of an infestation of rats. Mistress Drewitt was concerned that rats could get into the hospital. She has a dislike of the creatures, it seems.'

'Why is it not so simple an answer?'

'Because he caught many, but we still have a problem. Maybe it is because there is a dead animal somewhere nearby out on Ackworth Moor.'

'And what did he do with the dead bodies?'

'He hung them about the priory to try to deter any other rats. I fear we may have to summon him back again.'

'How long ago was this?'

Prior Norbert sucked his lower lip as he considered. 'Oh, about two or three weeks ago or so.'

'So the hanging rats are quite old?'

'They are, Sir Richard. You will see them if you look around the priory.'

'I will take a few away. They may be of some value to me.'

Prior Norbert looked puzzled, but he smiled affably. 'The Lord truly works in strange ways. Perhaps if you take some away, that will cause the live rats to go elsewhere and take away our problem.'

How strange. That would be another facet of the principium transfero *principle that Doctor Flynn told me about. If it happens!*

'My lord, I had not expected our paths to cross so soon,' Hubert said as Richard came out of the chapter house.

'Nor I, Hubert. Have you been successful?'

'The Widow Clegg is much better, my lord. Her wen is almost gone. It is quite remarkable. With some gentle persuasion and an assurance that none will be in trouble, she told me the place where the healer can be found. I knew it had to be Mistress Myrtle Drewitt.'

'And did she make a salve for the prisoners?'

'She made a salve, Sir Richard. But she was told that it was for a horse and that the owner did not want people to think that they would mistreat a horse.'

'Did she give you a name?'

'She did, my lord. I was going to visit there straight away.'

Richard gestured to the novice who was hovering with the horses. 'Then we shall go together. When we get back I shall release Siward Trapp and Emmet Waller, as long as Doctor Flynn is content to watch over Waller's wound. Prior Norbert confirmed that Siward Trapp did work here and killed many rats some two weeks ago. They are hanging around the priory somewhere.'

'I noticed some when I came in, my lord.'

'Then go and get two and bring them with us.'

The Church of St Peter at Kirkthorpe was empty when Brother Fergus reached it.

Someone had left two turnips and a carrot before the altar, presumably as some sort of remembrance of the dead priest.

'Was it from a wench?' he asked himself. 'Is that in remembrance of the mighty genitals of a fornicating priest?'

The thought amused the friar, but only for a moment. He did not generally permit himself the luxury of amusement. And having taken the vow of celibacy when he had entered the monastic life for the first time, he did not allow himself the dubious satisfaction of fornication, although he knew that many priests did.

'But I think you were not that sort of priest, were you, Alban? You were a rigid man of God. You hated sinners with a passion; that much I know from the little time I knew you. But you were methodical. You told me how you recorded the confessions of all those sinners. Just as you recorded what penitence you ordered each one as set out in that penitential book you swore by and held in almost as much reverence as you held the Bible. You just didn't show me them.'

He spied the small door where Father Alban had told him he often stayed at night.

'Is it here? Please God, let it be so, as I did not find it in your humble home in Wakefield.'

It did not take long to find it. It was no grand thing, but a plain wooden box containing a series of rolled up pieces of vellum. The priest's writing was small and cramped, for he had been economical with his precious vellum, but it was legible.

'But there are riches here,' Brother Fergus said as he sat and began to read of the confessed sins of the God-fearing rich and the poor of the area.

A cold smile crossed his lips as he found the answer that he had been seeking for so long.

'It will not be long now. After the mortal sins I have committed myself, here I will be able to continue my quest until I have rooted out these malign beings.' He permitted himself a single laugh. 'And then I shall cross the waters and deal with the bastard demon child of Satan once and for all.'

With the box secreted in a sleeve of his habit, he let himself out of the church and started on the trail to St Leonard's.

He had not walked more than twenty paces from the door of the church before he heard a twanging noise, immediately followed by an excruciating pain in the small of his back. He pitched forward onto the earth, groaning in agony. He managed to reach behind him and felt the shaft of an arrow, which was already sticky with his blood.

CHAPTER TWELVE

'Do you think these rats will tell us anything, my lord?' Hubert asked as they rode back through Wragby on their return towards Wakefield.

'I want to compare them with the dead rats that were found in Wakefield. Were they used with demonic purpose by witches, or were they planted to make us think so?'

'Do you think there are witches at work, my lord?'

Richard chewed his lip. 'I am not sure, although I have no doubt that it is entirely possible. We know from experience that there are those who practise sorcery, but I was doubtful that their spells and enchantments were anything more than blind desire. Then as the friar Brother Fergus said as he preached in the Church of St Peter in Kirkthorpe, the world knows that spells were cast against King Edward the Second and against the Despenser Lords. The King has been taken prisoner and deposed and the Despensers both executed. Perhaps those spells just needed time and they actually worked.'

They rode in silence for some minutes, passing fields where labourers wearing cloths to cover their mouths and noses were working with wooden rakes to spread night soil over the ground. Richard and Hubert followed their example and drew up their neckcloths and held their breath for as long as they could to minimise their exposure to the stench.

At last, after a long, slow climb towards a crest, they saw the tower of the Church of St Peter at Kirkthorpe. 'But you disposed of all their paraphernalia, my lord. How could they then work?'

Richard shrugged. 'Mayhap the deed was done and the means of casting the spell no longer mattered. It all seems very similar to the Widow Clegg's treatment by Mistress Myrtle Drewitt, and to Doctor Flynn's treatment of my father-in-law, Sir Thomas. Her healing and the doctor's physic have much in common.'

'So mayhap witchcraft and sorcery can indeed send demons and sprites to bring disease, misfortune and death to others?'

'That remains to be seen, Hubert. We shall go —' He stopped suddenly and stood up in his stirrups. 'What is happening there? Close by the church!'

They saw a horse, and beside it a man was kneeling over another. Even at that distance they could see blood.

They spurred their mounts into a gallop and soon reached the scene.

'Sir Richard, thank God. I … I didn't know what to do,' said Matthew Drewitt the manciple of St Leonard's. He was kneeling over the prone body of a friar wearing the black mantle over a white habit of the Dominican order. In his bloody hand, Matthew held the shaft of an arrow. 'It is Brother Fergus.'

'Is he dead?' Hubert demanded, jumping down.

'No. Not yet, but I fear he is close to it. He is not talking, and I did not know what to do, except pull the arrow out. Only … only —' He held the shaft up, shaking his head helplessly. 'I don't know how long he has lain here. I just came across him and I have not seen any footpads.'

'He lives yet, my lord,' said Hubert, kneeling and placing a hand near the friar's nose. 'He breathes, but only shallowly.'

Richard looked at the blood-soaked habit and the hole that still oozed blood in the small of his back. 'You have pulled the shaft free from the arrowhead, Master Drewitt. You would have done better to have left it or to have broken the shaft.'

'Should ... should we take him back to the priory to see my sister? She could make him a remedy.'

'He sweats like a pig, my lord,' Hubert said.

Richard felt the friar's brow. 'He burns up. I fear this is not merely an arrow wound.' He pulled off his neckcloth and made it into a ball, which he pressed hard against the site of the wound. Pulling the cord about the friar's waist up and over the cloth, he tightened it.

'Let us hope that staunches it and he does not lose too much blood. If he is to have a chance at survival, we must get him to Doctor Flynn. We shall drape him over a horse and two of us will ride on one.'

'Or take mine, my lord, and I shall walk.'

'No, Hubert, Master Drewitt and I shall ride with Brother Fergus and you go and alert the physician that we are bringing him another patient in need of his ministrations. We must find out more about this murderous attack.'

Doctor Flynn had been out on his rounds, including a visit to see the Widow Clegg. After Hubert found him and they rode to his home on the Warrengate, he told him of the success of his treatment. 'My cautery irons have shrunk her wen until it is no more than a shrivelled scar, and my bosh water tonic, made from the blacksmith's quenching tank, is restoring her strength. I think it is marvellous how red-hot iron plunged into cold water imparts the power of iron to the water.'

Hubert said nothing about Mistress Myrtle Drewitt's treatment to the physician, who would undoubtedly have branded it witchcraft.

They were waiting for Richard and the manciple to arrive with Brother Fergus and were alerted by the noise of a crowd of urchins and loafers that had inevitably congregated around the two horses, one ridden by two men and the other carrying the friar over its back.

Hubert shooed them away and helped Richard to carry the friar into the physician's chirurgia and treatment room, before Richard dismissed him on the errand they had set out from St Leonard's on. Before he did so, Hubert brought in Richard's saddlebag at the judge's request.

With the friar laid face down upon the table where not long before the physician had removed an arrow from Emmet Waller, Doctor Flynn made a cursory examination of the patient. He put a burnished metal mirror before Brother Fergus's mouth and noted how much it misted up. Then he slid a hand over the chest to feel the heart.

'He is gravely ill and has a fever, he is lathered in sweat, but yet his breathing is shallow and his heart is slow. That is strange. I need to examine this wound.'

He released the cord about the waist and removed Richard's blood-soaked neckcloth. Then, with Richard's help, he slid the habit up to reveal the ugly jagged entry wound of the arrow. He grimaced at the sight of it before dipping his hand in the water bucket placed in readiness, then he inserted his digit into the wound and felt.

'It is deep and not far from the spine,' he announced. 'And it is barbed.'

'Can you extract it as you did with Emmet Waller's?'

The physician shook his head. 'I could not get an extractor loop beyond the tip, nor could I get forceps to grasp the end that joined to the shaft. It has barbs on it, and they are designed so that it cannot be withdrawn.'

'I … I thought I was doing the right thing by pulling it out,' Matthew Drewitt said from the side of the room. He was pale and looked as if he might be sick.

'There is not a lot that could be done, Master Drewitt,' said the physician. 'But there is worse here.'

'You mean the arrow was poisoned?' Richard queried.

Doctor Flynn nodded. 'And I have little idea about what sort of poison was used. His body is trying to remove the malefic humour, hence his perspiration, but it is slowing his heart and breathing so that it may stop and then he will die.'

'Is there anything that can be done?' Richard asked.

The patient suddenly let out a long groan. Immediately, the doctor placed the mirror to his face and noted the increase in mistiness.

'There may yet be a chance. I will need to try to get some physic in his mouth and hope that he is able to swallow.'

He went to a shelf and took down two painted jars. From one he took out a dirty brown spherical object the size of a man's fist. 'We will begin with the bezoar stone. I have used this several times with good effect. It is a stone from the stomach of a deer. It may start to draw the poison. While I prepare a mithridate potion, I need you to hold this against the open wound and keep turning it round and round.'

Richard took the bezoar and applied it to the wound as directed while Doctor Flynn set about pulling more jars down and adding different ingredients to a pestle and mortar.

'Mithridate potion has over fifty ingredients, but fortunately, I already have various mixtures containing several of the herbs, spices and minerals needed. I have frankincense, myrrh, ginger, saffron, adder's tongue and toadstones, to name but a few.'

'Toadstones?' Matthew Drewitt repeated. 'My sister Myrtle uses only herbs in her concoctions at the hospital.'

'Partial knowledge can be risky,' the physician replied with a hint of disparagement. 'I removed these toadstones myself from the heads and the stomachs of several toads. When ground up and mixed in honey or wine, they act like bezoars to absorb poison. In this case I will use wine, for he needs the potion to be mostly liquid.'

Working quickly, the physician was soon mixing his ingredients with wine. 'Now let us turn him on his side, and while I try to get him to drink, keep rotating that bezoar in the wound.'

Matthew Drewitt took over with the bezoar rotating and Richard helped Doctor Flynn to open the friar's mouth enough to drip some of the potion in. After a few moments, they saw the Adam's apple slowly move up and then down.

'He has swallowed that much, at least. We will now wait. Best to lay him on his front again and just leave the bezoar stone on the wound.'

While they waited, Richard opened his saddlebag and took out the two dead rats by their tails. 'What do you make of these, Doctor Flynn?'

'Ugh! By the look of them, I would say they have been dead at least two weeks.'

'And what do you think of this arrow shaft?' Richard asked, pulling out the headless arrow that Matthew Drewitt had pulled from Brother Fergus's back.

The physician took it and shook his head. 'I am no expert at archery, Sir Richard. It is a common enough looking arrow.' He pointed to a corner of the room. 'Not unlike my own.'

Richard crossed and drew out an arrow from a quiver and held it beside the offending headless weapon. 'A pretty good match, I would say. Is it made of ash?'

Doctor Flynn nodded. 'It is. Simon the fletcher made it, and the bow. Even I as a physician must practise every week in case called upon by one noble or another.'

'Do you practise, too, Master Drewitt?' Richard asked.

The manciple held up his right hand, which was missing the forefinger and the end joint of his second. 'I do, Sir Richard, but I have not much power or much accuracy on account of losing these fingers to a dog when I was a child.'

So Brother Fergus was shot with a different type of arrow from Emmet Waller. They could still both have been fired by the same archer, but it seems unlikely that whoever it was would use two different arrows. Their weights would be very different, and they would not fly quite the same way.

A few moments later, the friar groaned and then his eyelids fluttered. The three men bent to look at his face. They saw him blink, and then his eyes moved to focus unsteadily upon Richard.

'F-Father!' he muttered.

'We must get more mithridate into him,' the physician said. 'He still burns with fever and he is covered in sweat.'

They turned him on his side again and slowly, a few drops at a time, they managed to get him to swallow the whole amount from the goblet.

'Bless me … father —' he breathed, trying to focus on Richard, '— for I have … sinned.'

Doctor Flynn laid the goblet aside and whispered, 'I think he believes you to be a priest, Sir Richard. He also must know that he is close to death.'

Richard nodded and bent close to the friar.

'Brother Fergus,' Richard said to him. 'Can you tell us who did this to you?'

The friar tried to reach out, but his hand merely twitched. 'Father … my name is not Fergus. It is … Connal. I was a monk at Bangor. Help me, Father… Please, hear my confession.'

Richard made an exaggerated sign of the cross. 'How have you sinned, my son?'

'I … have blood … on my hands!'

'You have been wounded, Connal.'

The friar tried to shake his head. 'No! I … have killed … men!' His eyes fluttered closed and his head slumped down on the table.

Doctor Flynn was adamant that the wounded friar needed to be left to sleep for a while. 'He has barely any strength left, Sir Richard. It is best to let his body build up strength through sleep. To try to revive him and press him now could be fatal. I will watch him.'

Richard nodded. 'Very well, I would like to have words with Master Drewitt in private anyway.'

The manciple followed Richard into the hall. 'Private words, Sir Richard? About what?' he asked.

'About you and your sister.'

He looked worried. 'She is very skilled, Sir Richard. She is a natural healer.'

'I know this,' Richard replied. 'But what I want is the truth. She is not your sister, is she?'

The manciple's eyes darted back and forth like a frightened coney.

'What is your relationship?' Richard demanded.

'We… We are man and wife, Sir Richard.'

'Why such secrecy?'

'We… We… I mean, I would not be able to be the manciple at St Leonard's. We could be brought before an Ecclesiastic Court.'

'Other orders have married couples living in their grounds,' Richard replied. 'There is something else, isn't there? The truth now.'

Matthew Drewitt swallowed hard. 'Myrtle was once a nun, Sir Richard. She — absconded, which is a sin according to Church law. If we were brought before a Church court, we would both be excommunicated.'

Richard looked at him for a few moments. 'Then we had better ensure that there is no reason for an Ecclesiastic Court to know.'

The manciple's shoulders slumped, as if a great weight had been taken from them. 'Oh thank you, Sir Richard. I ... we —'

'I think it would be as well if you returned to St Leonard's now. Tell Prior Norbert that Brother Fergus has been shot and wounded, but say nothing more. I think he is rambling, that is all.'

Matthew Drewitt hesitated. 'Before I go, I have a small confession to make, too.'

'Tell me.'

'After the feast of St Julian, after Father Alban, yourself and many of the guests had gone, I did hear someone talk to the franklin, Geoffrey Hopwood. It was Brother Fergus, or Connal. I heard him say that he knew they were here.' He wiped a bead of perspiration from his brow. 'That is all I heard him say, Sir Richard, I swear. But Master Hopwood seemed most agitated then.'

'Is there anything else you heard after the feast?'

'I heard Master Hopwood whisper to Lady Rowena that he would have to go to Wakefield to warn his friend.'

'Did he say who this friend was?'

'No, Sir Richard. Just his friend.'

A few moments later, Richard watched the manciple ride away on his horse.

But is the friar rambling, or is he truly the person responsible for all these murders?

Cedric of Sharlston was inside his barn milking his cows. As a fairly wealthy yeoman, he had servants to do such tasks yet enjoyed working with his animals himself, so he had sent the servants home as the day went on.

He liked to talk to the cows as he milked them. 'I just have those dullards to get rid of and then I have no more worries,' he said to the cow as he squirted milk into the bucket beneath it. 'Then she will either do as I wish or I will make sure she is thrown to the dogs.'

He had not heard his assailant creeping closer until he heard him run across the intervening space, aiming an arrow at his heart.

'Dullards now, are we?' Jay Groff snarled.

Cedric of Sharlston eyed him nervously. 'I know not what you mean, friend Jay.'

'Friend now? Dullard friend, mayhap.' He waved the bow and then resumed his aim at the big man's chest. 'On your feet. You are going to give me all your money.'

'Money for what? You have done nothing for it.'

'I shot my friend. The finest piece of archery ever, with just enough power to wound, but no more.'

'But the plan. Remember the plan, friend Jay. You are to kill them when they are released. Once you have done that, then I shall pay all.'

'Drop your dagger at your feet and kick it towards me. Then put your hands above your head, you evil bastard.'

The big yeoman did as ordered, then through gritted teeth, he said, 'Watch your words, friend.'

'I have the bow and I choose the words. It is up to you only to answer and speak when I say. First of all, who is she that must do as you wish?' His hand twitched the bow to emphasise his seriousness.

'The Plowman woman.'

Jay Groff snorted. 'The Plowman woman? Why, what is she to you?'

'She was mine, years ago. She — refused me and had a child with the franklin.'

'So?'

'The franklin was married, a rich man. She had refused me and married a dullard that she knew I hated.'

'Another dullard? They plague you, it seems, Cedric.'

'I vowed to get even with her. To take everything she has. Well, I took her husband!'

'Killed him yourself, did you? That's not your usual style. You usually get the likes of dullards like us to do your dirty work. Like we killed Bryce-a-Green on your orders. And like we blamed Quinn, who was unable to convince that fool of a judge that he was not guilty. Why, Cedric, why?'

'My business!' the yeoman replied angrily.

'Why were you so keen for Bryce to be killed and then for Quinn to be hanged?'

'Bryce-a-Green was a thief and a damned nuisance who had stolen sheep and cattle from me more than once. His life didn't matter. As for Quinn of Ryhill, the bastard slept with my sister and got her with child. She died in childbirth, so he had to die.'

'And you managed to get yourself on the jury and persuaded the others that he was guilty and we were not. But we still had a week in the Tolbooth and a flogging from that bastard Judd of Alverthorpe.'

'I got you salves for your backs, didn't I? And I paid you all when you got out. That should have ended it, but for that fool Siward Trapp.' Cedric of Sharlston's face had gone red as his temper had risen, but now, he forced a smile. 'But come, friend Jay, let us keep to our plan. Your new plan. Deal with the other two and I'll make you wealthy.'

Jay Groff shook his head. 'Change of plan, friend Cedric. You're going to pay me now — everything you have — and you are going to beg for your snivelling life. I've decided that I have a talent for killing and wounding to order. I'm going to travel where my talents will serve me best.'

Neither of the men had heard the barn door open further until a voice called out.

'Drop that bow or I'll break your head, you scum!'

Jay Groff spun round to see Hubert standing inside the barn, his sword out. The bowman released his arrow, but Hubert merely moved sideways and it imbedded itself in the barn door.

'I should have told you, arrows avoid me!' Hubert said, rushing forward before the archer could reach for another arrow from his quiver.

He brought the pommel of his sword down on Groff's head, sending him sprawling.

Cedric of Sharlston roared and charged at Hubert only to meet a fist in the face that sent him staggering backwards with a stream of blood following him from a broken nose.

'I heard everything, you evil great toad,' Hubert said, grabbing the big yeoman's tunic, and again he brought his sword pommel down on his head. Before the big man fell backwards, Hubert tipped the bucket of milk over his head.

As he looked around for some rope to tie the two men together, he grinned to himself. 'And I didn't even have to ask you to confirm that you got the salve from Mistress Drewitt.'

He tied them up. 'But I wonder, if you didn't shoot the friar, who did?'

CHAPTER THIRTEEN

Doctor Flynn had removed the bezoar stone and dressed the wound on the friar's back with a piece of leather from a jar. It was covered in mildew with green spots.

'I find that leather that has this mould seems to reduce pus. I dare not try to seal the wound with cautery while the arrowhead is inside him. His best chance is for the mithridate potion to act against the poison. If he survives, I may attempt to open the wound to get to the arrowhead.'

'Has he come round again?' Richard asked.

The physician shook his head, but at the sound of Richard's voice the friar stirred.

'Father ... can you hear me?' he said, his voice barely more than a whisper.

Richard bent close to his face. He had no option but to let the friar believe he was listening to his confession. 'I hear you, my son. What did you mean that you had killed men?'

'I am the ... avenger. Alice Kyteler and her demon familiar ... Robin Artisson ... left my sister to be tortured and ... burned as a witch.'

'Petronella de Meath? She was your sister?'

He nodded, his brow oozing beads of perspiration. 'I was a monk ... at Bangor Abbey. I did not hear until just before ... they burned her at the stake. I was there ... saw them laugh and take pleasure in her death. I became a clerk ... and worked for two years for Arnold le Poer, her brother-in-law, the Seneschal of Kilkenny. He ... never knew my real identity. He ... kept in touch with the cursed Alice and Robin Artisson through ... a messenger.'

'You blame Alice Kyteler for your sister's death?'

'She abandoned her and … disappeared. I found out later … that she had gone to London and there met a knight of the shire from Yorkshire.'

'Was this the franklin, Geoffrey Hopwood?'

He nodded. 'He arranged for them to go to … Wakefield. He was … a usurer like her! But there was no way … that I could follow until —' His voice trailed away and his eyelids fluttered as if on the verge of sleep again.

'Until, what, Connal?'

He rallied. 'Until I overheard the seneschal in conversation with the abbot say … that Black Friars from the Black Abbey were to be sent around the country and to England. I heard that Brother Fergus … who had advised Bishop Ledrede was to go to St Leonard's Priory. It was he who had been there when Petronella was murdered … and did not give her confession … at the stake. Instead, he spat on her. So, I planned my revenge.'

'Revenge on whom?'

'On Dame Alice Kyteler and Robin Artisson … and those who were involved. I … killed the messenger from Wakefield … so they could not be warned about Brother Fergus coming. Then I got him alone and strangled him … hid his body in the river … weighed down with rocks … and took his identity. As a monk myself … it was easily done.'

'Did you plant the rats?'

'I did … as bait. And I preached … and set my trap. I knew they were in Wakefield … but I knew not who they were.'

'And who have you killed in Wakefield?'

He gasped in pain. 'No one.' He reached out his arms. 'Bless me, Father…' Suddenly, his strength gave out and his head slumped down again on the table. An arm fell over the edge and a small wooden box dropped from the sleeve of his habit onto the floor.

'Is he dead, Doctor?' Richard asked as he bent to pick up the box.

Doctor Flynn put the mirror close to his face. 'No, he hangs on by a thread, I think. Again, better that you let him sleep for now.'

Richard nodded as he opened the box and found rolls of vellum with small and cramped writing on them. Taking them out one by one, he started to read, his interest piqued. Then he read two that had been folded separately.

'Is there something of interest there, Sir Richard?' Doctor Flynn asked.

'There is illumination here, Doctor. I begin to understand.' He looked at the friar. 'If he dies, send to the Tolbooth for Ranald Brigg to take his body there.'

He ran from the room, leaving the perplexed physician and the dying friar.

Richard rode like the wind to Kirkthorpe Manor in the fading light. Candles had been lit inside, and the door was locked. After beating upon it, he was admitted by the maidservant who had discovered Master Hopwood in the dovecote.

'Where is the Lady Rowena? I must see her urgently.'

'I am sorry, Sir Richard, but she left with Sir Basil and Lady Katherine de Roxford. They came in a covered coach for her. Lady Katherine herself came in while Sir Basil sat in the coach. She did not want the Lady Rowena to stay another night on her own after all that has happened.'

Richard did not wait; he ran and mounted his horse and spurred it on the circuitous trail around the wetlands and the great East Moor towards Stanley Manor. The horse was tiring fast by the time he arrived, and it was starting to get dark. He saw that the manor itself had candles lit, but the covered coach was drawn up at the base of the nearby hillcrest where Sir Basil's windmill stood.

Walking his horse to the coach, he saw that a figure was sitting inside on the seat, leaning against the frame. It was Sir Basil de Roxford.

He did not respond when Richard said his name, and when he reached over and touched his arm, he fell backwards into the coach. He was dead.

Dismounting and tethering his horse to the coach, Richard advanced to the door of the mill. He pushed it open and saw that it was dark inside. With his hand on his sword, he entered.

Without warning, he felt a thunderous pain in his head and then he was plummeting headlong into a deep, dark pool of unconsciousness.

Water splashed full in his face and a hand slapped him on the cheek, knocking his head sidewards and splitting his lip.

'How good of you to call on us, Sir Richard Lee,' came a female voice. 'And just a word of warning before you attempt to call out or do anything so foolish: Robin so dislikes displays of disobedience that he will be forced to hurt you. And he is an expert at doing so without leaving any marks. There are so many soft, delicate parts of the body.'

Richard shook his head to try to clear it and blinked his eyes open. It was dark apart from the light thrown out from several oil lamps. The first thing he was aware of was that he was bound to a chair of sorts and the imposing figure of Lady Katherine de Roxford was standing before him. Behind her was a table littered with all sorts of paraphernalia, including flasks, jugs and jars, pestles and mortars. Herbs and dead animals hung from rafters and around the great grinding stones, which were also used as surfaces for equipment. The wooden walls of the mill could not be seen, as bales of hay were placed against them from floor to ceiling.

'Do you like my little workroom?' she asked. 'Sir Basil has been so kind in letting me use this old mill for my private studies of herbs and plants and the occult.' She pointed to the hay bales. 'These keep it warm, and they stop noises being heard from outside.'

He felt a squirming movement behind him and heard a groan. Straining his head round, he saw that Rowena was tied to another seat behind him, so that they were back to back. Unlike him, she had been gagged.

'Dear Rowena had to be kept quiet when we saw you coming,' Lady Katherine said. 'She quite threatened to scream, just as she did when she found my dear husband was no longer with us.'

'Your real name, I take it, is Dame Alice Kyteler?' Richard asked.

'Yes, I thought you would know that, although how you do we are not exactly sure.'

'Brother Fergus, or rather, Brother Connal — who is actually Petronella de Meath's brother — told me.'

Alice Kyteler's beautiful dark eyes flashed in anger. 'He should be dead!'

'He was as good as dead,' came a man's voice. A moment later, Aiken the butler stepped into the light and put an arm about her slim waist.

She looked up at him accusingly. 'You should have finished him off properly.'

He laughed. 'I was disturbed by that blasted manciple. It was either leave him or finish them both off. I thought killing him could have further risks. Anyway, your poison on the arrow will have done its work by now. Just as your poisonous concoction will work with these two.'

'You mean the same way it did with Sir Basil?' Richard asked.

Alice Kyteler laughed as if she had just heard a fine jest. 'Oh, he was none of my doing. He keeled over from apoplexy earlier today when he found Robin and I abed. That is what the coroner would say — except that since you are the coroner, it will have to wait until they find a new one. I am afraid that you will also be dead. Poison, of course, but none will know as your deaths will be staged. The rape of a young girl by an older man, frustrated because his wife is with child. Strangulation afterwards, but then the man being shot with an arrow through the heart when discovered — how do you lawyers say it — *in flagrante delicto*! My poor dead husband will have fired the bow and then keeled over with the strain and the shock of it all.'

She giggled. 'The scandal of it all will travel far and wide. Imagine it, a circuit judge and coroner committing such felonies. The friar exposed as the murderer of the real Brother Fergus — we heard from my brother-in-law by another trusted messenger this very day, and we know what Petronella's brother has done. All this will nip this nonsense about witchcraft in the bud.'

Both Alice Kyteler and her lover Robin Artisson laughed.

Richard felt Rowena's hand touch his, and her questing fingers opened his fingers. And then, very slowly and gently, he felt her nimble fingers edge something metal into his hand. It was a pair of scissors, such as she used to snip plants and herbs.

'Robin, bring the funnel. I think we shall deal with Rowena first,' said Alice Kyteler.

'I understand that you murdered three of your four husbands,' said Richard, anxious to delay them. 'Brother Connal said that you bewitched all four, but only three succumbed to your poisons.' He worked the scissors round in his hand until he found the rope that bound him. He started to work the blades, trying not to indicate what he was doing by making any movement other than of his hands.

Alice Kyteler pouted in mock disappointment. 'It should have been four, but my last husband, John le Poer, had the constitution of an ox.' She picked up a jug and swirled its contents round and round as her lover brought a leather funnel.

'The franklin, Geoffrey Hopwood, was totally innocent,' Richard stated. 'I know that he arranged your marriage with Sir Basil de Roxford.'

'Basil needed money, and I needed somewhere that I could live according to my station and have my lover close by. Master Hopwood was only too happy to make the arrangements. Perhaps his only mistake was in getting that fool Father Alban to marry us. He insisted on me making confession first.'

'And rather than confess to your poisonings and your witchcraft, you —'

'I do not practise witchcraft,' she interrupted. 'I am interested in occult arts and alchemy.'

'And rather than confess to your felonies, you merely confessed to your usury, which is a felony in itself under ecclesiastic law.'

'The franklin and the priest knew nothing of all that, of course. They merely knew that I was a usurer in Ireland. But I persuaded Father Alban that he could dispel my crime of usury by giving me a penance.' She pouted suggestively. 'He was entirely happy with the arrangement, even if he did flagellate himself to expunge his own guilt at denying my crime. And then when he told me, he let me flagellate him, which suited us both very well.' She looked up at Robin Artisson as he passed and blew him a kiss. 'Fortunately, Robin and I have never been possessive of one another.' She suddenly looked suspiciously at Richard. 'But how did you know that?'

'Father Alban wrote many of the confessions he heard down on vellum. I have a box full of them.'

'That must have been what the friar was doing at the church,' said Alice Kyteler's lover, snapping his fingers. 'But enough of this, Alice. I will put the funnel down the girl's throat and you pour your poison down.'

'Wait,' said Richard. 'You have not told me all. You followed the franklin into town and saw that he went to warn his friend Father Alban that you were none other than Alice Kyteler and Robin Artisson, or Robin, son of Art. Then you drugged them both somehow and strangled Father Alban. In the morning, you staged the murder and stabbed the priest ten times, before you cast Master Hopwood into the street and started the hue and cry.'

'Very good,' said the butler. 'Exactly right.'

'But you had also threatened the franklin, hadn't you? I imagine you threatened to do something to his daughter, Rowena.'

'It was necessary,' Robin Artisson admitted. 'He was easy to scare.'

Alice Kyteler harrumphed. 'I had told him to deal with both, but he disobeyed me.'

Her lover gave her an angry stare. 'I told you, Alice, do not use that word with me. I am not a servant.'

Richard felt several rope fibres break apart and he began to cut deeper. 'But then he said nothing to me when I questioned him. I thought he looked drugged or dazed, which of course he would still have been. I suspected that he would claim Benefit of Clergy, for under ecclesiastic law there is no death penalty.'

'We couldn't take that risk, so I asked Robin to deal with the situation.'

Robin Artisson snorted with derision. 'Bribing the turnkey was simplicity. He was not one with the sharpest of wits. I told him that I would be his protector and make him rich beyond his wildest dreams. On that morning, he let me in to help the franklin escape. The only complication was the oaf in the other cell, whose throat I had to slit.'

Through the gag, Rowena gave a muffled scream.

'That young man happened to be Geoffrey Hopwood's son. Rowena's half-brother,' Richard stated.

Alice Kyteler's face seemed to register momentary surprise, but it was soon replaced by one of irritation. 'We waste time, Robin. The funnel.'

Richard felt more fibres give. 'And then you persuaded Master Hopwood to go to his home and wait in the dovecote. But there you strangled him and staged his self-murder by hanging. And you left Judd of Alverthope's dagger there.'

'The jailor didn't know what to do and put himself in my hands,' went on Robin Artisson enthusiastically. 'I had already left a basket of provisions in that sheepcote on the Heath, all beautifully prepared with Alice's best and least detectable poisons. All I had to do afterwards was go and hang his dead body from the timbers and leave the silk purse.'

'I expect you were angry when Brother Connal left those rats about the town?' Richard asked.

'Of course,' Alice Kyteler admitted. 'It meant that he had to die. Which he will have done by now. Now, no more delay.'

Her lover approached Rowena and pulled down her gag. She immediately opened her mouth to scream, but he roughly jammed the leather funnel into her mouth so that she gagged.

Immediately, Richard pulled his hands apart, breaking the bonds that held his wrists. He lashed upwards and stabbed the scissors into Artisson's hand, then before the butler could react he stood up and punched him hard in the face, sending him reeling backwards.

Richard's feet were still bound, and he started to use the scissors properly to cut through his ropes. But before he could free himself, Alice Kyteler had launched herself at him, throwing the contents of the jug in his face and then throwing the jug at his head. Whatever was in the jug stung his eyes, and he was momentarily unable to see properly. The jug bounced off his head and stunned him, but sensing an attack by Artisson he lashed out right and left, making contact with what felt like a jaw. That momentarily allowed him to wipe at his eyes and blink to see slightly more clearly.

Another voice suddenly called out, 'Halt!'

Standing unsteadily in the door of the mill stood the friar, the man that Richard had thought would by now be dead. In his hands he had a bow with an arrow nocked and aimed.

'By Beelzebub!' gasped Robin Artisson, clutching his jaw. 'You should be dead!'

'You mean like you will be,' he replied, firing straight at Artisson. The arrow struck him in the chest, lifting him off his feet to crash into the table, where he lay writhing amid the shards of broken jugs and flasks, releasing all manner of noxious odours.

'Robin!' cried Alice Kyteler. 'My love.'

'You witch … I have come for you. You caused the death of my sister … and I shall not rest until you and he are dead.'

She raised her hands. 'No, stop, please. I will do anything. You can do anything with me. I can make you rich.'

'I had intended … to go to Avignon … and deal with the Pope … but I am almost done … here shall be my pyre!' With an effort, he scooped up one of the oil lamps and threw it at the bales of hay, which being bone dry immediately caught fire. He nocked another arrow. 'And this, you witch, shall be … your stake!' He aimed it at Alice and shot her through the thigh. An arc of blood spurted from it. She screamed and tore at the arrow as she slumped to the floor. The dying friar turned to Richard. 'Take the girl and go! These two and I must take this doorway to hell.'

Richard sliced through the rest of the ropes and picked up Rowena, chair and all, and dashed past Connal de Meath out into the night.

He heard the door bang shut behind him and then bolted from within.

Swiftly releasing Rowena, he saw a horse trough nearby and ran to plunge his head into it, feeling relief as the water soothed the burning of the poisonous liquid. He heard shouting from the manor house and running feet as servants hurried towards the mill.

When he finally turned to see how Rowena was faring, he was surprised to see her smile as the old windmill turned into a raging inferno.

'I have never seen such a fine fire!' she said softly. 'My poor father and half-brother were both innocent.'

EPILOGUE

Sir Thomas and Wilhelmina sat on either side of the great log fire in the manor house in Durkar and listened as Richard recounted his rulings after the final inquest into the deaths in Wakefield and the surrounding district. He explained how the man they had known as Brother Fergus had rallied while Doctor Flynn was out of the room and plucked up his bow and quiver of arrows and managed to mount the doctor's horse outside.

'Had he not risen from death's door, there could have been a different outcome for Rowena Hopwood and I. As it was, justice was served and he avenged his sister, Petronella. The Lord will decide the fate of his soul for the murders he committed.'

'But now I am relieved that there need be no more mention of witchcraft,' said Wilhelmina, cradling her hands over her increasingly gravid abdomen. 'And I am so relieved to see how well Doctor Flynn's treatment has worked, Father.'

Sir Thomas rubbed his beard and looked down at the milk in his mug. 'I must say that I do feel better and have developed a taste for this white liquid.' He took a sip and then asked Richard, 'What of Quinn of Ryhill?'

Richard frowned. 'His body has been taken down from the Agbrigg gibbet and he will receive a pardon and a Christian burial. So too will Father Alban, Peter Plowman, Geoffrey Hopwood and Judd of Alverthorpe.' He scratched his cheek. 'I am not sure quite what to do about the bribe the jailor took, nor that taken by Ranald Brigg, but they will be matters that I will consider in court when I deal with the whole case of

Cedric of Sharlston and those three scoundrels from Ryhill. Murder was done, and the law must be upheld.'

Wilhelmina shivered. 'What of Rowena?'

'She is a young lady with a good head. She has already arranged for Mistress Plowman to be given a position and shelter in Kirkthorpe Hall. It will not be easy for them, but they will help each other by sharing each other's grief.'

Wilhelmina gave her husband a knowing smile. 'And what of the other "relationships" you told me of, husband?'

Richard held his hands up. 'I see little good in exposure, Wilhelmina. Not when good work is being done.'

Sir Thomas harrumphed, for he did not know exactly what relationships they talked about. He drank some more milk, then asked, 'Where is your good man, Hubert of Loxley?'

Richard smiled. 'He is teaching a young lad some of the finer points of archery.'

A NOTE TO THE READER

Dear Reader,

Thank you for taking the time to read my novel. *The Franklin's Felony* is a work of fiction, yet as with the two novels before it, *The Pardoner's Crime* and *The Summoner's Sins*, the locations, some of the characters and certain events are historical facts around which the story was woven.

King Edward II was captured by the forces of his wife, Queen Isabella and her lover Roger Mortimer, Lord of Wigmore and Earl of March. They had Hugh Despenser the Elder executed in October 1326 and his son, Hugh Despenser the Younger in November 1326.

The King was deposed in favour of his son, King Edward III, in February 1327. Allegedly, and as depicted in Kit Marlowe's play, *Edward II*, he was murdered most cruelly in Berkeley Castle in September 1327.

Pope John XXII was apparently the object of attacks by witchcraft, and he did issue a papal bull called *Super Illius Specula* in 1326, which made the practice of sorcery and witchcraft a heresy. This profoundly influenced Bishop Richard Ledrede.

Dame Alice Kyteler was born in 1280 into a noble Kilkenny family. She married four times, but three of her four husbands died. Her last husband, Sir John le Poer, and her children from earlier marriages accused her of using poison and witchcraft to bewitch him, intending his death. They petitioned the Bishop of Ossory, Richard de Ledrede, in 1324, who investigated and concluded that Alice Kyteler and her followers had rejected the Christian faith and practised witchcraft.

Bishop Ledrede wrote to the Chancellor of Ireland, Roger Outlawe, to have Alice arrested. Outlawe was actually her brother-in-law from her first marriage and he refused. Quite remarkably, the bishop himself was imprisoned for seventeen days by Sir Arnold le Poer, Dame Alice's brother-in-law from her last marriage.

Dame Alice vanished and was never heard of again. It was believed that she escaped to London with her lover, or her alleged familiar, Robin Artisson. Unfortunately for her followers, Bishop Ledrede vindictively pursued them instead. Dame Alice in her absence was found guilty of witchcraft and heresy.

Her maidservant Petronilla de Meath was thrown into prison, tortured and flogged mercilessly until she confessed to being a witch, further implicating Alice and the others. She was burned at the stake in 1324, the first person in Ireland to be burned for heresy.

In the novel I have outlined the Doctrine of Humours, the dominant medical theory of medieval times. It was believed that there were four fundamental humours or body fluids (from the Latin *umor* or *humor*, meaning 'moisture' or 'fluid'), which determined the state of health of an individual. These humours were blood, yellow and black bile and phlegm. Treatments aimed to remove excess of illness-producing humours by bleeding, purgation and the use of emetics, all of which my medieval physician, Doctor Flynn, uses.

Also mentioned are the *principium sympathiae*, the sympathetic principle and the *principium transfero*. The first means using an image or an effigy to form a link with the patient. The second means to transfer a disease to a creature. Both were principles of medicine — and also of magical practice! As you will have seen, there was little difference in the two practices.

A wen, such as the one that Lorna Clegg had in the novel, was the name given to any lump or lesion in medieval days. A wart, cyst or lesion on the skin could have been treated by cauterisation. Although the physician Doctor Flynn suspected that it could be a canker (a malignancy), it could have been any number of benign conditions. His use of bosh water in a tonic, from the quenching tank of the blacksmith, could have helped treat anaemia, which so many people were likely to have suffered in those days. And, of course, the various treatments given would all have had a powerful placebo effect.

If you have enjoyed the novel enough to leave a review on **Amazon** and **Goodreads**, then I would be truly grateful. I love to hear from readers, so if you would like to contact me, please do so through my **Facebook** page or send me a message through **Twitter**. You can also see my latest news on my **Website**.

Keith Moray

keithmorayauthor.com

Sapere Books is an exciting new publisher of brilliant fiction and popular history.

To find out more about our latest releases and our monthly bargain books visit our website:
saperebooks.com

Printed in Great Britain
by Amazon

40933285R00139